Stud Rites
Black Ribbon
Ruffly Speaking
Gone to the Dogs
Paws Before Dying
A Bite of Death
Dead and Doggone
A New Leash on Death

Susan Conant

Animal

Appetite

A Dog Lover's Mystery

D O U B L E D A Y
New York   London   Toronto   Sydney   Auckland

PUBLISHED BY DOUBLEDAY
a division of Bantam Doubleday Dell Publishing Group, Inc.
1540 Broadway, New York, New York 10036

DOUBLEDAY and the portrayal of an anchor with a dolphin are
trademarks of Doubleday, a division of Bantam Doubleday Dell
Publishing Group, Inc.

Library of Congress Cataloging-in-Publication Data

Conant, Susan, 1946–
Animal appetite: a dog lover's mystery/Susan Conant.—1st ed.
   p. cm.
1. Women journalists—Massachusetts—Fiction.   2. Women dog owners—
Massachusetts—Fiction.   3. Dogs—Maine—Fiction.   4. Indian captivities—
Fiction.   5. Massachusetts—Fiction.   6. Detective and mystery stories.
gsafd.   I. Title.
PS3553.04857A82   1997
813′.54—DC20   96-9622
CIP

ISBN 0-385-47725-2
Copyright © 1997 by Susan Conant
All Rights Reserved
Printed in the United States of America
April 1997
First Edition

10   9   8   7   6   5   4   3   2   1

To Kobi and Rowdy—Frostfield Firestar's Kobuk,
C.G.C., and Frostfield Perfect Crime, C.G.C., Th.D.:

Yea, though I walk through the valley of the shadow
of death, I will fear no evil: for thou art with me.

Psalms 23:4

Blessed above women shall Jael the wife of Heber the Kenite be, blessed shall she be above women in the tent.

He asked water, and she gave him milk; she brought forth butter in a lordly dish.

She put her hand to the nail, and her right hand to the workmen's hammer; and with the hammer she smote Sisera, she smote off his head, when she had pierced and stricken through his temples.

At her feet he bowed, he fell, he lay down: at her feet he bowed, he fell: where he bowed, there he fell down dead.

Judges 5:24–27

Acknowledgments

Many thanks to Tina Fuller, Kathleen O'Malley, and Carolyn Singer of the Haverhill Historical Society, Haverhill, Massachusetts, for help in researching the background of this book. For encouraging a dog writer's interest in colonial history, I am especially grateful to John Demos.

Thanks also to Jean Berman, Judy Bocock, Fran Boyle, Dorothy Donohue, Fran Jacobs, Roseann Mandell, Emma Parsons, Geoff Stern, Margherita Walker, and my wonderful editor, Kate Miciak.

The late and greatly mourned Alaskan malamute called Attla (Canadian Ch. Black Ice's Shear Force, W.T.D.X., W.W.P.D.X.) appears with the permission of his breeders and owners, Shilon and David Bedford, Black Ice Kennels.

Animal Appetite

One

I first encountered Hannah Duston on a bleak November Sunday afternoon when my car died in the dead center of Haverhill, Massachusetts. A handsome woman of monumental build, Hannah towered above me. She wore a long, flowing dress with sleeves to the wrists. Her hair fell in waves over broad shoulders and down a muscular back. With her right hand, she maintained what looked like a familiar grasp on a hatchet. Her left arm was outstretched to point an index finger of apparent accusation at my two Alaskan malamutes, who were relieving themselves within the precincts of the Grand Army of the Republic Park. The dogs ignored her. Rowdy, my male, continued to anoint a nearby tree, and Kimi, in the manner of dominant females, lifted her leg on a Civil War cannon directly ahead of Hannah, who stood frozen in her rigid, athletic pose. Although Hannah had every right to object—my dogs were, after all, on her turf—she said nothing. Finding her bland expression impossible to read, I studied the massive stone base on which she stood:

HANNAH DUSTON
WAS CAPTURED
BY THE INDIANS
IN HAVERHILL
THE PLACE OF HER NATIVITY.
MAR. 15, 1697

A bas-relief showed a house from which two women were being led by a pair of men depicted as just what the words said, Indians, as opposed, for example, to Native Americans.

With the dogs now on short leads, I moved to Hannah's left, directly under her pointing finger. Here, eight children clustered behind a man on horseback. He aimed a gun at a half-naked and befeathered figure. I read:

HER HUSBAND'S DEFENSE
OF THEIR CHILDREN
AGAINST THE PURSUING
SAVAGES.

Continuing my counterclockwise circuit, I found beneath Hannah Duston's back a trio of people in colonial dress, two women and a boy, and on the ground outside a wigwam, ten prostrate forms rendered in a manner that would not have pleased the American Indian Movement. The words cut into the stone were:

HER SLAYING OF HER
CAPTORS AT CONTOOCOOK
ISLAND MAR. 30, 1697
AND ESCAPE.

The last bas-relief, the one located under Hannah's hatchet, simply showed two women and a boy in a canoe. The engraved words, too, were simple:

HER RETURN.

In 1697, Hannah Duston had been captured by Indians. She had slain her captors. She and two companions, a woman and a boy, had come back alive. I felt immediately drawn to Hannah: In her place, I thought, my own Kimi, my dominant female, would have done the same. I felt ashamed to find myself the helpless damsel who waited for Triple A under the shadow of Hannah's bronze figure. My shame increased when my deliverer diagnosed the problem: The fuel gauge had broken. My car had run out of gas.

That same evening, when I'd finally reached Cambridge, fed the dogs, and unloaded half the firewood I'd been hauling back from my father's place in Owls Head, Maine, my friend and second-floor tenant, Rita, and I sat at my kitchen table splitting a pizza and drinking her contribution, an Italian red wine far better than anything I could have supplied, meaning, at the moment, anything costlier than tap water.

"It did seem to me," I told Rita, "that I was getting *awfully* good mileage." I chewed and swallowed.

Bizarre though this may sound, Rita was eating her pizza with a knife and fork, and from a plate, too, not from the carton. Furthermore, ever since her last trip to Paris, she's been keeping her fork in her left hand instead of transferring it to the right to get food to her mouth. Even when she was first learning the technique and accidentally stabbed her tongue with the tines, I didn't laugh except to myself. Ours is a friendship of opposites. You could tell at a glance. For instance, if you'd magically peered in at us sitting at that table, you'd have noticed that Rita's short, expensively streaked hair had been newly and professionally cut, whereas my unruly golden-retriever mop showed the signs of having been styled by a person, namely yours truly, with considerable experience in grooming show dogs. From Rita's brand-new navy blue cashmere sweater and coordinating pants, and my Alaskan Malamute National Specialty sweatshirt and holes-in-the-knees L.L. Bean jeans, you'd have drawn your own conclusions.

As you'd soon have guessed if you'd listened in, Rita is a clinical psychologist. A Cambridge psychotherapist. I train dogs. I also write about dogs, not just for fun but for a pittance that *Dog's Life* magazine passes off as money. Perhaps you've read my column? Holly Winter? So Rita and I deal with identical problems—mismatches, lost love, inappropriate conduct, needless suffering, failures of communication, and all the rest—but Rita gets paid more than I do because her job is a lot more complicated than mine. In Rita's profession, everyone is always fouled up. In my work, it's usually clear right away that an emotional block, a lack of moral fiber, or, in most cases, fathomless ignorance is causing the owner unwittingly to reinforce undesirable behavior in a potentially perfect dog, which is to say, almost any dog at all. In other words, even deep in her heart, Rita has to suspend judgment. I, too, can't go around voicing blame. Instead, I mouth the same shrink dictum Rita does: "It's not your *fault,* but it is your *responsibility.*"

But I digress. This story is supposed to have almost nothing to do with dogs. So let's magically let you peer at us again and conclude what you will of us. Can you guess that I have a mad crush on my vet? That he, Steve Delaney, is my ardent lover? And that Rita, in her prolonged longing for a human male soul mate, constitutes consummate proof of the unutterable density of men? If you are perceptive, perhaps yes.

So, with European delicacy, Rita was carefully transferring morsels of crust from her fork to her mouth and, as usual, listening to my complaints, which moved from my foolishness about the gas gauge to the advanced age of my Ford Bronco to the failure of the proud yet humble profession of dog writing to pay enough to feed one human being, never mind myself and two big dogs. What I expected her to say in reply was the kind of thing she always says: She'd interpret dog writing as a symbolic representation of a withholding maternal imago, demand to know whether I'd been abruptly weaned, or inquire about some other such developmental crisis that it was thirty plus years too late to fix.

But she didn't. In fact, Rita astonished me by putting down her knife and fork, looking me directly in the eye, and asking a radically practical question: "Holly, has it ever occurred to you to take a break from dogs and, for once, write about *people* instead?"

A large lump of mozzarella stuck in my throat. To save my life, I was forced to wash it down with a big slug of wine. "Well, yes, of course, Rita, but it's like what Robert Benchley said about exercise—sometimes I feel the impulse, but then I lie down, and the feeling passes."

"Has it ever occurred to you," Rita demanded, "that you are selling yourself short?"

I was suitably insulted. "Of course not!"

"Or that, by your own account, the book you want to write about the sled dogs of the Byrd expeditions will take you ten years to finish and will have a maximum possible readership of maybe two hundred people?"

I inched my chair back from the table. My eyes drifted to Rowdy and Kimi, whose ancestors went with Byrd to Antarctica. I looked back at Rita. "It's still worth doing."

"Or," she persisted, "that, in fact, your only practical alternatives are—"

"A real job," I finished. "No!"

"Or," Rita said gently, "economic dependence on someone else."

"I am *NOT* getting married! You are worse than Steve! And even if I did marry him, I would never, ever even think about marrying him or anyone else for—"

"Money," Rita said.

"Money," I echoed. "Rita, really! I am staggered that you would even suggest—"

"I was not *suggesting* anything, Holly. I was merely pointing out your options."

"Well, that one is totally unacceptable."

"Then," said Rita, swallowing a sip of wine, "you'd better get serious about expanding your readership."

"I am serious *now!*" I countered. "And I do not appreciate your condescending hints to the effect that I need to grow up!"

"What you are," Rita informed me, "is afraid you can't do it."

"Can't do what?"

"Write about people. Or, for that matter, anything else that has nothing whatsoever to do with dogs."

I dug my incisors into a juicy slice of pizza. When I'd finished ingesting it, I daubed my mouth with a paper napkin, drank more wine, and said defiantly, "That is not true! I write about dogs because, in case it isn't overwhelmingly obvious, dogs *are* what I'm interested in. Furthermore, as you know, I happen to be a person with a mission, namely, animal welfare."

Rita sipped her wine, cocked her head, and sighed lightly. "Well, isn't this just wonderful! Tell me, all of a sudden, are all of us free to earn our livings by pursuing our interests and following our missions? Do I, for example, get to cancel all tomorrow's patients and spend the day researching whatever takes my fancy?"

"You think"—I divided the remaining wine between Rita's glass and mine—"that just because I love my work, I don't really work at all."

"What I think," said Rita, "is that you are failing to actualize your potential."

"My potential, Rita, is strictly canine."

"You're scared," she whispered. "You're afraid you can't do it."

"I can write about any damned thing I choose." After emptying my glass, I added, "Even including, if need be, *people!*"

"I bet you can't!"

"How much?" I demanded.

"Five hundred dollars. Plus, of course, whatever you get paid for whatever it is you write. If, of course, you do."

I stretched my right hand across the table. Rita reached out with hers as if we were going to arm wrestle. If we had, the outcome would have been immediate and unambiguous. Rita has one Scottie, and I have two Alaskan malamutes. I'd have won hands down. Instead of arm wrestling, however, we shook on the deal.

"Five hundred dollars," Rita said, "for anything that has nothing to do with dogs."

"Nothing whatsoever," I replied. "Five hundred dollars." Then I rashly described the statue in the center of Haverhill.

And that's how I came to write about Hannah Duston.

Two

The next morning, of course, I tried to weasel out of the bet. I persisted for the rest of the week. I was letting Rita off the hook, I told her. We'd both had a lot of wine. I'd been exhausted. If I'd been thinking straight, I would never have agreed. She was my friend. It would be wrong for me to take her money.

There was no reason to believe that the deal would cost her a dime, she stubbornly replied. Or had I already finished the piece of writing I had contracted to produce? As to my unwillingness to accept her cash, I was, after all, a professional writer, wasn't I? I didn't just create for art's sake, did I? Besides, a bet was a bet. We'd shaken on the deal. She was not letting me out.

The dispute, I might mention, took place not in the smooth, continuous way I've presented it, but in staccato bursts. Arriving home from work, Rita would rap her signature tune on my door and merrily inquire about the progress I was making with Hannah Duston. Returning from a walk with her Scottie, Willie, she'd start in again, and Willie, as usual, would fly at my ankles and yap out what sounded remarkably like a translation of Rita's challenge into the scrappy language of terriers. By Wednesday, I felt sorry for Rita's patients. By Friday, I heartily pitied them. On Saturday morning as I hurried out of the house on my way to a bat mitzvah, I ran into Rita and finally relented. "But *when* I win this bet," I warned her, "I am donating the money. I am *not* becoming the object of your charity."

Rita's eyes crackled remarkably like Willie's. "Splendid! It will give me great pleasure to know I'm rescuing homeless malamutes." She paused. "As well as to read about Hannah Duston."

"This hostility is completely unlike you," I snapped. "And totally unnecessary. Writing about Hannah Duston will be entirely my pleasure."

As it turned out, Marsha Goldbaum's bat mitzvah offered me not just one, but two, independent opportunities to begin my research. It was also at Marsha's bat mitzvah that I learned of the murder of Jack Andrews. I have, however, leaped ahead of myself. Marsha, I should first inform you, was what in Cambridge would be called a mentee of mine, meaning that her parents had hired me as her mentor in the world of dog obedience competition. A few years earlier, the family had bought a bright, charming sheltie—Shetland sheepdog, and, no, appearances to the contrary, never, ever "miniature collie." The dog, Nickie, was supposed to be a family pet. To train him to be a good one, the Goldbaums sensibly enrolled Nickie in puppy kindergarten, where he and Marsha emerged as the stars of the class. (What *is* puppy kindergarten? I feel like a dope saying so, but remarkably enough, it's kindergarten for puppies: rudimentary manners, socialization with people and other dogs.) To continue Nickie's résumé: After graduation at the top of the puppy kindergarten class, he and Marsha entered a basic pet obedience class, then advanced pet obedience, and continued to shine. In the meantime, Marsha started teaching Nickie an impressive repertoire of tricks. All on their own, Marsha and Nickie worked out a wonderful little routine that tickled Professor and Dr. Goldbaum, and turned Nickie into the perfect, nuisance-free canine companion.

The nuisance part emerged when Marsha hit the dog-book section of the Newton Free Library and learned of the existence of American Kennel Club trials, titles, and ribbons, and of the various other rituals and honors of what I pursue as the religion of my own ecstatic choice. So Marsha started plaguing her parents, who had no idea what she was chattering about, but eventually located someone who did. Consequently, in addition to classes with a religious scholar, she got lessons from me. With her other teacher, she read the Torah. With me, she studied Barbara Handler's *Successful Obedience Handling: The New Best Foot Forward.* Barbara *Handler?* Truly, she is a real person, an obedience judge as well as what her name proclaims. Here in dogs, we take for granted these little signs of meaning and harmony in an otherwise random and dissonant universe. I told Marsha so. In a rather different fashion, perhaps her temple conveyed the same message.

To become a bat mitzvah, Marsha had to wait for an arbitrary date, her thirteenth birthday. Nickie, however, earned his C.D.—Companion Dog title—in three straight trials. Twice in the ribbons. Brag, brag. Although my principal contribution to Marsha's success had been to drive her to and from the scenes of triumph while enjoying her company—she was a really cute, bright kid, and the dog was brilliant—she was irrationally grateful to me.

So that's why I got invited to Marsha's bat mitzvah, which took place in a temple in Newton so Reform that its spacious interior was almost indistinguishable from a Congregational church, except, of course, for the absence of crosses and the presence of what to my New England WASP eye looked like an astonishingly large number of people for any day other than Christmas or Easter. But I'm no expert. I spent most of my childhood Sundays in the company of golden retrievers under the revival tents of dog shows, and except for switching to malamutes, I've stuck with the family faith.

I'd attended only a couple of other bar and bat mitzvahs, so I'm unqualified to review Marsha's and will limit myself to reporting that there was more English and less Hebrew read aloud at hers than at the others and that everyone, even the rabbi, refrained from referring to the deity by a gender-specific pronoun, but consistently talked about God and God's whatever, instead of His, Hers, or (heaven forbid!) His or Hers, as if speaking about revered sets of monogrammed towels. The high point of the service arrived, I thought, when Marsha walked as confidently and briskly to the pulpit as I'd taught her to do in the ring and delivered the speech she'd written. Her topic was the gory story from the Book of Judges about Jael, the wife of Heber the Kenite, who slew her husband's enemy, Sisera, by driving a nail through his head. Indeed, just like Hannah Duston! As far as I knew, Hannah, however, was a heroine, plain and simple, who'd killed her captors to survive, whereas, according to Marsha, the ethics of Jael's deed merited deep debate. Only later did I realize that I'd missed the essence of Marsha's interpretation and thus perhaps the quintessence of Judaism—that the ethics of absolutely everything were always subject to end-less reexamination. Debate and reexamination were, in fact, Marsha's specialties. As she'd patiently explained to me, a certain portion of the Old Testament had to be read on schedule everywhere in the world on a given Saturday. The yearly cycle began in the fall, and the portion about Jael would be read in January or Febru-ary. Consequently, Marsha had had to concoct a compli-cated explanation to justify a bat mitzvah topic that didn't really correspond to the allotted portion for this Saturday in November. As I'd told Marsha, I under-stood perfectly: The American Kennel Club, too, had a yearly cycle of dog show weeks, and I had been compa-rably inconvenienced when, for example, the schedule made the Ladies' Dog Club show fall annoyingly close to Memorial Day weekends that I'd otherwise have spent with my father in Maine.

After the ceremony, the guests were invited to what turned out to be a sumptuous catered lunch in a big hall in the temple. The tables were elaborately set and had beautiful centerpieces of flowers, as well as carefully let-tered place cards. I knew only three people in the big crowd, Marsha and her parents, who were making their way to what was obviously a family table, where I didn't belong. Milling around, I eventually located my name card at a place to the right of a handsome elderly man with twinkling blue eyes. He rose, helped me to my seat, and graciously introduced himself as George Foley, a name so legendary in the world of dogs that I did a momentary and, I hope, imperceptible double take. The dog man—the *real* George Foley, as I at first thought of him—presided over the Foley Dog Show Organization, published *Popular Dogs,* and was a charter member of the Dog Writers Association of America. It didn't sur-prise me at all to have the name crop up anomalously attached to someone else. As I've said: meaning and harmony. Or as the bumper sticker on Steve Delaney's van reads: Dog Is My Copilot.

Fortunately, I'm not shy, and neither was this George Foley, who turned out to be Marsha's mother's maternal great-uncle and lived on Fayerweather Street in Cambridge, not far from my own house. Within a minute or so, we'd established an area of common interest, and I heard all about his late bulldog, Winston. As I was sympathizing, an attractive-looking young couple appeared. They greeted my new friend as Professor Foley and took seats to his left. During the introductions, I learned that the newcomers, named, incredibly, Dick and Jane (was Spot at home?), were graduate students in the Harvard history department, from which Professor Foley had recently retired. Jane said that she was Marsha's cousin. I said that I was Marsha's dog trainer.

As the four of us exchanged the usual remarks about how well Marsha had done, I felt so outclassed that I let fall what was meant to be an impressively casual comment about the subject of Marsha's speech, Jael, who, I said, had made me think of Hannah Duston. Dick and Jane didn't seem to recognize the name. Professor Foley, however, not only knew who Hannah Duston was but—in contrast to the ignoramus who'd raised the subject—actually knew something about her.

"Taken captive six days after the birth of a baby. One presumed motive: The infant was killed almost immediately. Curious episode," he told me with what appeared to be genuine, even childlike, interest.

An admission of ignorance felt like my only defense: "Actually, I know practically nothing about Hannah Duston."

When George Foley smiled, happy lines radiated upward from his eyes and from the corners of his mouth. "The beginning of knowledge."

I asked, "Would you happen to know if there's a book about her?"

"Well," he replied, "you'll want to check Coleman, of course, *New England Captives Carried to Canada*—she's in there somewhere—and then Thoreau discusses her, Whittier, Hawthorne, June Namias's *White Captives.*" He mentioned a few other names. "But your best bet if you're just getting started is Cotton Mather. *Magnalia.* Mather draws the same parallel you did: Jael, Hannah Duston. There's a sermon, too, I believe. Mather's about as close as you'll get to a primary source: Hannah told her whole story to him. Oddly enough, though, I was discussing Indian captivity at a conference only a week or two ago, and someone told me about a privately printed book dating back to the thirties, if I recall correctly. I've been meaning to track it down. Probably something by one of her descendants or commissioned by the family, something of the—"

As I was about to pull out a notebook to jot down authors and titles, the arrival of two new people cut Professor Foley off. Actually, only one of them did. A woman named Claudia Andrews-Howe dramatically seized upon my last name, Winter, to relate the circumstances surrounding the death of her first husband, Jack Winter Andrews.

Claudia's appearance so unambiguously proclaimed her place of residence that if I'd encountered her on a street in Bangkok, in a restaurant in Buenos Aires, or in a car on the Trans-Siberian Railroad, I'd have stepped right up to her and announced, "Hi! I'm from Cambridge, too!" Marsha and her parents, I now realized, had considerately placed me at a table where I'd feel at home. Although Claudia must have been close to sixty, her gray-streaked brown hair hung limply halfway down her back and was held away from her makeup-free face with the kind of handcrafted leather barrette that looks nailed to the crown of the head by a dowel driven through a hefty chunk of scalp. Her flowing multicolored handwoven garments were what peasant women would wear if they had tons of money and no desire to rise above their station, and her big gold earrings, necklace, and bracelet bore deliberate hammer marks. To a bat mitzvah in Massachusetts in November, Claudia wore open-toed Birkenstock sandals over bright green stockings. In Cambridge, comfort is everything.

Her late husband, Jack Winter Andrews, she informed me, had been murdered eighteen years earlier by a business partner greedy for Jack's insurance money.

At a loss as to what to reply to Claudia's announcement, I said simply that, as far as I knew, the victim and I hadn't been relatives.

"Jack was poisoned," she proclaimed, as if she'd only seconds ago discovered how he'd died. "I was the one who found him!"

"That must have been terrible for you," I murmured.

By now, we'd been served salads of radicchio, arugula, and avocado, and I was more interested in enjoying mine and in pumping Professor Foley about Hannah Duston than I was in listening to Claudia, especially if she moved on to unappetizing details, as she promptly did.

"There were rats in the building," she informed me.

"Damned Yankee Press," Professor Foley interjected.

"Oh, the guides," I said. The series was (and still is) popular: *The Damned Yankee in Maine* and so forth.

Claudia ignored our efforts. "That's what this partner of his used—rat poison slipped in Jack's coffee. Jack was addicted to caffeine, always kept a thermos of coffee on his desk."

"Jack was a very fine man," Professor Foley informed all of us. "Student of mine. We always stayed in touch. A dear friend."

"Fine man," agreed a deeply tanned, bald, muscular fellow about Claudia's age whose style was so entirely different from hers that I'd been surprised to hear him introduced as her husband, Oscar Fisch. He wore a conventional dark suit, a white shirt, a paisley tie, and no jewelry and nothing even vaguely reminiscent of Chinese rice growers, American factory workers, medieval serfs, or any other Cantabrigian icons. To judge from Claudia Andrews-Howe's last name, though, it must have been Oscar Fisch who'd adapted to her world. Among Cambridge intellectuals, it is considered inexplicable, even somewhat bizarre, for a woman to assume the surname of her husband. Hyphens are still acceptable—Howe must have been Claudia's maiden name—but I predict that they're doomed, too. If the trend spreads throughout the country, the only creatures in the United States to share family appellations will be interrelated show dogs who bear the names of famous kennels. I wondered whether the pleasant-looking Oscar Fisch minded that his wife had retained Jack Andrews's name and failed to add his. If so, he showed no sign of the resentment. On the contrary, he sat quite close to Claudia and eyed her proudly, as if she were an exotic bird that he hoped would perch on his arm.

As servings of poached salmon arrived and were consumed, the conversation became general, and I learned that Claudia was an associate professor at what Cambridge calls "the" Ed School, as if there were none other—the Harvard Graduate School of Education. Her field was child care policy. Oscar taught at what is invariably called "the" Business School. Dick and Jane, of course, were in "the" history department; George Foley, as I've mentioned, was a Harvard professor emeritus of history; and except to insert vegetable sticks and heavily laden pieces of silverware, I for once kept my mouth shut and wished that my magazine subscriptions extended beyond approximately thirty thousand dog magazines. If that had been the case, maybe I could have contributed something more intelligent than the sound of my incisors ripping through carrots and celery.

After a while, though, Claudia, in what may have been a peculiar effort to include me in the conversation, returned to the topic of her first husband's murder. By then, she'd learned that I train dogs. "We were supposed to believe that Jack committed suicide," she announced. "We were meant to. And at first we did. But Shaun made one major error!"

"Shaun McGrath," Professor Foley murmured. "Jack's partner. Died before he went to trial. Never even arrested."

"His murderer!" Claudia corrected fiercely, as if Professor Foley had declared Shaun McGrath innocent. "Jack had a *dog,* you see," she continued in the tone appropriate to proclaiming that the dead man had doted on a pet tarantula. "And the dog went everywhere with him. Everywhere! But when Jack was alone in his office, the dog was always running around loose. It was only when Jack had someone else there that he tied it up."

I nodded.

"To keep it from bothering people."

I nodded again.

"And that's how we eventually realized that Jack hadn't committed suicide."

"Yes?" I asked.

"He'd been murdered!" Claudia again proclaimed. "We knew! Shaun tried to disguise it as suicide, but we knew! We knew someone else had been there! Because when we found Jack's body, the dog was still tied to his desk."

"Oh," I said. Then, without censoring what must have sounded like an odd query, I asked the question that's a reflex with me: "What breed of dog was it?"

Claudia blinked.

I clarified: "What kind of a dog?"

"A golden retriever," she answered, raising her hand and pointing a finger in a manner that reminded me of the statue of Hannah Duston. "It was a golden retriever."

My parents raised golden retrievers. I, Holly Winter, grew up with the breed. Jack *Winter* Andrews. A *golden*. Claudia's Hannah-like gesture felt like the finger of fate. The finger pointed directly at me.

Claudia brandished an empty fork. "Everyone knew. There was no mystery about it. As soon as we saw that it was murder, we knew immediately that it had to be Shaun McGrath."

"It's common knowledge," said Oscar Fisch.

"Written up," Professor Foley commented. "Chapter in a book."

Claudia almost leaped on him. "A dreadful book! Written by the prototype of the pompous ass!"

"All I meant, my dear Claudia, was that Shaun McGrath had been identified in print." Professor Foley paused. "Not that it matters at all."

"Certainly not," said Oscar Fisch. "The man was undoubtedly guilty. In any case, one can't libel the dead."

Three

The canine press abounds with stories of dogs that detect drugs or arson, rouse trauma victims from comas, or entice children from autistic states. *Dog's Life* alone must have published two dozen articles about family pets that awakened households when the smoke alarms failed, valiant canines who dragged sleeping infants from flame-licked cribs. In revealing Jack Andrews's apparent suicide as murder, however, his golden retriever had served humankind in what struck me as a fresh and publishable way. I should be able to whip off a little piece about the heroic golden in no time at all. Hannah Duston represented a radical career change; dog writing was my real métier. Until people writing started to pay off, I couldn't afford to quit my day job, not yet.

On Sunday, the day after Marsha's bat mitzvah, I checked the phone book for Claudia and found her listed ("Andrews-Howe, Claudia & Oscar Fisch") on Francis Avenue in Cambridge. Our Fair City, as it's known, has two fancy neighborhoods. The famous one, the area surrounding Brattle Street, is only a few blocks from my house, but on the patrician side of Huron Avenue. Francis Avenue and the other streets that begin at Kirkland and run back toward the American Academy of Arts and Sciences are a sort of quiet version of Off Brattle. The houses are just as discreetly immense, the vegetation just as lush, the residents just as reliably university-affiliated, and the walk to Harvard just as short as from high-traffic Brattle Street. Furthermore, there's no disguising the monied exclusivity of Brattle Street; but from Francis Avenue, it's only a couple of blocks to a decidedly working-class section of Somerville, so if you're both very rich and very egalitarian, you can take comfort in your proximity to those who work with their hands.

When I reached Claudia and asked how she'd feel about my writing up the story of Jack and his revelatory dog, I made the mistake of saying "heroic," and she churlishly pointed out that the dog hadn't actually *done* anything at all, really. Rather, in remaining tied to the desk, the dog had been nothing more than a piece of passive evidence. My readers would not object, I assured her. Did I have her permission to write the story? I did. We made an appointment for eleven o'clock the next morning at her office. She promised to bring a photograph of Jack and, if she could find one, a picture of his dog, too.

Claudia's office was on Appian Way, only a few blocks from Harvard Square, in Larsen Hall, a peculiar-looking mid-sixties fortress with high, blank walls of red brick and, except in a sunken courtyard, almost no windows. The architect's message, as I read it, was that at the Harvard Graduate School of Education, one had definitively arrived and thus need look nowhere else. The design did, I suppose, minimize hard feelings about who got stuck with offices in the interior of the building. Claudia's was an airless beige cube to which she'd added personal touches evidently selected to create the illusion that she worked in Santa Fe. Woven into the red-patterned ethnic rug was a faded yellow motif of what looked like interlocked swastikas. A Hopi pot on her desk held pens and pencils. On one wall hung a large framed poster of a desert landscape with prickly pears in bloom. There wasn't a toy in sight. Go to any canine training center you like, any dog show, any small-animal veterinarian's office, and take a wild guess at what the decorations depict, usually in bewildering number and variety. The objects in my own home-office are precisely what you'd expect: a gold-framed copy of Senator Vest's Eulogy on the Dog; photographs of Rowdy, Kimi, and my late goldens; snapshots of dogs sent by people who read my column; ribbons and trophies; and, on top of a bookshelf, a wooden urn containing the ashes of my last golden retriever, Vinnie, with a leather collar fastened around it and a little brass plate that bears her name and the years of her birth and death. Nothing in Claudia's office, however, even remotely suggested an interest in children. Not that I expected cremated remains.

The door to her office had been open when I arrived. When I tapped lightly and entered, Claudia looked up from her computer, removed her glasses, and gestured to a hard plastic chair by her desk. "My office hours," she said. "We may be interrupted." She wore a one-piece khaki safari outfit, a sort of boilersuit, and a necklace strung with such heavy-looking chunks of polished rock that the giant-size bottle of ibuprofen next to her keyboard made sense. Her long gray-streaked hair was held back by the same barrette I'd noticed at the bat mitzvah. The style is popular among women handlers:

The clump of hair above the barrette provides a convenient place to stash the comb needed for last-minute touch-ups on the dog. I didn't say so to Claudia. Just as my mother taught me, I made no personal remarks. I'll tell you, though, that the bright overhead lights were unkind to Claudia's face. The skin under her eyes was bluish, and deep lines cut her mouth and chin off from the rest of her face, as if her lower jaw were hinged in the manner of a marionette's.

I sat. "Thank you for seeing me. I guess my request must have seemed a little strange."

She shrugged. Her left hand opened and closed as if she were kneading a fat lump of putty.

The contrast with the driven volubility she'd shown at the bat mitzvah was so sharp that I felt ill at ease. I pulled a steno pad and pen out of my purse, settled into the chair as best I could, and smiled. "I wonder if you could tell me what happened."

She cleared her throat. "Jack was a publisher. He ran a small press. In Cambridge. Damned Yankee Press. They did travel guides. New England guides. Books on the Alcotts, Lexington and Concord, Paul Revere. Before personal computers were, uh, fashionable, before the computer revolution hit, when it was just beginning, Jack saw the potential, especially for small presses, not only for the actual publishing but for direct marketing, mail order, all that sort of thing." Claudia looked not at me but at her keyboard. She cleared her throat. "So at that point, he got connected with this dreadful little moon-faced man, Shaun McGrath, who was billed as some kind of computer whiz." She transferred her gaze to me. "But what Shaun McGrath was, was a mindless technocrat! A complete philistine. He'd gone to some little business college, and . . . Jack himself was an acquisitions editor, really. His grasp of the business side of things wasn't what it could have been. So he ended up taking in this sleazy little person! And somehow or other, McGrath talked Jack into signing a life insurance policy with himself as the beneficiary!"

I nodded. "So that's how you suspected—"

"We did not *suspect!* We *knew!* Once we learned about the insurance policy, we put it together with the dog and the desk, and it was perfectly obvious. The police knew, too. Everyone did. It couldn't have been anyone else. Everyone loved Jack. And it had to be someone who worked there."

I raised my eyebrows.

"They'd had rats in the building."

When I was growing up, the local dump had rats. Remarkably enough, even after it became a sanitary landfill, it still had rats. Until a few months earlier, I'd never seen one anywhere else, unless you counted a few ailing white rats in cages in Steve's waiting room. My own neighborhood, however, was now experiencing what *The Boston Globe* called a "rat invasion," a sudden and occasionally visible proliferation apparently attributable to construction on Huron Avenue, where a new water main and gas line were being installed. In Owls Head, Maine, target-shooting rats was a socially acceptable, if gruesome, local sport. As a new Cambridge pastime, however, it had all the promise of pre-Columbian proto-soccer played with a human head. We'd been warned not to poison the rats, either. Cambridge being Cambridge, we were probably supposed to conduct an ethological study of rodent behavior in a natural urban environment.

"Rats," I echoed.

Claudia nodded. "Jack foolishly decided to deal with the problem himself. He got hold of this horrible, very powerful poison. Everyone knew it was there—everyone at the press. And Shaun McGrath laced Jack's coffee with it. He planted a couple of letters that purported to be suicide notes. But when we found the dog tied to the desk, well, that was the first hint we had. Once we saw that, we realized that Jack couldn't possibly have been there alone."

"He always took his dog to work?"

"Always."

"This was a golden retriever."

"Yes."

I wished she'd expand. I had the sense that without the audience she'd played to at Marsha's bat mitzvah, she'd lost interest in dramatizing the murder.

I prompted, "A male?"

Claudia nodded.

"And what was the dog's name?"

She looked startled. When she ran a finger slowly back and forth over her lips, I saw that her nails were chewed to the quick. "Skip," she finally said.

"And what happened to him?" It goes without saying, I hope, that I meant the dog.

"Oh, everyone knew he was guilty, but before the police could arrest him, he ran his car into a tree. He was killed instantly."

Reluctantly shifting my mental gears back to Shaun McGrath, I asked, "Suicide?"

"No, there were dozens of witnesses. It was on Memorial Drive, actually, only a few blocks from here. He was driving a convertible. He was speeding, and he wasn't wearing a seat belt. He swerved to avoid something and ran head on into one of those trees by the river."

"And when did this happen?"

"Eighteen years ago. Almost to the day."

"Do you remember the exact date when . . . ?"

"Jack died on November fourth. It was a Monday.

Monday evening. He didn't come home, and I ended up going over there. And that's when we found him. Monday, November fourth."

A tap sounded on the door. Claudia sighed. "Office hours. Come in!"

A young woman's head appeared.

"Another two minutes, Cynthia!" Claudia told her. "I'll be right with you." Fishing around in a canvas tote bag crammed with books and file folders, Claudia produced a manila envelope. Thrusting it at me, she said, "The pictures I promised you. Is that everything?"

"Just one last thing. Skip?"

Claudia looked puzzled.

"The dog," I reminded her. "I wondered whatever became of the dog."

"Oh," Claudia said blithely, "I found him a good home."

After thanking her for her help and accepting her assurance that I could call if I had any questions, I departed. I took the elevator to the first floor. Among the various notices taped to its walls was one that advertised a career panel for Ed School women about balancing career and family. One of the four speakers would be Associate Professor Claudia Andrews-Howe. I'd never even asked whether she and Jack had had children. She hadn't mentioned any.

When I got outside, the wind tunnel around Larsen Hall was roaring, and a cold rain had started to fall. Instead of going home on foot, I walked to Garden Street and caught the bus, which was almost empty. Seated alone, I removed my gloves and opened the big manila envelope Claudia had given me. I was eager to see Skip. And Jack Winter Andrews, too, of course. The top photo in the pile was what I took to be a college graduation picture. It showed a handsome, affably smiling young man whose character was not written on his face. He bore no resemblance, I might mention, to me or to any of my paternal relatives. So far as I know, there's not a single cleft chin in our lines, or if there is, it gets obscured by the Yankee lantern jaw that Jack Andrews had lacked. Also, mainly because of the thick eyebrows that predominate on my father's side of the family, he and his kin appear far more ferocious than affable.

Next, a blurry Polaroid showed an older version of the same pleasant-looking man with his arm around a woman I recognized as Claudia. Then, in a family picture taken by an amateur, Jack, Claudia, and two children posed against a background of rhododendrons. The boy was ten, perhaps, the girl four or five years his junior. Jack's hands rested on the little girl's shoulders. Her head was tilted backward, Jack's downward: Father and daughter exchanged grins? Jack and the little girl were on the left, Claudia in the middle, and the boy on the right, next to Claudia, but his shoulders were angled away from her and he wore a grimace. He looked ready to flee the family group.

The photograph on the bottom of the pile made me catch my breath. It was larger than the others, in sharp focus, and shot from close up. A man's body lay awkwardly sprawled facedown on a wood floor. The legs were twisted. The right arm was extended, its fingers bent. Beyond the hand, a coffee mug lay in a puddle of liquid.

Claudia Andrews-Howe had given me a crime-scene shot of Jack Andrews's dead body.

Four

Ever heard of McLean Hospital? Well, if you happen to
be a famous Cambridge poet, a rock star, a billionaire
novelist, or a Harvard professor, and if you also happen
to have cracked up, it's probably where you went to get
patched together. McLean is in the Boston suburb of
Belmont, conveniently close to Cambridge, and in the
days before managed health care, the hospital looked
like a cross between an exclusive country club and a
ritzy college: golf course, riding stables, the whole bit.
Rita, who did her internship at McLean, went out there
recently for a conference about a patient. She returned
sighing about such sad signs of decline as peeling paint
on the woodwork and weeds in the gravel paths. Hard
physical work, I reminded her, was excellent therapy. If
the stables and putting greens were no more, the patients need not languish in idle madness, but could be
put to work scraping paint and pulling crabgrass, thus
building sound minds in sound bodies.

Anyway, the more I thought about Claudia, the more I was reminded of a prominent sign located only a block from McLean that shows an arrow pointing toward Cambridge and reads, in really big letters, HARVARD SQUARE. My idea was that the heavy traffic in both directions called for a corresponding sign in the middle of Harvard Square with an arrow pointing toward Belmont: McLEAN HOSPITAL. Really, it's a two-way street. A crime-scene photo of her first husband's dead body?

On Monday afternoon after I got back from seeing Claudia, I drove to the Brookline Public Library. The first thing I did when I got there was to go to a terminal and type "A = ANDREWS-HOWE, CLAUDIA." She'd written a couple of books about child care policy, and when I found them on the shelves and skimmed through them, they appeared perfectly sane: She hadn't slipped in any odd chapters about her first husband's murder, and there weren't any illustrations at all, never mind crime-scene photos that had nothing to do with her topic. The reference lists in both books contained numerous articles she'd published in scholarly journals. The bios on her dust jackets didn't mention a psychiatric history, of course. What I learned from them was that after serving as the director of a Cambridge child care center, she'd gotten her doctorate at the Harvard Ed School. She'd been an assistant professor when the first book was published and was an associate professor by the time the second came out. My Cantabrigian reflexes reminded me that as a mere associate professor, Claudia didn't have tenure. At Harvard, few women did. According to both dust jackets, Claudia was a nationally recognized authority in her field.

Then I turned to the task that had taken me to Brookline, namely, hunting through microfilm for Jack Winter Andrews's obituary. I am a minor authority on local libraries. The best (maybe the best in the world) is Harvard's library system, and my cousin Leah, who's a freshman, will let me borrow her ID card, but I don't exactly look like an undergraduate, so I'm always afraid of getting caught and landing Leah in trouble. Harvard takes crimes involving the printed word with the utmost seriousness. Defacing, stealing, or plagiarizing a book is on a par with murder. Cheating on exams is, by comparison, a misdemeanor. Remember Ted Kennedy's Spanish exam? So I usually ask Leah to get books for me. The Observatory Branch of the Cambridge Public Library is on Concord Avenue directly across from my house. That's where I go for fun reading. The Newton library has by far the best air-conditioning around; it's my pick for hot weather. The Boston College Law School Library serves as an especially complete U.S. Government documents depository, as does the BPL—Boston Public Library—which has, in fact, only one big disadvantage: Because it's located in Copley Square, there's no place to park. Like the BPL, Brookline had *The Boston Globe* on microfilm as far back as the year of Jack Andrews's death, and on a weekday afternoon, I had no trouble in finding a space in its underground garage.

I hate microfilm. I'm convinced that the technology was invented by someone who loathed reading and wanted to stop other people from doing it, the kind of vile person who'd probably been kicked out of Harvard for tearing up books. Every time I sit in front of one of those machines watching the pages whirl by, I get dizzy, and my head aches. After shoving the correct spool of microfilm into the machine and struggling to start the tape, I fast-forwarded through old comics, news stories about forgotten scandals, and promises of special deals on new cars now, eighteen years later, rusted and crushed to oblivion.

Jack had died on Monday, November 4. He hadn't come home, Claudia had said. She'd gone to his office. She must have gone Monday evening. There was nothing about his death in Tuesday's paper. In Wednesday's, his name appeared in the list of death notices. Thursday's *Globe* carried the obituary. JOHN W. ANDREWS, PUBLISHER, it was headed. Because we'd shared a name—Winter—and a breed—the golden retriever—I was curiously unsurprised to find that he'd been born in Haverhill. Indeed, when I read the information, I felt almost as if I'd been expecting it, or at least something similar. Hannah Duston, of course, was Haverhill's local heroine. What solidified my sense of connection to Jack Andrews, however, was that Bradford, a section of Haverhill, just so happened to be the birthplace of my own Rowdy, whose breeder, Janet Switzer, still lived there. Janet was the reason I'd been driving through Haverhill at all and thus had ended up by the statue of Hannah Duston: Before running out of gas, I'd intended to pay Janet a short visit.

But back to the obituary. Jack attended the Haverhill Public Schools and Harvard College. After graduation, he worked for a well-known Boston publishing house and then went on to found Damned Yankee Press. He was a member of the Friends of the Arnold Arboretum, the Friends of the Mount Auburn Cemetery, and the Friends of the Avon Hill School. I concluded that he'd been a friendly guy. Generous, too. He was survived by his wife, Claudia Andrews-Howe; a son, Gareth; and a daughter, Bronwyn. The funeral was to take place the next day, Friday, at Christ Church, Cambridge. The obituary gave no cause of death.

Fighting off vertigo, I searched through the reel for

an article about the murder investigation or simply for Shaun McGrath's obituary. Finding nothing, I succumbed to my headache, rewound the microfilm, and turned off the machine.

All public libraries in the Metro-Boston system let you access the computer listings of the whole system, but after standing at a terminal and entering every relevant term I could think of—Jack's name, McGrath's, murder and Massachusetts—the best I came up with were a few call numbers in the section of the library devoted to true crime. Poking around among the actual books, I found nothing about Jack's murder.

My computer search for anything about Hannah Duston was equally unproductive, but in the short time I had left before I needed to get home to take care of the dogs, I browsed in the shelves devoted to colonial Massachusetts and found a few short write-ups, one in an old history of the commonwealth, the other in a book called *Travels in New England and New York* originally published in 1821 and written by Timothy Dwight, who'd been the president of Yale.

Let me summarize what I learned that day about Hannah Duston. According to Dwight, on March 5, 1697, Thomas Duston was working in a field. His wife, Hannah, was at home. She'd had a baby six days earlier. With Hannah was her nurse, Mary Neff. A midwife? Suddenly, a party of what the books stubbornly called "Indians"—what tribe?—attacked Haverhill and approached the Duston house. Thomas evidently got there too late to rescue Hannah, Mary, and the baby, or maybe he just didn't feel up to the task. I couldn't tell. Still, he managed to mount his horse and round up his seven other children. (On the Haverhill monument, hadn't there been eight?) I couldn't tell whether he'd gone to the field armed or had entered the house in time to get his gun. In either case, returning the fire of his attackers (or, according to some sources, holding his fire), Duston defended the children all the way to a distant house—a garrison, maybe—where this part of the Duston family found safety.

Meanwhile, another group of what I am forced to call Indians broke in, plundered and burned the house, and departed, taking Hannah, the baby, and Mary Neff as captives. Before the little band had gone far, the infant was snatched from the nurse's arms and killed: dashed against a tree.

So much for *Dances with Wolves*.

According to Dwight, late April 1697 found Hannah Duston and Mary Neff near what is now Concord, New Hampshire. (Hadn't the Haverhill monument said March 30?) By then, the women were traveling with a group of twelve Indians and another captive, a young English boy, en route to a remote settlement where, Hannah was told, the prisoners would be stripped naked and forced to run the gauntlet. Instigated by Hannah, the English boy, who had been taken captive some time before, questioned his master about where to strike to kill someone instantly. In the middle of the night, as her captors slept, Hannah Duston used the knowledge the boy obtained. With the help of Mary Neff and the boy, she "dispatched," as Dwight delicately phrased it, ten of the twelve Indians. The other two escaped. Hannah Duston returned to Haverhill with ten scalps.

Now that's what I call tough.

Five

It's almost impossible these days to find a really good vet who makes house calls like Steve Delaney's. At ten-thirty that night, we got out of bed to finish the take-out seafood lasagna he'd brought for dinner, and as we ate it, I started to ask, "Steve, if I'd had a baby six days ago and—"

"Are you breaking the news?" Steve has a really beautiful smile. His blue-green eyes change colors. He has a pointer, Lady, and a shepherd—German shepherd dog—India, but if he wanted a breed to match his looks, he'd own a Chesapeake Bay retriever. His brown hair waves like a Chessie's, and he's muscular, with no fat.

"Let me finish! It's strictly hypothetical."

"Damn."

"I'm serious. Suppose I'd had a baby six days ago, and suddenly the house is surrounded by hostile Indians. Algonquins. Native Americans. Someone. I don't know who they were yet. Anyway, you're out in a field, and then you discover that there I am, baby to my breast, about to be murdered and scalped."

"I grab my sickle, slay them all, and rescue the damsel in distress."

"That," I said, "is exactly what Thomas Duston didn't do. He supposedly despaired of saving Hannah and the baby, and rescued their other kids instead. Seven, I think. Possibly eight. These experts can't get their stories straight. Anyway, if I'd been Hannah, I'd have been none too thrilled to see him rushing off, leaving me to be taken captive."

I waited while Steve ate some lasagna. He had a grandmother or maybe a great-grandmother who was apparently the world's last believer in some nutty health craze called "Fletcherizing." She made him chew everything thirty times before he swallowed. After a long while he said, "If they had seven or eight children, he must have figured out by then that Hannah could take care of herself without any help from him."

I subsequently learned that Nathaniel Hawthorne had had an identical take on Thomas and Hannah Duston. Thomas Duston, Hawthorne wrote, probably "had such knowledge of the good lady's character as afforded him a comfortable hope that she could hold her own, even in a contest with a whole tribe of Indians."

"There is that," I agreed. "Killing and scalping ten people doesn't just come out of nowhere. And, of course, she had ample motive. She'd watched them murder her child, and she was terrified of what was going to happen when they got to the settlement, wherever it was. Canada. But lots of people were taken captive, lots of women, and I've never heard of anyone else who did what she did."

"You're going to take Rita's money after all?"

"I'm a freelance writer. Besides, this is going to be

more work than I planned. By the time I'm done, I'll have earned five hundred dollars."

"Round-trip plane fare to Minneapolis is—"

"No! I'm donating it to Malamute Rescue. That's the deal I worked out with Rita. Besides, for the millionth time, if you won't go to Owls Head with me, I am not going to Minneapolis with you, especially since I have *already* celebrated, if you can call it that, an early Thanksgiving with my father. And I am not doing Thanksgiving here and then going to Minneapolis for a late Thanksgiving—"

"We could still try to get tickets for—"

"No! It's too late to fly, it's the busiest travel time of the year, and I'm not driving all that way, and you know that your mother would much rather see you without me around, anyway."

I'll spare you the rest.

The next morning, I was the first one up. After letting the dogs out in the yard for a minute, I leashed Rowdy at one end of the kitchen and Kimi at the other. Food is the one thing they'll fight over, food and anything that resembles it. Rawhide. Dead squirrels. Rats, too, I suspected. I hoped that none of my neighbors was putting out poison. As soon as I opened the closet door to dish out the kibble, the dogs started yelping and screaming. As I added fresh Bil Jac from the bag in the refrigerator, both dogs were lunging and plunging and bawling. The bedroom door opened. Steve emerged and remarked at the top of his lungs, "Still starving them, huh?"

After breakfast, he checked what I was relieved to hear him pronounce a nicely healing wound on one of Rowdy's front paws. See? Steve really does make normal house calls. Then, without kissing me good-bye, he left for his clinic, and when I'd tidied up, taken a shower, and walked the dogs, I called the police. I call the police all the time, not because I'm one of those nuts who are always hearing imaginary burglars, but because my next-door neighbor and friend, Kevin Dennehy, is a Cambridge police lieutenant. Sometimes I need to reach him at work.

Even at home, Kevin refuses to answer the phone with a cordial hello. Instead, he barks out his last name as if he were responding to a military roll call that grated on his nerves: "Dennehy!"

"Kevin, it's Holly," I said.

He softened. "Hey, how ya doing?"

"Fine. Listen, could I ask you a favor? I'm writing a story about a guy who was murdered in Cambridge eighteen years ago."

"Girl reporter. You get sick of dogs?"

"Never. When the guy's body was found, he was in his office, and his dog was tied to his desk. It was supposed to look like suicide, but the dog gave it away. When the guy was alone there, the dog was always loose. His business partner murdered him for some insurance money. The partner died in a car accident before your boys could arrest him. Officially," I added, "I suppose it's still unsolved."

Kevin lapsed into a mock-Irish accent. "Eighteen years ago, I was but a slip of a lad meself."

"Yes, Kevin, but miracle of miracles, records were presumably kept even before you joined the force."

"Of sorts," he conceded.

I gave Kevin names—John Winter Andrews, Shaun McGrath—and the date of Jack's murder.

"Relative of yours?" he asked.

"Not that I know of," I answered.

After that, I made a trip to the main branch of the Cambridge Public Library and returned home with a pile of photocopies and a stack of scholarly books that had nothing whatsoever to do with dogs. After dumping the Xeroxes and the tomes on the kitchen table, I made a pot of coffee and spent a few minutes savoring the sense that after all these years in Cambridge, I finally fit in. Until now, while other Cantabrigian writers were spinning dizzying theories about the causes of social revolutions, interpreting statistical factors related to contextually based aspects of psycholinguistic variation, and revealing latent feminist themes in the rediscovered works of nineteenth-century women novelists, I'd been scribbling about flea infestations and explaining, for the millionth time, how to get your dog to come when called. (Short answer: Use food.) Ah, but now? Fledgling Cambridge intellectual that I was, I preened with the pride of the newly hatched. Elizabeth Coleman: *New England Captives Carried to Canada*. June Namias: *White Captives*. John Putnam Demos: *The Unredeemed Captive*. And *A Week on the Concord and Merrimack Rivers!* Henry David Thoreau! Dog writer no more, I settled down to transform myself into an esteemed authority on Hannah Duston.

Disillusionment set in as soon as I opened the Coleman volume to the section about Haverhill. Indian attacks, it seemed, were part of what she called Philip's War. Wasn't it King Philip's? But I didn't even know who Philip (king or no king) was, who'd fought his war, or what it had been about. Beginning the section about Hannah Duston, I was pleased to discover the name of the boy-captive who'd assisted her: Samuel Lenorson. He'd been snatched two years earlier from his father's farm near what is now Worcester. Two years! No wonder he'd been able to converse with his captors! The next sentence bothered me. After Hannah and Mary Neff were taken prisoner, in Haverhill, the two women supposedly traveled for a hundred and fifty miles before

reaching the island where Hannah carried out her famous deed. Hold it! From Haverhill, Massachusetts, to
Concord, New Hampshire? Eighty miles? Unless by a
very circuitous route? Furthermore, according to Coleman, the expert, although Hannah and Mary were told
otherwise, running the gauntlet was a form of torture
reserved for men; there was no evidence that women
had ever been subjected to it.

Then came the killer, so to speak: Until now, I'd
imagined Hannah's captors as tall, strong men. As it
turned out, of the twelve Indians, two escaped. One was
a woman, who was badly wounded. The other was a boy
Hannah and her companions had meant to spare. Of
the ten remaining "savages," only four were adults.
Hannah Duston had killed and scalped six children.

And that's not my idea of heroism.

The more I read, the worse it got. The band of twelve
people was a family consisting of two men, three
women, and seven children. The group had presumably
been headed for a large settlement near Montreal. Roman Catholic converts, the Indians prayed three times a
day. In between murdering infants and taking prisoners, I guess. I learned the name of the six-day-old baby:
Martha Duston. Taking captives did at least turn out to
be a practical, comprehensible activity: Indians held
their captives for ransom. If Hannah had stuck it out,
she'd probably have been exchanged either for guns or
for French prisoners held by the English. The other
thing Indians did with captives was adopt them into
their families. The boy, Samuel Lenorson? Had the Indian family felt him to be one of their own?

The scalping, I gathered, was not part of Hannah
Duston's original plan. Rather, it was a grisly after-
thought with a mercenary motive. It's midnight. The
Indians are asleep in the tent that everyone shares. The

Haverhill monument and some old engravings showed everyone in the cold outdoors, with the wigwam in the background. In New Hampshire in March? I think not. So, inside the crowded wigwam, Hannah, Mary, and Samuel, armed with stolen hatchets, strike as one. The attack begins, I believe, with the men. Hannah certainly assigns herself one. Mary or the boy, Samuel, kills the other. (Samuel's age? I did not yet know.) Simultaneously, someone crushes the head of one of the sleeping women. Another Indian woman is wounded, but escapes, as does the boy, who would have been spared. Who kills the third woman? The remaining children? According to the books, Hannah is the leader.

I can imagine the blood. I once saw my father's ax slip as he was chopping wood. The blade he was slamming into a log sliced through his boot. I'd never heard him scream like that before. I'd never have believed that my father would cry for help. And his ax dug only into his foot. And only once. But the gash was deep and ugly. The wound bled and bled. Miraculously, he didn't lose even a toe. Miraculously, one Indian boy survived, as did one wounded woman.

Their slaughter ended, Hannah Duston, Mary Neff, and Samuel Lenorson set off in a canoe. But they turn back. There actually had been rewards for Indians, not dead or alive, either. Just dead. Proof had been required. Scalping was primarily an English practice. The rewards have been canceled. Maybe Hannah doesn't know that. It is she who returns, she who wields the scalping knife. Soon after she reaches Haverhill, she and her husband take the scalps to Boston to petition for "publick Bounty." It is granted. On behalf of his wife, Thomas Duston receives twenty-five pounds. The same amount is divided between Hannah's companions in captivity "as a reward for their service in slaying divers of those barbarous salvages." Question: What did Thomas Duston do to deserve the money? Answer: Possess a Y chromosome.

In the midafternoon, I set aside my scholarly research on a colonial heroine to work on an article for a women's magazine about how to get your dog to come when called. Make yourself a good target, I advised. Open your arms to your dog. Your voice is important: Make it welcome your dog. And when your dog runs to you, don't grab him, don't run at him, don't invite opposition! Back up! Help him learn to move to the one who loves him. And when he gets there? Feed him. The way to a dog's heart is through freeze-dried liver.

I'm a convert to positive training, you see. I used to give a lot of corrections. That's a nice way of saying that I used to inflict pain. I now use gentle methods. I get results. But I am a captive only of dogs. I am a prisoner of love. My civilized advice had nothing to do with Hannah Duston.

Six

Two purported suicide notes lay on Jack Andrews's desk the night his body was found. One, handwritten in what reminded me of my own illegible scrawl, read as follows:

> I have slowly and reluctantly been driven to conclude that it takes more than the absence of faults to make a winner. Consequently, I am determined no longer to pursue what is obviously a lost cause. Your disappointment is my only regret.
>
> Love,
> Jack

The second note had been typed on what I guessed was an IBM Selectric. Like the first, it had no salutation.

> It is unfortunate that society judges some weaknesses more harshly than it does others. Far from desiring to create an embarrassing public

furor, I am eager that what must now transpire do so as privately as possible.

With regret,
John W. Andrews

Above the typed name was a scribble that I deciphered as "Jack."

I didn't know what to make of the second note and was unwilling to share with Kevin Dennehy what even I recognized as an eccentric interpretation of the first. I'll admit to you, though, that from my admittedly dog-obsessed perspective, it seemed to convey the decision to quit trying to finish a championship on a dog that no judge had looked at twice.

Kevin didn't bring me the original notes, of course. What lay on my kitchen table at five o'clock on Friday afternoon were photocopies. Kevin had just finished eating a lobster salad sandwich made from yesterday's leftovers. To try to brighten what had been shaping up as a gloomy Thanksgiving, Steve and I had decided on lobster in lieu of turkey. He bought double portions for each of us: four lobsters. When we got them out of the bag, I noticed that two were dead. If you, like Steve, happen to be from Minneapolis, I should inform you that the regional specialty here is boiled *live* lobster, okay? Not boiled dead lobster. And a veterinarian, of all people, should be able to see the difference. Unfortunately, I said so. We ended up overcooking all four lobsters. Steve pretended that his tasted fine. I accused him of lying. Mine, I insisted, was tough and flavorless. While we were arguing, Kimi filched one of the two remaining lobsters and dashed into my bedroom to devour her catch of the day in the long, narrow, inaccessible recess under the headboard of my platform bed. Naturally, I took it for granted that while I was luring

Kimi from her den, Steve would have the sense to re-
strain Rowdy. But just as I'd almost wrested Kimi's prey
from her jaws, Rowdy zoomed into the room, and still in
possession of the lobster, Kimi zipped back under the
bed. By the time I'd locked Rowdy in the guest room,
once again enticed Kimi out of her hidey-hole, and successfully traded a half stick of butter for the lobster, my
Thanksgiving dinner was cold, and Steve had finished
eating. We exchanged words about obedience training,
malamutes, and food. Then the inevitable happened.
The phone rang. One of Steve's clients was on his way to
the clinic with a beagle who'd been allowed to eat two
turkey legs, splintery bones and all, and was suffering
from what might turn out to be a perforated intestine. I
hadn't seen Steve since.

So Kevin had enjoyed the salad I'd made from the
fourth lobster and was now drinking Bud out of the can.
I'd drafted my *Dog's Life* column on Wednesday. Today,
in an effort to finish it and get it in the mail, as I'd done
an hour earlier, I'd consumed so much coffee that my
system was suffering from what may have been genuine
caffeine poisoning. Now I was drinking milk. Although
Kevin had finished eating, Rowdy and Kimi, who had
studied his habits, were still stationed eagerly at his
elbows. The dogs are wolf gray and white, with almond-
shaped brown eyes and beautiful stand-off coats. Kimi
has the dark facial markings that constitute what's called
a "full mask." Rowdy has an "open face," meaning that
it's white and very definitely not meaning that it in any
way resembles a Scandinavian sandwich. Kevin's hair is
red. His eyes are blue. His face, like Rowdy's, is white,
but covered with freckles, and his tongue wasn't hanging out of his mouth. Rowdy is a bit over the twenty-five
inches at the withers and eighty-five pounds that the
American Kennel Club standard calls for—let me just

report flatly that he's gorgeous—and Kimi is almost precisely twenty-three inches and seventy-five pounds. Kevin, in contrast, is far beefier than what's probably called for in the official standard of the Cambridge Police Department. For as long as I'd known him, he'd dealt with the stress of being a cop by near-daily long-distance running, but instead of becoming gazellelike, he increasingly reminded me of some impossible cross between a gorilla and a mastiff.

"Kevin, do not even think about giving them beer," I warned. "And do not tell me that you haven't been doing it, because the other day when Steve opened a can of beer, they both came flying, and Rowdy opened his mouth and practically begged to guzzle."

"Hey, hey," Kevin said to Rowdy, "didn't the three of us swear it was going to be our little secret?"

"Steve did not give them any," I said emphatically. "He knows better. So do you." Gesturing to the photocopied notes, I asked, "Any idea what kind of paper these were written on?"

"Yeah. The one about the faults, 'Love, Jack,' was on plain white paper. Torn across the top. The other was on business letterhead. Same paper the company used. Also with the top torn off. Typed on the machine in his office. That one'd been folded, to go in an envelope. The other one hadn't. The writing's his. No question."

"Neither one had been crumpled up?"

"Nope. He didn't do that. Just threw things in the trash. Didn't ball them up first."

"He didn't have a secretary?"

"Yeah, but he typed his letters himself."

"So anyone at the press could've kept going through his wastebasket for a letter that could pass as a suicide note."

"And the guy wrote a lot of letters, most of them telling people he wasn't going to publish their books."

"Most publishers just use a form letter. He must have been a nice guy if he bothered to write personal rejections. These aren't rejection letters, though. I guess the first one could be about a book he hoped would be a bestseller that didn't make it and that he wasn't going to promote anymore. But I don't think so. Damned Yankee Press doesn't exactly do bestsellers. Maybe he really did think about suicide. Hey, Kevin, Shaun McGrath was brought in to computerize the business. How come Jack was still using a typewriter?"

"Computers cost big bucks in those days. Or maybe he liked to type. I wasn't there."

"So tell me about this poison." I repeated the words Kevin had said earlier. "Sodium fluoroacetate."

"Colorless, odorless, tasteless."

"I've never heard of it."

"Banned for years. Licensed exterminators used to be able to get it. Your friend Mr. Andrews had an uncle in the pest-control business."

"In Haverhill?"

"Yeah. How'd you—?"

"That's where he grew up," I said. "You'd think the uncle would've just come and poisoned the rats himself."

Kevin tapped a sausagelike finger against his mammoth head. "Early stages of Alzheimer's. He'd quit the business. He just happened to have this stuff back on a shelf somewhere."

"I hope that no one around here gets any stupid ideas like that."

"You seen any of them around here yet?" Kevin didn't say "rats."

Neither did I. "No. Thank God."

"Saw one last night. Big as Rowdy's head." Kevin sounded as proud and happy as if he'd spotted a purple gallinule among the house sparrows at his mother's feeder.

"It wasn't," I countered. "The *Globe* says that they're sewer rats and that they practically never get bigger than a pound and a half."

"Five pounds if it weighed an ounce. Maybe ten. Big sucker." He grinned. Civic pride certainly takes some peculiar forms.

"Where?"

"Corner of Appleton and Huron. Ran under a car parked right there."

My house is at the corner of Appleton and Concord. Kevin's is on Appleton, right next to mine. Huron is the next major cross street.

"Dear God," I said.

"Don't hurt them, and they won't hurt you," Kevin proclaimed.

"Kevin, please!"

"You can catch a lot worse from a raccoon."

Rabies or no rabies, raccoons are cute. But rats? And somehow the knowledge that ours were mere *sewer* rats (as opposed to *what?*) was no comfort.

"So tell me exactly why Shaun McGrath killed Jack," I said.

"No proof he did. Ever heard of the presumption of innocence?"

"The people I talked to said that everyone knew Mc-Grath did it. His family. His friends. They said the police knew. And apparently there's a book with a chapter about Jack's murder, and it says that Shaun McGrath killed him. I just haven't been able to track it down yet."

Kevin shrugged.

"So, Kevin, *if* Shaun McGrath did it, what went on? I

heard it was for insurance money—that Shaun was the beneficiary on a policy for Jack's life."

"Thirty thousand dollars," Kevin said.

"So that was true."

"They tell you it was vice versa?"

"What was?"

"Two policies. These guys were business partners. Bought all this computer stuff. Took out policies on each other. Guy at the station who knows about this stuff says it's common practice."

"I didn't know that," I said.

"Yeah, well, strictly between us, neither did the asshole, pardon my French, who ran this investigation."

"Was that all there was to it? The insurance money—was that the only motive?"

"Naw, there were personal disputes. About business, but the thing turned personal. Jack was the good guy. Nice to everyone who worked there. Friendly. Gave everyone time off. Let 'em bring their kids to work. Brought his own. Brought his dog. Casual with the money. Transferred funds between the business account and his own, back and forth. Easygoing kind of a guy. Harvard grad: not safe out alone. McGrath was the bad guy. Wanted the business run like a business. Tight-assed nerd. Obvious suspect."

"But McGrath's death really was an accident?"

"No question. Happened right on Memorial Drive."

"I know. He swerved to avoid something and ran his car into a tree."

"Convertible. Dead on impact. They tell you what he swerved to avoid?" Kevin's tone was infinitely smug.

"No," I admitted.

"Siberian husky," Kevin informed me. "Ran into a tree so's he wouldn't hit a loose dog."

Seven

Just west of Boston proper, downtown, sprawls Allston-Brighton, which is actually two separate sections of the city, Allston and Brighton. No one except the U.S. Postal Service knows where one ends and the other begins, and it won't tell. Brighton Avenue is evidently an urban no-man's-land claimed neither by Allston nor by Brighton, nor by the City of Boston, or so I assume. What I know for sure is that no one assumes responsibility for filling the potholes. Even at twenty miles an hour, my old Bronco jounced and rattled so violently that the empty metal dog crates in the back were compelled to take up the cries of the shocks and springs, and I almost wished I'd brought Rowdy and Kimi along for ballast. For obvious reasons, auto body shops thrive in the area, but there are also lots of Irish bars, student nightspots, Vietnamese restaurants, Asian shops, and extraordinary Russian grocery stores where you can buy big glass bottles of sour cherries, whole dried fish in every size from minnow to the-one-that-got-away, and plastic containers of a sweet-cream version of sour cream so scrumptious that I wish I knew its name, but I don't, because my Russian vocabulary consists of three words—sputnik, babushka, and borzoi—and the grocers don't speak English.

Bronwyn Andrews's piano-moving business was located at the end of an alley off Brighton Avenue that must have been wide enough to allow the two big black moving vans parked outside to clear with maybe an inch to spare on each side. On the sides of the vans and on a black panel truck, gigantic gold letters spelled out:

MUSIC HAUL
HARMONIOUS PIANO TRANSPORT
KEYED TO YOUR RANGE

When I'd phoned Claudia to ask whether someone else in the family might have a picture of Jack's dog, Skip, Claudia hadn't mentioned the son, Gareth (whose name had appeared in his father's obituary), but had conceded that her daughter, Bronwyn, might have a photo. She'd given me Bronwyn's phone number. When I called to explain my quest, Bronwyn sounded gruff—her voice was hoarse—but she agreed to tell me about the dog and promised me a photo of him. Actually, I asked for a picture of Skip. She sounded offended. "You've got it wrong," she told me abruptly. "It was Chip, not Skip. Chipper. And he was, too."

Now, on Saturday morning, as I parked next to the black panel truck and opened the car door, loud barking emanated from behind a shiny black door set in the wall of a brick warehouse. Mounted next to the door was a glossy black sign with gold letters:

MUSIC HAUL
BRAT ANDREWS, PROP.

I knocked. The dog fell silent. The door opened, and there stood before me the most extraordinarily muscular woman I have ever seen. It occurred to me that Music Haul might have no employees whatsoever; the proprietor looked capable of bench-pressing a concert grand all on her own. She wore her straight black hair in a crew cut and was dressed entirely in black: a Music Haul T-shirt, jeans, and running shoes. Her eyes were a startling shade of intense violet-blue. So were the bold tattoos on her immense biceps. The tattoo on her left upper arm depicted a leaping Rottweiler dog. On the right was a close-up portrait of the dog's face. The model for both, a handsome male, posed like a sphinx in a down-stay about a yard in back of her on the floor of a cluttered office.

"Winter?" she demanded.

I nodded.

"Brat," she stated flatly. She did not smile. Now I understood why her voice was hoarse: from struggling to lower its natural high pitch. "Come in." She nodded to the dog. "Okay," she told him softly. "Good boy, Johann." She didn't bother to say that the dog wouldn't hurt me.

The unfriendliness of the reception compelled me to show off. I started with the dog's name, Johann. I'd have bet a thousand dollars on what it stood for. I'd have won. "J. S. Bark," I said.

Brat's nod was almost imperceptible.

"I have dogs, too." I smiled.

She didn't. She didn't offer me a seat, either. Johann came up and sniffed the pockets of my jeans. "Good boy," I told him. Ordinarily, I'd have asked permission to give him a treat, but I thought his owner wouldn't like it. "When you taught him to down," I informed Brat, "you taught a moving down. You didn't teach him to stop or sit first." I knew I was right. If you teach a dog to lie down by having him stop or sit and then lower himself, you don't get that haunches-up sphinx look. Rather, you get a slow drop into what the dog thinks is a boring, static position. Although she'd addressed Johann in English, I blandly asked, *"Schutzhund?"* It's a German system of dog training that consists of obedience, tracking, and protection work. It used to have a bad rep in the United States among AKC obedience people like me. We thought it was authoritarian. In truth, we were bigoted: What we really thought was that it was fascist dog training. Then we discovered—paws across the water—that while we, the good guys, had been hurting our dogs with choke chains and pinch collars, a *Schutzhund* trainer named Gottfried Dildei had been using fun and food. *Schutzhund* means "protection dog," and the "bite work," as it's called, training in aggression, still puts me off, but I've had to wonder who'd really been the fascist trainers?

A lot of people know about *Schutzhund*. Brat still wasn't impressed. I'd begun to make an impact, though. She backed up, took a seat in a battered wooden chair in front of a littered rolltop desk, and silently pointed a finger at an old green-upholstered armchair about three yards from the desk. I lowered myself obediently into the chair. Johann nuzzled my hands. I stroked his head.

"Beautiful dog," I said. Then I really, really showed off. "Sally Brand did a good job." I'd recognized Sally Brand's work the second I'd seen those tattoos on Brat's arms. Sally does genuine portraits. She has a great eye for a likeness. A great needle, too.

Brat finally cracked. For the first time, she looked like

the little girl in the old photograph, the child who'd craned her neck to return her father's grin.

"I wrote an article about Sally Brand once," I explained. "The one I'm doing about your father is mostly about his dog."

"Daddy wouldn't have minded that," Brat said. "Chip went everywhere with Daddy. Chip adored him. They adored each other." Her own Johann was at her side now. His worshipful eyes studied her face. Her hand rested on his powerful neck.

"I'm sorry I got Chip's name wrong."

"That was Claudia. She probably forgot it. She hated him. My parents fought about Chip all the time. Him and everything else. Or as Claudia always said, 'We don't have fights! We *discuss* things.' " The abrupt shift from gruff silence to intimate family matters made me feel slightly disoriented. Before I could ask an innocuous question about Chip, Brat leaned forward and confided, "Money was the other thing. Daddy was very generous. He was the original soft touch. I remember one time, someone came to the door asking for a donation to something, Greenpeace, some clean-water group, something like that, and Daddy wrote a check for a hundred dollars. And Claudia sat Gareth and me down and said that if we couldn't go back to school in the fall, it'd be all Daddy's fault. Gareth started crying and screaming. He took Claudia's side. He always did. It was a real scene."

"You both went to Avon Hill?" It's one of the most prestigious private schools in Cambridge. My cousin Leah once worked at the Avon Hill Summer Program. She taught a course in conversational Latin. That about sums up Avon Hill. I hastened to tell Brat that I'd read her father's obituary and that Avon Hill had been mentioned.

"Yes. We both went there. I didn't fit in too well. It

wasn't big on sports. But the music program was really good. That's why my father wanted us there. It was just Claudia who was always threatening that we'd have to go to public school. Her other favorite theme was that the gas and electricity would be cut off, and we'd have to sit in the dark eating cold sandwiches."

"You lived in Cambridge?"

"Yes. Not where Claudia does now, not on Francis Avenue. We had a house in North Cambridge, right off Mass. Ave. We lived on the first floor. A humble abode, but our own. Or the bank's. But it was okay. The yard was fenced. Chip was one of those goldens that go crazy for tennis balls. We had an old hammock out there, and I used to lie in the hammock and throw his ball for him. He loved water. You'd be in the shower, and he'd be trying to jump in with you. Claudia went wild over that one. One time in the summer, there was a heat wave, and we didn't have air-conditioning, and Daddy and I bought a wading pool. And when Chip ever discovered that! He was a really fun dog. High energy. He jumped on people. Daddy never trained him, and at the time, I didn't know how."

"Brat, when did your father get Chip?"

"Four years before he died." Her face looked pained. Her voice shifted to its little-girl pitch. "Four years before Daddy died."

"Your mother told me that your father's murder had been written up in a book." When I'd spoken to Claudia about a photo and been given Brat's number, I'd asked for the title of the book. Claudia had said she couldn't remember. I told Brat so.

"Bullshit. She has about a hundred copies of it. It's called *Mass. Mayhem.*"

"Do you happen to own it?"

She shook her head. "I read it when it first came out. I threw it away. It was a piece of trash."

"Do you remember the author?"

"Randall Carey."

"When was it published?"

"Ten years ago. Give or take."

"Brat," I asked tentatively, "did you know Shaun Mc-Grath?"

Her original immobility returned. Her eyes narrowed. Her jaw clenched.

"I shouldn't have asked," I said.

"No, it's okay. He was a little shit. Everyone hated him. Even Claudia had the sense to hate him. Gareth really hated him. We used to go over to Daddy's office. We'd fool around with the Xerox machine. We used the typewriters. Gareth would type his homework. Daddy would've let us use the computers, but Shaun didn't want us near them. We weren't babies! Gareth was sixteen when Daddy died. I was eleven. We wouldn't have hurt them. Shaun was just being a bastard about it, as usual. Daddy was the only one who got taken in by Shaun. Daddy was a soft touch about everything. Everyone liked him. He liked everyone."

Brat turned toward her desk, raised a tattooed body-builder arm, extracted two photographs from one of the overstuffed pigeonholes, and handed the pictures to me. One was the studio portrait of the young Jack Andrews that Claudia had given me. "College graduation?" I asked.

"Yeah. But it looks like Daddy. It's how I remember him."

The other, also a professional photograph, was a head study of a golden retriever.

"Brat, did your father show Chip?"

She looked pleased. "No, but he was a good-looking dog, wasn't he? Good bone. Nice head."

"Do you know where he came from?" I could tell at a glance that the dog wasn't from our lines—my mother's lines—but I was equally certain that he was from another show breeder's. "Do you know his registered name?" Little details—the dog's registered name, his breeder—would please the readers of *Dog's Life*.

"No idea."

"Would Claudia have his papers?"

"Not a chance. If she'd come across Chip's papers, she'd have thrown them out."

"Your mother told me that she found Chip a good home. I wonder if his papers might've gone with him."

To my amazement, Brat's violet-blue eyes filled with tears. She reached out for Johann and let him lick her muscular hands. I waited. Eventually, she said, "I don't know what Claudia told you, but let me tell you something. The night she found Daddy, the night he died, she didn't even bring Chip home. You know who she sent him home with? Shaun McGrath! She sent Chip home with Shaun McGrath. After the morning of the day Daddy died, I never saw Chipper again."

Eight

Returning from my visit to Brat Andrews, I took advantage of a second burst of Indian summer—am I allowed?—to tidy my yard, rake leaves, and work on my woodpile. If the stripped, skeletal branches of the trees and the blackened mounds of frost-killed impatiens hadn't given away the late-November date, the day could have passed for a warm October 1. If you know Cambridge, you've probably noticed my house, which is the barn-red one at 256 Concord Avenue, almost on the corner of Appleton.

What draws attention to my house is the little "spite building," as it's known, that occupies the actual corner of Concord and Appleton, and fences in one side of my yard. Although the spite building apparently memorializes the bitterness of some long-ago property dispute, the improbability of the long, narrow one-story structure adds charm and whimsy suitable to its recent reincarnation as a tiny toy shop. Vines grow thickly up the brick wall on my side of the spite building, and I keep my house and my wooden fences freshly painted. I clean up after the dogs every day, regularly fill in the holes left by Kimi's bouts of excavation, routinely prune the lilacs and roses, and apply gypsum in a doomed effort to undo the damage caused by dog urine.

This year, I added a park bench. It's been a big hit with the dogs. Consequently, I have to hose it down all the time, and it's already showing rust spots. The bird feeder was a disaster, at least from my point of view. Rowdy and Kimi saw it as a device to lure prey. Malamutes, I hereby testify, can catch songbirds on the wing. On the last day of the bird feeder's residence in my yard, Kimi turned out to have caught what I think had once been a house sparrow. She'd swallowed it whole. Enough said. I gave the feeder to Mrs. Dennehy. Even without it, however, the yard is on its way to becoming a little urban Eden.

A New Yorker by birth, Rita was seated on the perfectly clean park bench leafing through the *Times* and listening to me describe Brat Andrews. Rita wore a wool skirt, a good sweater, and leather pumps. I was on my hands and knees uprooting dead annuals. I had on torn jeans, a dirt-smeared sweatshirt, and a pair of the heavy leather boots with reinforced toes that I wear when I split wood.

"In most cases," Rita pronounced, "that particular defense against loss doesn't take quite such an extreme form. It does happen, though. Now and then, you hear of a man whose wife dies, and all of a sudden, he appears in public wearing a piece of her clothing, with no apparent awareness of the incongruity. It's a testimony to love, really. It's the best way he can find to keep her alive."

"Well, besides trying to turn herself into a man," I

said, shaking the dirt off nasturtium roots, "what Brat's doing is keeping herself Daddy's little girl. When she refers to Jack, that's what she calls him: Daddy. And she's really got it in for her mother. She never calls her anything but Claudia, and she spits the name out, too. Daddy was perfect. Everything bad was Claudia's fault."

"Polarized," Rita commented. "Really, it all sounds like an effort to preserve the moment just before this traumatic loss. What a shame that she never had a chance to work herself free of this extreme idealization of the father! Every child deserves the opportunity for disenchantment. Speaking of idealized figures, how is Hannah coming along?"

"Hannah! Well, damn, it's—"

"No, don't tell me! She owned a darling little lapdog, and—"

"No, she did not. That's why I picked her to begin with. The New England colonists had dogs—some of them did—but not as real pets. They were superstitious about dogs. They thought they were creatures of Satan. *God* spelled backward."

"Is that true?"

"Yes. I mean, I should've known there'd turn out to be something radically wrong with her! Rita, those so-called Indians she killed? Six of them were children. Hannah Duston murdered six children. I am really disgusted."

Folding up the *Times* and rising, Rita said, "Well, if you set out to do research, Holly, you've got to be prepared to suspend judgment."

"Not," I insisted, "if your previous research has consisted almost exclusively of documenting the perfection of dogs."

As Rita departed, my phone rang, and I dashed inside. I was hoping for a call from a professional portrait photographer named Violet Wish, who had long ago abandoned a successful career immortalizing children. She got fed up with mothers and switched to show dogs instead. With dogs, Violet claimed, she got very few complaints that there was something wrong with the mouth. When I'd dialed Violet's number, I'd heard only the recording: "Violet Wish Studio! Dogs only! *No,* repeat, *no* children! Leave a message!" Before the beep sounded, a pack of little dogs sang out a cheerful chorus of yaps. Violet has papillons. I'd left word for her to call, but on a Saturday afternoon, she and the dogs were probably at a show. There was one in Fitchburg, a conformation show with no obedience. I hadn't entered. Kimi wasn't the judge's type. Rowdy wasn't, either, and in any case, he was still lame from his pad cut.

In fact, the caller was a woman who wanted information about adopting a malamute. Alaskan Malamute Rescue is my unpaid job. I help to find adopters for homeless dogs. This woman's wonderful-sounding golden retriever had died recently. After I explained that malamutes are big and powerful, shed plentifully, clown around in the obedience ring, steal food, and exhibit a pronounced wild streak, she asked whether I happened to have the number of Yankee Golden Retriever Rescue. I did. Gee, and I hadn't even mentioned songbirds.

For most of the afternoon, in between sprinting to answer the phone, I worked on the unsplit wood I'd hauled home from my father's. My part of the house, the first floor, is an updated version of Cambridge student housing, but I renovated the second- and third-floor apartments when I bought the building, and Rita and the couple on the third floor expect the outside of the house to look decent. To my prosperous urban tenants, the pile of logs dumped at the far end of the driveway would suggest the imminent arrival of a rusted, doorless refrigerator and a flock of mite-infested geese. Splitting wood, like training dogs, is a meditative activity. On most of the logs, which were already cut to fireplace length, I used a big, sharp metal wedge that I drove in with a short-handled sledgehammer. The small pieces of birch just needed to be split with an ax. From time to time, I'd stop to stack the split wood under the flight of wooden stairs that leads up to the back door. I knew almost nothing about city rats. I hoped that, unlike chipmunks, they weren't attracted to woodpiles.

At four-thirty, Violet Wish returned my call. As I'd guessed, she'd been at the show in Fitchburg. One of her papillons had finished his championship. After offering congratulations, I asked Violet whether she remembered a guy named Jack Andrews. "Eighteen years ago, maybe more. He had a golden named Chip. Chipper. You did a portrait of the dog." Violet's name stamped on the back of Chipper's photograph was the reason I'd called her. I'd been surprised. Violet had always specialized in show dogs. I'd wondered how a pet owner like Jack Andrews had known of her existence.

"Oh, yeah. I sort of remember him. You used to see him at shows with that tall girl. What was her name?"

"I have no idea. I don't remember him at all. I didn't even know he showed." Showed *dogs*, naturally. What else?

"He was a nice guy, but he kind of stayed in the background. I only knew him, really, because I did those portraits. That was a long time ago. The girl was the one who handled. She finished Chip for him." (Translation: handled the dog to his championship.) "That's when he had the portrait done. What was her name? Tall girl with short brown hair. If you want to know about Jack, she's the one you ought to ask."

"Do you know how I'd get hold of her?"

"I haven't seen her for ages. Geez, Holly, it might even *be* eighteen years. Maybe more."

When we hung up, I made myself a cup of coffee and took it, together with Violet's portrait of Chip and Jack's graduation picture, out to the fenced side yard, where the dogs had been safely confined while I split wood. My goldens would've kept me company as I worked. When Vinnie was on a down-stay, nothing but the sound of my voice would persuade her to budge. Rowdy and Kimi might have held their stays, too. They might also have torn off after a squirrel, rounded the corner of Appleton, and ended up in the traffic on Concord Avenue. As obedience dogs, malamutes have many strengths: They're highly motivated, especially by food. They learn quickly. They have a long attention span. They work hard. They're lively and fun. In fact, the only thing wrong with them as obedience dogs is that they're, well . . . disobedient. They are, however, incredibly intelligent. I was hoping to absorb some of Rowdy and Kimi's brain power by osmosis. But if they had any brilliant insights about Jack Andrews and Chip, they kept their thoughts to themselves. When I went back inside, the dogs followed me.

"Not quite yet," I said, meaning dinnertime. Then, armed with the knowledge that Chip had been a show dog, I started to tap my extensive network for information about Jack Winter Andrews. To my annoyance, an infuriating number of people, including my father, had only vague memories of Jack. He'd owned two or three dogs, they thought. Yes, all goldens. The person I should be talking to, I was told over and over, was that tall girl. She dropped out of dogs a long time ago. What was her name? Tracy something, I finally learned. No one came up with a last name. Jack's family hadn't

known about his dogs, a few people told me. No one—
no one in dogs—was supposed to call him. His family
had thought Chip was just a pet.

The handwritten note found on Jack's desk? *It takes
more than the absence of faults to make a winner.* I hadn't
read an idiosyncratic meaning into that sentence after
all; Jack Andrews hadn't been writing about himself—
he'd really been writing about a dog.

Jack Andrews, I concluded, had led a double life. His
family had known nothing about his existence in the
world of dog shows and show dogs, which is to say, in
my own world. John *Winter* Andrews had had *golden retrievers.* The life he had kept secret felt weirdly like my
own.

Nine

On Sunday afternoon, Steve and I and our four dogs piled into his van for what proved to be a dismal trip to the island in the Merrimack where Hannah Duston had been held captive three centuries ago. Saturday's blue sky had turned ashen, and the temperature had dropped thirty degrees. The heavy rain that slicked the highway seeped into the interior of the van to reawaken the odor of every dog Steve had ever transported in it. By the time we reached Concord, New Hampshire, we'd had to stop twice to clean up after Lady, Steve's pointer, who sometimes gets carsick.

As the miles and minutes passed, my relationship with Steve smelled more and more like a sick, wet dog. Neither of us said anything about my father, his mother, Thanksgiving, or his impending post-Thanksgiving trip home to Minneapolis.

"If you'd fed her gingersnaps the way I told you," I said, "she wouldn't have thrown up."

He didn't reply.

"You should've given her Bonine. We should've stopped in Nashua or Manchester and found a drugstore."

"If I want a consult, I'll hire a consultant." He peered at the highway and leaned forward to wipe the fogged-up windshield. "With a degree in veterinary medicine."

"As a matter of fact, I wrote an article about car sickness, and obviously, I know more about it than you do. *My* dogs aren't throwing up." Neither was India, Steve's other dog. Furthermore, I hadn't fed Rowdy and Kimi gingersnaps, dosed them with Bonine, or done anything else to prevent a malady from which neither had ever suffered. Steve nobly refrained from saying so.

"Which exit is it?" he asked.

"Next one. Seventeen. When we get off, we follow the sign for Penacook, but we go only a half mile or so. The island's actually in a town called Boscawen. The parking area's supposed to be on the left."

And it was. When we turned in, the rain was pouring down, and I wanted Steve to stop so that I could take a picture of the green historic marker from inside the van, but he kept going. "You can get one on the way back," he said. "Let's get this over with."

"I didn't make you come! You volunteered. I could have driven here by myself. In case you've forgotten, we decided it would be a chance for us to spend some time together."

Steve parked next to a path that led down a hill toward the river. Rowdy, who hates to get wet, balked at leaving his crate. Once we were all out of the van, Kimi directed an unprovoked growl at India, who looked to Steve for guidance.

"You ought to get that under control," he said to me. "There's no need for it."

"If I want a consult, I'll hire a consultant," I snapped. "Preferably an expert in animal behavior, by which I don't mean a vet." Veterinarians don't necessarily know anything about dog behavior, but Steve is as good a dog trainer as I am. In some ways he's better because he's more patient than I am. India had her U.D.—Utility Dog title—and was working on her U.D.X. The X is for excellent, and excellent is just what she is. The title Perfect Bitch obviously belonged to someone other than India. In the eyes of Steve and all four dogs, I read the message that we should have stayed home.

Fortunately, as we started down the path, the rain stopped, the sky brightened, and our foul moods began to evaporate. When I'd called the New Hampshire Historical Society for directions, I'd envisioned the scene of Hannah's massacre as a small and perhaps inaccessible island in the middle of the Merrimack, which I imagined as wide, rocky, and turbulent, bubbling with the confluent waters of the Contoocook River. To my surprise, I'd been told that there was a footbridge. I pictured a narrow, rustic suspension bridge with footing that might prove treacherous to the dogs. By now, the entire episode of Hannah's captivity had acquired such significance in my mind that it never occurred to me that anyone would have marred the site by running railroad tracks straight through the island. In all my reading, I might mention, I'd come across only one other person, a man, Leslie Fiedler, who found Hannah as consequential as I did. According to Fiedler, Hannah's story represented the characteristically American and feminist recasting of the European myth of the damsel in distress. What weakened a lot of the points he made, however, was his failure to get the facts right. According to Fiedler, the Haverhill Hannah was a stone monument of a woman in a sunbonnet who held a tomahawk in a

"delicate" hand. Bronze, no hat, a hatchet, not a tomahawk, and a hand toughened by rough work. A hand, in
fact, like mine. Furthermore, central to Fiedler's argument was the image of offended motherhood's defense
of a male child. The murdered child, however, was a
baby girl.

But back to the island, which was barely that: a few
acres separated from the riverbank by marshy water and
nowhere near the center of the confluence. The Merrimack and the Contoocook were dark, flat, and not half
the width I'd imagined. The old iron railroad bridge
didn't even have to stretch hard to link land to island. As
we followed the tracks across, Steve said, "The river
would've been higher in March."

"Yes, but not all *that* much. In a pinch, you could swim
across."

"Maybe not at that time of year. And they probably
didn't know how to swim."

"True. The river was in flood, I think. And if they'd
gotten wet, they might've frozen to death."

I hadn't known or maybe had forgotten that there was
a monument on the island. I suppose I'd harbored some
crazy expectation of crawling around in the moldy remains of a skin-covered tent or unearthing the skeleton
of one of the birch-bark canoes that Hannah had scuttled before she fled. After three hundred years, needless
to say, no trace remained. The abandoned tracks and a
dirt path took us through a wooded area of bare-limbed
maples and low evergreens to a big clearing.

In the center of the clearing, near the river, rose a
monument much taller than the one in Haverhill and
far more funereal in appearance, a massive pillar of gray
granite topped with a gray granite Hannah. She leaned
forward in a way that reminded me of a figurehead on a
ship. The bodice of her dress dipped low, and her arms

were bare. Her left hand didn't point in accusation, but rested at her hip. In it she clutched what could have been an upside-down bouquet of wilted flowers with round, flat blossoms.

Scalps.

Her right arm hung at her side. The hand had once held a hatchet. The blade remained. The handle was broken. Most of Hannah's nose was missing.

On the four sides of the pillar beneath this Hannah were rectangular slabs with rounded tops. The panels looked like tombstones. There were no pictures on them, just words. The one on the front started out in Latin and switched to English:

HEROUM GESTA
FIDES JUSTITIA
HANNAH DUSTON
MARY NEFF
SAMUEL LEONARDSON
MARCH 30, 1697
MID-NIGHT

"Something about fidelity and justice?" I said to Steve. "Heroism?"

He shrugged.

On the tombstone under Hannah's right side was carved DONORS. Beneath was a list of names. Under Hannah's left arm and the scalps was what was evidently intended as poetry. It was all in capital letters and had no punctuation.

STATUA
KNOW YE THAT WE WITH MANY PLANT IT
IN TRUST TO THE STATE WE GIVE & GRANT IT
THAT THE TIDE OF TIME MAY NEVER CANT IT
NOR MAR NOR SEVER

68   SUSAN CONANT

THAT PILGRIM HERE MAY HEED THE MOTHERS
THAT TRUTH & FAITH & ALL THE OTHERS
WITH BANNERS HIGH IN GLORIOUS COLORS
MAY STAND FOREVER

At the bottom were five more names.

" 'Glorious colors'?" I said. "It's totally gray."

"Doesn't mean a thing to me," Steve said.

But the really weird inscription appeared on the back of the pillar, and before I present it, let me comment that there's nothing like real weirdness to heal a troubled relationship, so if you, too, ever find that the harmony between you and your lover has been marred, severed, or otherwise disrupted by mothers, fathers, national holidays, car sickness, or anything else, take a visit to Boscawen, New Hampshire, make your way around to the back of Hannah's statue, and read, just as we did:

MARCH
15   1697   30
THE WAR WHOOP TOMAHAWK
FAGGOT & INFANTICIDES
WERE AT HAVERHILL
THE ASHES OF
WIGWAM-CAMP-FIRES AT NIGHT
& OF TEN OF THE TRIBE
ARE HERE

I subsequently learned that on June 17, 1874, the day this monument was unveiled, between three thousand and six thousand people attended the ceremony, which was cut short by heavy rain. The reporter for the *Concord Monitor* who described the aborted festivities complained in print that the monument was "disfigured with some doggerel and other evidence of bad taste."

Steve and I gaped. I read the inscription aloud.

"It isn't English," he said.

"But 'faggot'?"

"Bunches of sticks. Firewood. Death by fire. They burned people alive."

"Not here. But I can't think what else it could mean. 'Infanticides' means her baby, I guess. Martha, her name was. But the rest? It's amazing that she isn't missing more than her nose and the handle of her hatchet. You'd think someone would've dynamited the whole thing by now."

" 'Are here,' " Steve read. "Are they?"

"An Indian woman and child escaped. The woman survived. There's a record of it. Maybe she sent people back." I wondered aloud about the burial practices of Hannah's captors, the converts to Roman Catholicism who had prayed three times a day. In the soggy ground beneath us, perhaps, were the bones of murdered children.

Infanticides, indeed.

Ten

Monday morning was rainy and dreary. Armed with the title of the book that had a chapter about Jack's murder and, thanks to Kevin Dennehy, with the date of Shaun McGrath's death, I went to the Brookline Public Library. As I approached, I noticed near the front of the building a Civil War memorial that I'd taken for granted in the happy days of yore when my professional interests had centered exclusively on dogs. Like most other public monuments in the United States, this one depicted a male Caucasian. He wore a uniform and rode a horse. The only public statue of a dog I'd ever seen was the one of Balto in Central Park. And Balto was a male. Men of color? On a frieze in Boston, a Civil War memorial to the 54th Massachusetts Volunteers. Women? One. Hannah Duston. Twice. In Haverhill. In Boscawen. I was in a good mood to read obituaries.

Shaun McGrath's was short. He'd grown up in Arlington, which is just north of Cambridge, and his funeral mass had been celebrated at a church there. The survivors were listed as his parents, James and Shirley McGrath, six brothers and sisters, and a variety of nieces and nephews. After graduating from a local business college, McGrath worked for a computer firm and then joined Damned Yankee Press. Interestingly enough, from his high school days on, Shaun McGrath had been an avid chess player. At the time of his death, he'd been the president of a local chess club. And this was a man who'd supposedly made no backup plan in case Jack's murder failed to pass as suicide! I also located the account of McGrath's fatal accident on Memorial Drive. It was a paragraph long and said only that he'd run his car into a tree. It didn't mention Jack Andrews, the police, or the Siberian husky Shaun had died to avoid hitting. It didn't say that this man, in whose presence Chip had supposedly been tied, had taken the dog home after Jack's corpse was found.

According to the catalog, the main branch of the Brookline Public Library owned *Mass. Mayhem*. The author was, as Brat had said, one Randall Carey. The publication date was ten years earlier. The book was supposed to be available. The call number, MASS 364.15 C something, sent me to the section about true crime in the commonwealth, the same section that I'd checked on my last visit. The book was not, however, in its allotted place on the shelf. I returned to the terminal and checked the entire Metro-Boston system. Eight local libraries owned, or at least had owned, the book. It was, however, listed as missing from six of the eight, including the main branches of the Boston and Cambridge public libraries. Brookline's copy, supposedly available, was, as I'd just discovered, not on the shelf. Newton's main branch was supposed to have a reference copy, one that did not circulate.

Before I left the Brookline library, I asked a librarian about what seemed to me the odd disappearance of *Mass. Mayhem* from so many places. She was a plump, intelligent-looking woman. When I told her the call number, she smiled knowingly. "So you're one of those three sixty-four fifteen types, huh?"

Momentarily flustered, I felt like explaining that I was actually a wholesome type whose professional interests focused on dog training and the polar regions, and whose recreational reading consisted mainly of novels by Charles Dickens, Barbara Pym, Elinor Lipman, and the inimitable Jack London. As I turned red and began to sputter, the librarian took pity on me. Many of the library's most irreproachable patrons, she assured me— upstanding members of the community, civic leaders, socially prominent mothers, even—never checked out anything except true crime. Hearing the news, I had to wonder what kind of place Brookline really was. Were comparable suburbs all across America also populated by citizens of guileless, upright appearance and de- meanor whose true passion was true crime?

As I drove along Route 9 from Brookline Village to Newton, the image stayed with me, and I viewed the innocent-looking mock-Tudors and Victorian arks with freshly alarmed eyes. Indeed, who knows what evil lurks in the hearts of suburban men and women? No, not the Shadow. How would the Shadow know? The one who really has the scoop on our foibles is the local librarian.

As I've mentioned, the main branch of the Newton Free Library is my summer pick because of its superb air-conditioning. Its bright central atrium also made it a good choice for this gloomy late-autumn day. Just off the atrium, which housed the reference room, was a wall of books about Massachusetts, books that couldn't be checked out. But could, of course, be lost or stolen. As in

Brookline, the copy of *Mass. Mayhem* was missing. *Mass. Mayhem* didn't appear in *Books in Print;* I'd be unable to order it unless I went to a search service for out-of-print books. Again, I consulted a librarian. This one didn't rag me about reading true crime. Rather, she clucked her tongue, called up the title on her screen, and advised me that the only available copy of the book was at the main branch of the Brookline Public Library.

"That one's missing, too," I told her.

I felt relieved when she agreed that the situation really was odd.

I had more luck in finding material about Hannah Duston than I'd had in locating Randall Carey's book. Among other things, in a rather recent article in *Yankee* magazine by someone named Sybil Smith and in an old book about the history of Haverhill, I read that the statue of Hannah Duston in the center of Haverhill was believed to be the first monument in the United States erected to a woman. So much for supposed expertise. I already knew that in 1861, Haverhill had erected a hefty marble monument, not a statue, in Hannah's honor, but that because of the Civil War, its sponsors had been unable to pay for it. Repossessed, the monument was later installed as a soldiers' memorial in Barre, Massachusetts. The Boscawen statue went up in 1874, Haverhill's bronze Hannah in 1879. The *Yankee* article gave repulsive details about scalping, but pointed out that Hannah Duston must certainly have wrung the necks of chickens and helped to slaughter pigs and cows. On-the-job training. Since I was already immersed in revolting subjects, I thought about trying to find some practical volume about rodent invasions *(How to Shoot Rats in the City Without Getting Caught?)*, but my stomach turned, and I gave up and went home.

When I got there, my answering machine had a message from my cousin Leah, who reported the good news that Harvard owned *Mass. Mayhem* and the bad news that it had been checked out by a professor who'd be entitled to keep it indefinitely. There were three other messages. Two were from dog people who said that they had no recollection of a tall girl named Tracy who used to handle goldens for someone named Jack Andrews. The last was from Mrs. Dennehy, Kevin's mother, who doesn't really like me, but loves dogs and approves of what she calls my "kindness to God's creatures." She is very religious. "Holly, dear," her voice said, "I have to tell you that when I went to take out the garbage this morning, a rat went scuttling away from the trash cans! O-o-o-o-h! It gave me the willies! Watch out! They're right here on Appleton Street!" And not exactly God's creatures, I took it.

I wondered whether rats liked dank weather. In the late afternoon, when I walked the dogs, the rain had stopped, but a combination of dark clouds and evening filled the sky. Rowdy insisted on detouring around the puddles, and he and Kimi kept coming to prolonged halts to sniff city smells intensified by the dampness. Because the construction on Huron Avenue was supposed to be the source of the rats, I headed in the opposite direction, down Concord, around the observatory, back up Garden Street, and, eventually, to Donnell, which meets Concord across the street from my house. When the traffic finally let us cross, we hurried, but as I made my way down the short stretch of sidewalk next to the spite building, the dogs' ears suddenly went up, the hair on their backs rose slightly, and they hit the ends of their leads. Ahead of us, just beyond the Dennehys' house, a small animal scuttled across the sidewalk and slithered under a parked car. Although I'd been reading and hearing and talking and thinking about the invasion for weeks, it took me a second to realize exactly what the small animal was. Once I knew, it didn't seem so small anymore. Rowdy and Kimi had known right away. The dogs had smelled a rat.

Eleven

Ah, Cambridge! I love you! Across the street from Emma's Pizza—The New Emma's Pizza: new owners, but the same fabulous crust and peerless sauce—is what has officially been rechristened the Bryn Mawr Book Store, but for at least the next decade will still be known throughout Cambridge by its original name, the Bryn Mawr Book Sale. Although "Sale" suggests a one-day fund-raiser, the store is a permanent used-book shop run by alums for the benefit of the college. Whenever I'm in danger of having my entire living space taken over by books, I enter the Bryn Mawr Book Sale with a couple of bags or cartons of literary discards, receive a little slip proving that I've made a tax-deductible contribution, and promptly buy the precise number of books I've just given away. I've found some great bargains on dog books there, and I always scan the works on Antarctica, which reside directly across a narrow aisle from a little notice that reads

DEATH IS NOW LOCATED ABOVE SELF-HELP

I can never decide whether the news is heartening or depressing.

So that's where I finally got a copy of the elusive *Mass. Mayhem:* at the Bryn Mawr Book Sale. If you're a book on the lam, avoid Cambridge. Around here, you can run, but you can't hide for long.

By the time I got my hands on it Tuesday morning, I'd convinced myself that its chapter on the murder of Jack Andrews held the key to the identity of his real murderer. At Marsha's bat mitzvah, of course, when I'd first heard of the murder, Claudia had told me that the book named and blamed Shaun McGrath. I didn't care what the author, Randall Carey, had pronounced in print or what Claudia Andrews-Howe or anyone else believed. Sprinting home from the Bryn Mawr Book Sale, stopping here and there to peek at the chapter, I was confident that it contained a hidden clue. With luck, it would also expose the whole story of Jack's secret life in dogs and reveal the last name of the tall girl, Tracy, who'd dropped out of dogs and whose last name no one remembered. So excited was I that when I got home, I delayed the thrilling moment of discovery by making a pot of coffee and setting out on the kitchen table a pen and the fresh yellow legal pad on which I, Holly Winter, the Nancy Drew of dogs, would inscribe the name of the real murderer.

Well, was I ever disappointed. Whoever this Randall Carey was, he'd known less than I did about Jack Andrews. It seemed to me he'd cared far less than I did, too. Maybe his middle name wasn't Winter. Maybe he hadn't grown up with golden retrievers. If Carey had ferreted out Jack's hidden life, he'd kept Jack's secret. The chapter said only that Jack's dog was a golden retriever; it didn't even give Chip's name. According to the book, Jack had had a lot of style, and Claudia none. After her father's death, Bronwyn had become increasingly masculine, the book said. The son, Gareth, was described as eccentric. For all I knew, he was. I did learn the names of some people who'd worked at Damned Yankee Press. At the time of Jack's murder, his secretary, Ursula Pappas, had been on vacation in Greece. A temp named Estelle Grant was filling in for her. The chapter referred only to rat poison in the coffee; it didn't specify sodium fluoroacetate. The only really new information was the suggestion that Shaun McGrath had forged Jack's signature on the insurance policy; Claudia had not mentioned forgery, nor had Brat or Kevin.

The themes of the chapter, to the minor extent that it had any, were betrayal and, appropriately enough, disappointment. In the author's view, Jack had betrayed his children by frittering away money needed for their private-school tuition. Claudia, who came across as lazy and feckless, had let her husband down by working in child care instead of pursuing a lucrative career. The masculine Bronwyn and the eccentric Gareth would've been a disappointment to their father, or so the author maintained. Even so, Shaun McGrath had cheated Jack of the chance to see them grow up. When Jack had founded the press, he'd duped everyone, including himself, into believing that he could run a publishing house. Discovering the sloppy way the business actually operated, Shaun McGrath had felt cheated. Even the vacationing Ursula Pappas came across as betraying Jack. If she'd stayed at work and not gone gallivanting off to the Mediterranean, the chapter implied, Shaun wouldn't have dared to poison her caffeine-addicted employer. The hint was that Jack Andrews had betrayed even himself: If the man had refrained from coffee, he'd be alive today.

I dialed Kevin's number at the station.

"Dennehy," he bellowed, as if I'd charged him with being someone else.

"Kevin, Holly. The report about Jack Andrews: Was there anything in there about Shaun McGrath's forging Jack's signature on that insurance policy?"

"Hey, hey, so we're on a first-name basis now," Kevin replied.

"As it happens, we are. Was there?"

"No," said Kevin. "Not a thing."

With a growing sense of futility, I consulted the phone book in search of a number for Shaun McGrath's parents. Boston is more Irish than Ireland. Seriously. I've heard that there are more Irish people here than in Dublin. Consequently, even in one of the suburbs, Arlington, I expected to find a few dozen J. McGraths. To my surprise, there was a listing for James and Shirley. The number got me an answering machine. I left a brief message asking to have my call returned. I hoped that the McGraths didn't assume I was dunning them about a credit card payment or trying to persuade them to have their carpets cleaned.

Then I took another look at *Mass. Mayhem*. It wasn't much of a book, but it was a hardcover, and the copy I'd bought still wore its dust jacket. On the back flap were a photograph of the author, Randall Carey, and a biographical sketch. The picture showed a bland-looking young man with a pipe in his hand. He wore a corduroy jacket. Behind him were shelves of books. The image was too small to let me read the titles. Maybe they weren't scholarly books at all. Maybe they were nothing but junky would-be potboilers like *Mass. Mayhem*. According to the bio, Dr. Randall Carey had gone to Harvard College, held a Ph.D. in history from Harvard University, and taught at Newton North High School. Around here, it's not unusual to find a Harvard Ph.D. teaching in a secondary school, including a public school. Actually, in the Square, it's not all that unusual to find a Harvard Ph.D. driving a cab. What does salary matter? Proximity is all that really counts. As these people see it, they're like electric cars that can travel only a fixed distance; if they don't keep going back to the power source all the time, they'll sputter and quit. A call to Newton North High School told me that Randall Carey no longer taught there.

I followed a hunch and checked the phone book again. Dr. Randall Carey's address wasn't far from mine. As I'd done with the McGraths, I left a message on his machine asking him to return my call. I wanted to find out where Carey had heard that Shaun McGrath had forged his partner's signature. I also wanted to hear anything Carey might have learned about Jack's murder in the ten years since he'd published his book.

By now, my work life felt divided between the people I thought of as *my* murderer, Hannah Duston, and *my* victim, Jack Andrews, and I was learning to shift rather smoothly from the distant horror of 1697 to the horror of a mere eighteen years ago. As Kevin had noticed, Hannah, Jack, and I were now on a first-name basis. Or I was with them. Whether they called me or each other anything at all was, of course, the ultimate mystery that I certainly couldn't solve.

While I waited for the McGraths or Randall Carey to return my call, I went over my notes about Hannah. Nowhere in anything I'd read was there a single indication of the particular group or tribe that had abducted her. Most accounts just called the people "Indians." An alarming number used what I read as racist obscenities: "squaws," "redskins." Cotton Mather had had lots of names for Hannah's victims: "idolaters," "persecutors," "formidable salvages." Not that I myself would have called them, say, "lovely human beings." In the raid on Haverhill, the attackers had killed twenty-seven people, including fifteen children. Hannah and Mary were two of thirteen people taken captive or, as the old accounts phrased it, "captivated by the salvages." As far as I could tell, Hannah and Mary were the only two to survive. It was common practice among Indian captors to kill the very old, the very young, the weak, and the infirm: those who wouldn't survive captivity anyway. Consequently, my wish to call these people something other than "Indians" did not stem from some romantic vision of Hannah's captors as noble savages. Rather, although I knew almost nothing about particular tribes, I did understand that all tribes weren't alike. To call all of them "Indians" made as much sense as using "European" to lump together the seventeenth-century English and French. Also, like Hannah, I had a pecuniary motive. If I wanted to sell whatever I wrote about Hannah to a magazine as well as to Rita, I'd do well to avoid a word that would bother people. The terminology of political correctness, however, did nothing to solve my problem. I could hardly write that Hannah had been "captivated by Native Americans."

So that's why I got in touch with Professor George Foley, who, in his own way, had captivated me. As he'd told me, he lived on Fayerweather Street, which, as it happens, crosses Huron Avenue conveniently near Emma's and the Bryn Mawr Book Sale. His name was in the phone book. I dialed the number. He was at home.

After polite preliminaries, I posed my question.

"Coleman doesn't say?" he asked.

"No, she doesn't. And I can't find it in anything else I've read."

"Hmm. Well, to hazard a guess, I'd say they were Abenaki. Yes, I'd say there's a ninety-five percent chance they were Abenaki."

The Abenaki were once widespread throughout what is now Maine, New Hampshire, Vermont, and Massachusetts, he told me. Few survived the epidemics of smallpox, bubonic plague, and other diseases brought by the Europeans. I'd had no idea who they were. George Foley, I realized, must have been a wonderful professor, a gifted teacher. Instead of making me feel ashamed of my ignorance, he seized on my curiosity. He also invited me to tea. He promised that on Friday at four o'clock we'd have a long talk about Hannah Duston and the Abenaki. As I hung up, I made a silent vow that Professor Foley and I would also have a chat about Jack Andrews.

Twelve

After my conversation with Professor Foley, I put on my heavy leather boots, a wool shirt, and pigskin work gloves, and went out to split and stack wood. The sky was the blue of bleached denim, the sun was a pale buttery yellow, and the air was wintery. When I'd been out there for an hour or so, the phone rang, and I dashed inside to grab it. Dr. Randall Carey's voice was even more supercilious than deep. I explained that I'd read his chapter about the murder of Jack Andrews and wondered whether he'd be willing to discuss the subject with me. According to the phone book, I said, we were practically neighbors. He lived on Walden Street, didn't he? I was at the corner of Appleton and Concord. Yes, the red house next to the spite building. Smitten as I was with Professor Foley, I imitated him: I invited Dr. Randall Carey to tea.

Dr. Randall Carey refused, and not very graciously. He was very busy. He worked at home, but he *did* work.

He did not say what he did. I worked at home, too, I announced. I was a writer. I did not inform Dr. Randall Carey that I wrote about dogs. Not that I'm ashamed of being a dog writer; on the contrary, I'm proud. It's just that around here, when I say what I do, people get this funny look on their faces. I wished I'd had credentials of some sort to present to him. Dropping Professor Foley's name would probably have worked, but it would also have felt like a betrayal of my harmless infatuation. So I fell back on the reliable skills honed by a lifetime of training dogs. I'd made the beginner's mistake of asking a question: *Come, Rover? Rover, come? Come to Mommy?* I corrected my error: "I'm taking my dogs for a walk late this afternoon," I informed Dr. Randall Carey. "I'll be passing right by your house. We'll stop in."

Life with malamutes has sharpened my sensitivity to power plays. When I encountered Dr. Randall Carey, I intended to emerge one up. Consequently, I dressed for success in a uniquely Cantabrigian manner: I wore my same old jeans, wool shirt, and heavy boots. At the highest levels of academe—Harvard, where else?—the So-and-So Professors of Such-and-Such are always getting mistaken for maintenance workers. Dr. Randall Carey would take one look and decide I was brilliant and eminent—unless he wrote me off as an unemployed lumberjack with the bad manners to go around inviting herself places she most definitely wasn't welcome.

Rowdy and Kimi were already dressed for success. Under the streetlights, their wolf gray coats gleamed. On the block between Appleton and Walden, a neighbor greeted them by name. As we waited for the traffic light at Walden, two little boys admired the dogs, who dropped to the sidewalk and rolled on their backs so the kids could scratch their furry white tummies. On the first block of Walden, we paused while I chatted with a fellow dog walker, and Rowdy and Kimi exchanged full-body sniffs with her greyhound, Gregory, a retired racing dog adopted off the track. Rowdy sometimes gets tough with other males, but never with Gregory. As Kimi checked out the gentle dog, her face wore an expression of motherly accusation: "Just where have *you* been? And what have *you* been up to?" Not much, she decided. Nothing to get alarmed about. Where Walden crosses Garden Street, Kimi snatched a discarded paper cup from the leaf mush in the gutter and paraded along showing off her trophy. Rowdy pretended to ignore her. From behind a chain-link fence, one of Rowdy's neighborhood enemies, a black cocker, yapped out a challenge. Kimi dropped the cup. Rowdy's hackles rose. "Leave it!" I told him. "That dog is none of your business." I felt guilty. As a convert to positive methods, I should have found a way to reward him for behavior I wanted.

Although Walden Street is perfectly pleasant, it isn't grand. Even so, Randall Carey's resonant Harvardian tones led me to scan the street numbers in expectation of a comparatively august residence, perhaps a majestic Victorian divided into renovated condos. To my surprise, I found the number on a three-story house with weathered brown shingles. The bare yellow bulb of a bug light illuminated a sagging porch crammed with paper grocery bags and recycling bins in which newspapers, glass, milk bottles, metal cans, and other discarded items had been carefully sorted. The thick black paint on the three mailboxes was chipped to reveal a hideous aqua. The one marked DR. RANDALL CAREY was empty. His name appeared again on a hand-printed card under one of three door bells: DR. RANDALL CAREY. I rang the bell. "Sit," I told the dogs. Correctly sizing up the porch as something other than an AKC obedience ring, they obeyed.

A door with alligatored paint opened inward. The temptation to address Carey as "Mr." almost got the best of me. Alternatively, I could've asked him to remove my appendix. But I behaved myself. "Hi!" I said. "I'm Holly Winter. Dr. Carey?"

In person and a decade after the publication of *Mass. Mayhem,* Randall Carey looked just as nondescript and academic as he had when the photo was taken. He hadn't aged much. In his hand he held what may have been the same pipe. His brown hair was longer than in the picture and cut in an English-schoolboy style reminiscent of the early Beatles. His eyes were a washed-out hazel. He wore khakis, a cream-colored turtleneck, and a tweed sports jacket with leather elbow patches. The main difference between the image on the dust jacket and the man who opened the door was that this guy looked uncomfortable. Also, he seemed vaguely familiar. In response to my greeting, he raised the pipe to his thin lips and puffed. You can always tell who's gone to Harvard and who's gone to Dale Carnegie.

"I called," I reminded him. "I have a few questions about Jack Andrews."

"Come in," he finally said.

I hesitated. "You don't have a dog, do you?" I asked. "Or a cat?"

"God, no," he replied.

"You don't mind if . . . ?" Rowdy and Kimi's tails were thumping the old boards. Their eyes were bright. They love making new friends.

"I'd prefer that they stay on the porch."

"Then maybe we'd better talk out here," I said. "It'll just take a second. Really, Dr. Carey, I just wanted to know where you heard that, on the insurance policy, Shaun McGrath had forged Jack Andrews's signature."

"Randall." He said his own name in a peculiar way, stretching out the syllables, almost as if he were making fun of himself. "Huh. The wife, I think. Claudia. Maybe someone else. Sorry, it was more than ten years ago. The details aren't fresh in my mind." Either the impeccable behavior of my dogs or the cold wind softened him. "You'd better come in, Ms. Winter."

"The dogs will behave themselves. They're trained." Smiling, I added, "And I'm the alpha leader around here." To the dogs, I said, "Okay! This way."

A common recommendation in the vast literature on how to establish yourself as your dog's alpha leader is that you, alpha, must always precede your dog. In particular, when you enter or leave a building, you go through the door first; the duly impressed Rover humbly follows. If he's as big as Rowdy and Kimi, he's humbled all right! The poor guy's tail is always getting mashed when the door shuts. Consequently, the dogs followed Randall Carey into his first-floor apartment, and I trailed after them.

The first thing I noticed once we got inside was that, even apart from the tobacco smoke, the place smelled peculiar. I never did identify the source of the odor. There was no cat, so it couldn't have been a litter box, and if there'd been a cage of gerbils or guinea pigs, Rowdy and Kimi would certainly have noticed. The dogs and I entered what had been built, I thought, as a living room, but was now a study crammed with a minimum of ten trillion books. The desk was a door that rested on trestles. On it sat a Brand X computer, a decent-looking printer, and a neat stack of manuscript. The bookshelves were brick and board. A wide archway opened to what had once been a dining room. The built-in china cabinet held books, and on the industrial metal shelves that lined the walls were books, books, and yet more books. The wooden trim around the windows and doors was chipped off-white. The walls might have been any color at all: fuchsia, geranium, aquamarine. I don't know. I saw nothing but books. In Cambridge, normal apartment decor consists of an overwhelming display of the printed word: everything from ancient volumes to textbooks to how-to manuals to paperback thrillers to whodunits with lurid covers in languages so foreign you can't guess what they are. The only unusual feature of what Randall Carey probably referred to as "my library" was a predominance of hardcovers and a corresponding scarcity of paperbacks.

"I know where I've seen you!" I burst out. "The Bryn Mawr Book Sale."

"Bryn Mawr."

"The Bryn Mawr Book Sale," I repeated.

"Bryn Mawr," he said again.

I finally caught on: Randall Carey was correcting my pronunciation. My consonants were okay, I think; it must have been the vowels that irritated him. I didn't try again. If I want language lessons, I'll pay Berlitz.

"I thought you looked familiar," he admitted. Now that we were indoors (need I say that the light was adequate for reading?), he scanned me as if I were a work of fiction he'd decided not to buy. His eyes lingered on my heavy boots.

"Down," I told the dogs. "Stay!" To Randall Carey I said, "I really shouldn't have barged in on you. Especially with big dogs."

"Huskies," he said.

Ten trillion books on the shelves and . . . !!

"Alaskan malamutes."

Standing corrected—he hadn't taken a seat and

hadn't offered me one—he remarked that the dogs seemed well-behaved.

"Thank you. They'll just stay there. And they're perfectly friendly."

Seating himself on an old leather swivel chair, he gestured toward what I thought of as an analyst's couch, a heavily padded, leather-covered chaise longue raised at one end. A potted palm dangled its fronds above the head of the couch. The source of the odor may have been the pieces of furniture rather than musty books. I remembered reading somewhere about an American tourist who'd brought home a hassock from some exotic place and discovered that it was filled with camel dung. Or possibly Dr. Randall Carey fed the plant with fish emulsion.

"Your chapter on Jack Andrews was very helpful," I lied. "I haven't had a chance to read the rest of the book yet."

Between the swivel chair and the analyst's couch sat a steamer trunk that served as a coffee table. Prominently displayed on it was a new and highly publicized translation of Dante's *Inferno*. I understand that the *Inferno* is literature, okay? I'm not a total philistine. But strictly between us, I never have trusted Dante. I mean, it's your choice, of course, but if the guy ever invited *me* home to see his etchings, I'd dream up some excuse to bolt. Dante: the blind date from hell. Cambridge disagrees. When the translation first appeared, it immediately sold out at every bookstore in the Square and popped up on coffee tables all over the city. In normal places, a coffee table book is a gorgeous edition of Audubon's *The Birds of America* or maybe a photographic study of Monet's garden, Cape Cod, or the south of France: things you'd like to see, places you'd like to go. In Cambridge, it's Dante's *Inferno*. You work it out.

"Sherry?" he offered. With an author, flattery will get you anywhere.

I don't know which kind of sherry I hate more, dry or sweet. "I'd love some," I said enthusiastically.

He rose, crossed the room, and passed through the book-filled dining room to what I assumed was the book-crammed kitchen. I noticed that he had the build of a little boy: short, with a round head, and plump in the middle. When he moved, he rocked a little from side to side. In his absence, I tiptoed to his desk and snuck a glance at what proved to be the title page of the manuscript. It read:

Dent-U-Stick Industries:
An American Corporation
by
Randall Carey, Ph.D.

I now knew how Randall Carey earned his living: He wrote corporate histories on contract. His present subject was a famous manufacturer of dental adhesive. I returned to the couch. If he found out the true subject of my usual literary endeavors, he'd probably smirk, too.

Returning with a bottle of dry sherry and two actual, if not very fancy, sherry glasses, Randall poured a drink for me and one for himself. Raising his glass, he said, with a note of self-mockery, *"Santé!"* He downed the sherry in his glass.

"Santé!" I took a sip. Yick.

"In memory of Jack Andrews," Randall Carey said.

"Yes. You knew him?"

"Met him once. Very briefly."

"Well, I'm working on a little article about his murder, and a couple of things have come up that bother me. One is this whole business of the dog being tied up."

"Dog's," he said absently.

"What?"

"Possessive with the gerund. 'Dog's.' Preferably, 'the dog's having been tied up.' "

"Well, yes," I conceded. "Anyway, it just doesn't gibe. Brat—Bronwyn, Jack's daughter—told me that on the night Jack was murdered, after his body was found, the dog went home with Shaun McGrath. And then the way Shaun McGrath died. What happened was that he ran his car into a tree to avoid hitting a loose dog. I mean, if he liked Jack's dog, Chip, well enough to take him home, and if he sacrificed his life to save a dog he didn't even know, why did Chip have to be tied up when Shaun was in the office?"

"Holly—may I?"

"Of course."

"I'm sorry not to be more helpful, but the book came out ten years ago. My publisher made a lot of promises and then never did a damned thing to promote it. The ludicrous title, by the by, was not my idea. And then they let it go out of print before it went on sale."

Randall was, I saw, attempting a joke. I attempted a chortle. I sympathized about the difficulties of being a writer.

"The book must have sold okay, though," I told him. "At least, a lot of local libraries bought it. Strangely enough, though, it's missing from all of them."

At his insistence, I gave him the details. He seemed genuinely mystified. Although I hated to tackle those vowels again, I admitted that I'd finally located the book at the Bryn Mawr Book Sale. Giving up on finding the opportunity to pour my sherry into the potted palm, I heroically drained my glass and started to thank Randall for letting me barge in. "Oh, I had one other question,"

I said. "Did you know that Shaun McGrath played chess?"

"Barely remember a thing about him," Randall confessed. "So, is this what you do? You devote yourself to true crime?"

Should it seem that I make fun of my fellow residents of Our Fair City, hear this! In ridiculing Cambridge, I am surely mocking myself. In the ever so Cantabrigian atmosphere of Dr. Randall Carey's stinky library, I let slip a word or two about my interest in Hannah Duston. Randall Carey knew exactly who she was. He was impressed. Releasing Rowdy and Kimi, praising them, feeding them bits of liver, I said not a word to Carey about *Dog's Life* magazine.

Cambridge gets to everyone.

Thirteen

"Claudia's child is in pain," confided Oscar Fisch.

Karma: In the long run, fair is fair. Sometimes in the short run. No sooner had I returned from Randall Carey's than Claudia Andrews-Howe's second husband, Oscar Fisch, phoned to insist on paying me a visit. I tried to put him off. I said I was busy. In fact, Rowdy and Kimi hadn't eaten. Neither had I. I'd missed lunch. For once, I felt like cooking myself a real meal. Besides, I'd been skipping my prayers: Hannah Duston's abductors had said theirs three times a day, yet here it was, Tuesday, and I hadn't trained my dogs since Saturday morning. Nonetheless, in our little skirmish, Oscar Fisch won. I later learned that his specialty at the Harvard Business School was the art of negotiation.

I, the loser, hung up and bustled around microwaving some frozen eggplant parmigiana for myself, tying the dogs at opposite ends of the kitchen, doling out their combination of dry kibble and fresh Bil Jac, and waiting the two or three nanoseconds it took them to eat. Tonight, as soon as I freed Rowdy, he headed for Kimi's dish, and as soon as I untied her, she dashed to his. While the dogs scoured each other's empty bowls, I changed out of my boots and into running shoes, replaced the wool jacket with a respectable-looking fleece pullover, and ran a brush through my hair. Then I tidied up the kitchen and the living room, and ate my eggplant.

Just as I finished washing my plate, the bell rang, and the dogs went flying to the front door and stood by it grinning in happy expectation and silently wagging their plumy white tails. So inexpressibly useless are they as guard dogs or watch dogs that I always forget how they look to a stranger who doesn't know dogs. How do they look? Big, dark, and scary. When I opened the door to admit Oscar Fisch, instead of striding after me, he flattened himself against the nearest wall. So taken were Rowdy and Kimi with this fascinating behavior that they sniffed Oscar's feet, nuzzled his hands, and otherwise tried to determine what was wrong with him. The fear of big dogs was beyond their ken.

I took pity on Oscar, whose tan had vanished. His face was now a deeper green than the patina on the bronze Hannah Duston. Ordinarily, I'd have put the dogs in the yard, but our neighborhood rat invasion was making me slightly paranoid. For one thing, my dogs are very affectionate. I didn't like the idea of a post-rat lick on the face. Besides, for all I knew, rats carried horrible diseases that could infect dogs. I reminded myself to ask Steve. My great fear, though, was that one of the dogs would eat a rat that had ingested poison. A dog who has eaten the kind of rodent poison you buy at the supermarket can be treated with vitamin K, but the treatment has to start promptly, and, of course, you have to know that the dog swallowed the poison and precisely what it was. Alone in the yard, my dogs might silently murder a dozen rats larded with who knows what toxic materials.

"I'll put the dogs away," I told Oscar Fisch. When I'd shut them in my bedroom, I took Oscar's overcoat, hung it up, invited him to take a seat in the living room, and offered coffee. The couch being the only place to sit, that's where he sat, but he refused the coffee. I brought a chair from the kitchen and joined him. Now that the dogs were locked up, his color had returned. His almost complete baldness somehow added to the vigor of his appearance. The trousers of his pin-striped three-piece suit were tight over the knees; he wasn't the kind of man who took care to preserve the creases.

"I am here," he began, "to appeal to your good nature."

"I have none other."

"Let me speak frankly." He reminded me of tapes of Richard Nixon: Next he'd want to make one thing *perfectly* clear.

"Do," I said.

"Without meaning to, you have been harassing my wife."

After mulling over the disappearance of all those copies of Randall Carey's book, I'd certainly felt like harassing Claudia. According to Brat, her mother had "about a hundred" copies of *Mass. Mayhem.* "If I've been harassing her," I said, "it has been entirely unintended. When I met both of you at Marsha's bat mitzvah, Claudia seemed more than willing to tell me about Jack Andrews's murder. I never intended to do anything except take her up on what felt like an invitation."

And that's when Oscar leaned forward and, in low, confiding tones, said, "Claudia's child is in pain."

Bronwyn was in her late twenties. Gareth must now

have been about thirty-four. Neither was my idea of a child. Could Claudia and Oscar possibly have had a baby? Had I grossly overestimated Claudia's age? If not, the couple might still have adopted. In that case, though, why was he referring to the little one only as Claudia's? Could she have had a husband between Jack and Oscar? "I'm very sorry," I said, envisioning a toddler hospitalized with some cruel illness. "How old is the child?"

"Hers is only four," he reported. Brightening, he added, "Mine is about nine."

About? I wanted to ask. *Your own child, and you don't know?*

Before I said anything, Oscar went on. With a rueful little shake of his head and a knowing look, he said, "Conflict there! Happens in all couples when there's an age discrepancy between one partner's child and the other's."

As I'd now worked it out, after Jack's murder, Claudia had remarried, produced or adopted a third child, and then either been divorced and granted custody or again been widowed. When she'd married Oscar, he, too, must have been a parent.

"Well," I said, "with dogs, a big age difference can work either way. Sometimes the older ones simply can't accept the little ones, but sometimes they're really rejuvenated, or they get very maternal."

Oscar's face took on a look of amazement. His whole muscular body seemed to surge with energy. "Why, that's astonishing!" he exclaimed. "Dogs, too?"

"In terms of their emotional lives," I informed him, "they're very much like people. They're social animals. They have attachments, rivalries, love . . . everything."

"But *children?* How would one ever know?"

As a professional dog writer, I am an expert on the general public's boundless, staggering ignorance about dogs. Moreover, I'd often noticed that many people who knew absolutely nothing about dogs were highly educated types who knew a lot about everything else and consequently assumed that they knew a lot about dogs, too. But how on earth could Oscar fail to realize that dogs had puppies?

"Well," I said, "by observation, I suppose."

"I'll have to tell our group about this," Oscar said. Once again sharp and rather grim, he said, "The group brings me back to the point of this visit." Responding to what must have been my baffled expression, he added, "Claudia and I are both recovering."

That's when I finally caught on. The child of Claudia's he'd said was in pain was not Bronwyn, not Gareth, not the third child I'd imagined. All along, Oscar had meant only the *inner* child.

Claudia, Oscar informed me, had been the victim of what he called "financial abuse" at the hands of the late Jack Andrews. Jack wrote checks on the couple's joint account, failed to record them, and blamed Claudia when the checks were returned. Claudia now understood, Oscar reported, that in struggling to make ends meet, she'd been an *enabler*. Bronwyn and Gareth, Oscar claimed, had been raised in an atmosphere of constant insecurity. "Never knew from one semester to the next whether they'd be pulled out of Avon Hill."

Heavens! If the trend continued, we'd soon have recovery groups for people who'd been traumatized by having to attend public school.

"Jack Andrews enjoyed the good life," Oscar went on. "Drained the family purse traveling to promote those guidebooks." Oscar's tone made Jack sound like a purveyor of pornography.

And wherever Jack went, I thought, there just so happened to be a dog show.

"The fact is," Oscar continued, *"nil nisi bonum* aside, if Jack Andrews hadn't died when he did, things would have been even worse than they already were. His insurance was the only thing that got that family through—his insurance and Claudia's spunk."

"The picture you're presenting," I remarked, "is quite different from the impression I had."

The bald head and heavy shoulders gave Oscar a bullish appearance. In an accusatory tone, he said, "There is no need for anyone to turn that son of a bitch into some kind of local hero."

"I have no such intention."

"Destructive excuse for a human being! Look at what's happened to Bronwyn! Christ, look at Gareth!"

"I've met Bronwyn." I felt guilty about using a name other than the one Brat preferred. "I liked her. I've never met Gareth. I don't know anything about him."

"Go to the Square. That's where he lives. Refuses to take his medication. Hangs around the rubbish bins foraging like a wild animal."

If I wanted to see Jack Andrews's true legacy, Oscar declared, all I had to do was take a look at Gareth.

Fourteen

My dog training club meets on Thursday nights in the Cambridge Armory, which is on Concord Avenue right by the Fresh Pond traffic circle, not far from my house. One subzero Thursday last winter, we'd arrived to find the far end of the hall, where the advanced class meets, cordoned off and occupied by homeless mothers and children taking shelter from the cold. The floor space where we usually spread our mats and set up our jumps was lined with rows of folding cots. As we trained our dogs in the front half of the hall, the women and children sat on these flimsy beds, which weren't even their own, to wait until we'd left so that they could go to sleep.

The true contrast between the haves and have-nots would have been far greater at a fancy tennis club, a new-car dealership, or an expensive restaurant than it was at the shabby armory. What made it poignant was the simultaneous presence of the dogs and the children. The next day, my dog-training friend Hope Wilson started to volunteer at a soup kitchen located in the basement of a church in Harvard Square.

On Wednesday morning, I called Hope to ask whether she knew anything about a man named Gareth Andrews. Before I'd even said that he was Caucasian and must be in his mid-thirties, Hope interrupted me. "Oh, Lord, Gareth! Yes, everyone knows Gareth. You've probably seen him in the Square. He always wears an aqua backpack. You see him at the corner of Mass. Ave. and Bow Street."

"What does he look like?" I asked.

"Tallish. These days, he's wearing a purple parka. On his good days, he has on earmuffs. On his bad days, he doesn't, because he thinks that's where the voices come from. On his really bad days, he doesn't even need the earmuffs: The voices come from the fillings in his teeth."

I wanted to consult Rita, but she was at her office seeing patients. To me, Gareth's evidently severe disturbance sounded far worse than what you'd expect from a childhood trauma that consisted of the fear of having to leave private school. Maybe it was the result of growing up in what sounded like a miserable family. Claudia and Jack, I believed, really had fought about money and about the dog, Chip. Rita would undoubtedly say that those topics were stand-ins for underlying issues of love and control. Brat had memorialized her father by becoming, in one person, both Daddy and Daddy's little girl. Gareth had been Claudia's son. In the family photo, he'd looked as if he were trying to bolt. When Jack was murdered, Brat had been eleven, she'd told me, and Gareth sixteen. A father's murder would obviously have a powerful impact on any child. I wondered whether Gareth's evident madness could have anything to do with knowledge, spoken or unspoken, of his father's death.

Although a few homeless people share Harvard Square with their dogs, most street people back away from Rowdy and Kimi. The alarm in those people's eyes doesn't look irrational; it looks like the kind of fear that's based on reality. The genuine need to be wary of big dogs always saddens me. The partnership between people and dogs goes back tens of thousands of years. *Homo sapiens* and *Canis familiaris* evolved together. To sever the bond with dogs is, I think, to lose humanity. All this is to explain that when I went searching for Gareth Andrews, I left Rowdy and Kimi at home.

Empty parking spaces in Harvard Square being almost nonexistent, I took a chance in driving, but the wind was ferocious, and the sky was spitting rain. I lucked into a spot on Mass. Ave., as it's called—Massachusetts Avenue—just around the corner from Quincy Street and opposite Bow Street. One high brick wall of Harvard Yard runs between Quincy and the Square itself. On the opposite side of Mass. Ave. are dozens of businesses that cater to students: clothing shops, a bookstore, an ice cream place, and restaurants, including one that's reputed to house a brothel upstairs. Maybe the rumor is just one of those urban legends, like the story about giant albino alligators in the sewers of New York. (There really aren't any, are there?) Anyway, at eleven o'clock in the morning, the only streetwalkers were jaywalking students bearing armloads of books and notebooks both ways across Mass. Ave. After nearly getting hit by a car, I made it across, checked out the area where Gareth Andrews was supposed to hang out, and saw no one with a purple parka and an aqua backpack. To escape the cold, I went into the Harvard Book Store. There I hunted around downstairs among the used history books for anything that might have to do with Hannah Duston, but didn't find her in any of the indexes I checked. Out of curiosity, I looked for *Mass. Mayhem.* It wasn't there.

After a while, I went back outside, wandered around the Square, fought the wind along Mount Auburn Street, and eventually wound my way back to my car to feed the meter. Wishing that I'd called Leah to arrange to meet her for lunch, I again crossed Mass. Ave. and went alone to Bartley's Burger Cottage, where I battled the miasma of steamy heat and sizzling hamburgers, and ordered and ate a tuna sandwich made the way tuna's supposed to be: dripping with mayonnaise. Then I left Bartley's and again checked the corner of Mass. Ave. and Bow Street.

Right on the corner, just a few steps from the ice cream store and a few doors down from Bartley's, was a big trash barrel. Bending into it was a man in a purple parka. He didn't wear the small aqua daypack I'd somehow imagined, but an internal-frame backpack, its numerous compartments neatly fastened. Lashed to the bottom of the pack was a compact bedroll. With bare hands, the man was frantically and ferociously stuffing his mouth with soggy ice cream cones, discarded french fries, and hunks of half-eaten burgers. So rapidly did he shovel the remains of other people's lunches from the trash barrel to his mouth that he couldn't possibly have examined the debris before ingesting it.

I stepped toward Gareth. He continued to shove fistfuls of refuse into his mouth. From close up, I could see that he was cleaner than I'd expected. Except for some smears of grease and ketchup around the cuffs and on the front, the purple parka looked new and expensive. He wore neither earmuffs nor a hat. His wavy dark hair wasn't matted or dull, and he'd had a recent haircut. If he'd been strolling down the street instead of raiding the trash with the appetite of a starving dog, he'd have been easy to mistake for a hiker at the end of a long trek. All that gave him away was the twisted quality of that ravenous greed. When parents refer to teenage sons as "human garbage disposals," they are only kidding. Twice a day in my own kitchen, I witness raw animal appetite. I joke about it. Turned loose on that trash barrel, Rowdy and Kimi would have fought over the greasy rubbish. If Gareth had paused, I wouldn't have been surprised to see him lift his leg on the barrel, or raise a foot and try to scratch an ear. I also had no doubt that if I reached in to snatch a french fry, he'd bite my wrist.

Knowing no other way to approach Gareth, I returned to Bartley's and ordered a cheeseburger with fries to go. As I waited for the food, the sight of ordinary people chewing food turned my stomach. Never again, I resolved, would I laugh at Rita for eating pizza with a knife and fork. From now on, I'd do the same myself.

Back outside, I had to remind myself that in buying sustenance for a homeless man, I was doing nothing wrong. I tried to think that I was offering him the dignity of eating his very own food instead of jettisoned burgers and fries that bore other people's tooth marks and saliva. What rattled me was the familiarity of my own behavior. I train my dogs with food. I had a horrible sense of treating Gareth as other than human.

By now, he was standing upright. I got my first look at his face. For no good reason, I had envisioned him in the image of his father's graduation picture. In fact, he looked vaguely like Claudia. His expression, though, was weirdly passive and puzzled. Gareth had the vacant look of a man who's spent a long time waiting for an event that has never materialized—not the coming of Godot, either, but the arrival of a nameless something. He now stood a few feet from the trash barrel with his arms hanging limply at his sides and his feet spread. He wore new high-top running shoes. His face was clean: He must have wiped his mouth on something—his sleeve, perhaps, or someone else's discarded paper napkin. His cheeks showed only a few days' growth of beard. There was, I thought, a sort of lost sweetness about Gareth.

I thrust the paper bag of cheeseburger and fries toward him. "Gareth," I said, "my name is Holly. I brought you some lunch."

For obvious reasons, I expected him to tear open the bag and shove the food down his throat. But as he stared at the bag in his hands, his expression was mystified. His fingers trembled.

"It's a cheeseburger," I said, "with fries."

I should have expected the clear, educated voice. After all, he'd gone to Avon Hill. "Thank you. If you don't mind, I'll save it for later."

"It'll get cold," I remarked.

"I don't mind. And I've just eaten." He could've been referring to lunch at the Harvard Faculty Club. Fixing pale, innocent blue eyes on mine, he said rather intently, "They don't feed me at home. They threw me out on the street." Pointing to the backpack, he added, "I was forced to take the essentials with me."

"Oh," I said.

"Oscar Fisch blames me for the rats, you see," Gareth confided. "They're everywhere in the house these days. One can't avoid them. They scurry around in the walls. It's dangerous. They gnaw at the electric wires. Their teeth are sharp."

"It's amazing they don't electrocute themselves." I felt as if Lewis Carroll had written the line for me.

"Oh, but they do!" His voice dropped to a whisper. "The decay is everywhere. They die in the walls. The stench fills every room." Glancing nervously left and right, he continued in an undertone, "Oscar Fisch knows they're there. He won't admit it. So does my mother. But she lets men take advantage of her." After a pause, he said at normal volume and in a cheerfully matter-of-fact tone, "And rats, too."

"Rats," I echoed.

Gareth looked slightly alarmed. "You haven't come about the rats, have you?"

"Certainly not. I brought you lunch. Remember?"

Exactly as he'd done before, he said, "Thank you. If you don't mind, I'll save it for later."

"I don't mind at all," I assured him.

For a moment, his face went blank. Then his eyes brightened, as if he'd remembered something. "Uncle George bought rat poison," he informed me.

The elderly relative of Jack's? The retired exterminator who'd stupidly supplied Jack with the poison?

"Your Uncle George?" I asked.

"George Foley!" Gareth replied. He pointed across the street toward the brick wall of Harvard Yard. "Professor George Foley! My mother is a professor, too. So is Oscar Fisch. Oscar has been granted tenure. My mother has not." In a bland conversational tone, he remarked, "My mother collects books about mayhem. She interests herself in the topic. It is her chosen field of study." Once again, he lowered his voice. "Harvard maintains rat colonies for experimental purposes. At night, the rats are loose on the streets. Oscar Fisch knows all about it."

"Well," I said, groping for reality, "the psychology department probably has rats, but I don't think they use them at the Business School. Isn't that where Oscar Fisch teaches?"

Sounding disconcertingly sane, Gareth declared, "Oscar Fisch is a professional survivor. Oscar Fisch is high up in the recovery movement. Oscar Fisch runs *groups.*" He gave me a moment to appreciate the significance of the disclosure. Then he went on. "Jim Jones had groups, too. His groups all went to South America, and everyone drank Kool-Aid. Even the children." As if reading from a natural-history text, he reported, "Rats are heavily distributed throughout the world." Citing a reference, he added, "Uncle George says so."

Since we seemed to be getting nowhere except deeper into lunacy, I finally took the initiative. "George Foley was a friend of your father's, wasn't he?"

Mistake! Gareth's eyes blazed. "My father drank rat poison!" he shouted. Veering around to address the passersby, he roared at top volume, "My father drinks rat poison, and it's better than he deserves, the stinking son of a bitch! His name is John Winter Andrews, and he collects rat poison! And then he drinks it! And he falls down on the floor, and rolls around, and coughs up blood and vomit! And then he never, never *DIES!*" The muscles in Gareth's face were so tense that his head seemed to have ballooned. His arms were shaking. Brandishing the unopened bag of food I'd given him, he took a step toward me. Involuntarily, I backed away. Like a dog, he moved toward me. Again, I felt ashamed of seeing him as an animal.

"Rats!" he shouted, shaking the bag. "Oscar Fisch sent you with RATS!" Hurling the paper bag to the sidewalk, he lumbered toward me.

I turned tail. Groping in my pocket for the keys to my car, I bolted through the traffic, managed to get across Mass. Ave. without being hit, and ended up leaning on my Bronco for support. I dove into the car, threw myself in the driver's seat, and locked the door. Just as I started the engine, Gareth began to pound on the rear window. I don't know why it didn't break. The shouting alone should have cracked glass. As Gareth hammered his fists on the side window and bellowed about rats, poison, Oscar Fisch, and the father who hadn't died, I found a break in the traffic and tried to escape. Gareth chased my Bronco. Smack in the middle of Harvard Square, I got stuck at a red light. The rearview mirror gave me a nightmarish image of a shouting man dressed in a purple parka. Rage contorted his face. The light seemed to stay red for two or three hours. He reached the rear of my car. As his bare fist pounded the glass, the light turned green and the cars ahead of mine moved. The next traffic light was yellow. Sounding my horn at the pedestrians, I slammed my foot on the gas and narrowly missed hitting two kids. Only when I pulled into my own driveway did I make the connection. Desperate to escape, I could have killed those children: just like Hannah Duston.

Fifteen

"Psychotic rage," Rita diagnosed. "Now you understand why we want people like this to take their medication."

I'd snagged her when she'd arrived home between patients to eat lunch and walk Willie. We were in my kitchen. Dressed for work in a gray wool skirt with a white silk shirt and a bright scarf, she was feeding herself tiny spoonfuls of low-fat raspberry yogurt. She looked utterly civilized. I felt better already.

"But why don't they?" I asked. "I don't understand why someone like that wouldn't take his medication."

Rita shrugged. "I've heard people complain that when they do, they don't feel like themselves, which may sound laughable, but I think there's a sort of truth there, too. Sometimes, they're too disorganized, cognitively, to remember or to follow through and *do* it. Even if they're just supposed to have injections every week or two, sometimes it's too much for them to get to the doctor's office."

"If they were sane enough to take their medication, they wouldn't need it."

She smiled. "More or less. Actually, less. Plenty of people do take their meds and function very well."

"In dogs," I said, "rage syndrome is—"

"Please!"

"I'm serious! It occurs in springer spaniels. It's genetic. It's well documented in springers, but it's believed to occur in other breeds."

"Well, in an individual like this Gareth, there's undoubtedly some organic basis."

"I was sort of wondering the opposite. I wondered whether he hadn't been driven crazy by something to do with his father's murder. Plus, for all that his mother is a professor, there's something strange about her. She doesn't quite connect. It's also possible that she's a sort of, uh, strange kind of kleptomaniac. And giving me that crime-scene picture of Jack's body was really peculiar."

Rita nodded. "And the daughter—"

"Brat's eccentric," I admitted. "She's unusual. But when you're with her, you don't get that creepy feeling that you're off in space somewhere. You don't with Oscar, either—Claudia's second husband, the one she's married to now. That's something else I don't understand. Oscar is perfectly capable and focused. So why doesn't he see to it that Gareth is . . . I don't know. In a halfway house, maybe. Or a hospital? Rita, he really isn't—"

"It isn't as simple as that. These days, even for flagrantly psychotic people, the insurance companies don't want to pay for anything except brief hospitalizations. The family probably couldn't get Gareth hospitalized unless he was in the kind of state he ended up in today."

"Rita, he is really violent. He could kill someone."

"First of all, Holly, contrary to popular myth, most psychotic people aren't like that. Most of them are absolutely no threat to anyone except themselves. And this guy scared the daylights out of you, but he didn't actually do you any harm."

"Because I ran away! And even before that, Rita, you should've seen him eating out of the trash! He was shoveling garbage into his mouth. There was something so sick and so pitiful about it. And he has all these crazy ideas about rats and poison. Meanwhile, he's scavenging like a rat and probably getting botulism. I don't know why someone doesn't—"

"Holly, the family probably knows all that." Rita ate a bit of yogurt. "They probably try. Most of these families do."

"He's had a haircut," I conceded. "He's not all that dirty. And his shoes and his parka look expensive."

"Well, there you have it. The family probably does its best, but this guy can't be easy to help. With someone as disturbed as this, there are no simple solutions."

"I should never have mentioned his father."

"Anything could have precipitated it."

"Not just *anything*. His father really was murdered."

After Rita left for her office, I tried to settle down to my own work. Gareth's ranting about rats and poison seemed to haunt me. On inspiration, I consulted *The Merck Veterinary Manual*. It's a fat book, and in addition to chapter after chapter about the ailments that afflict dogs, cats, livestock, marine mammals, fish, and all the rest, it has a long section about poisoning, because, of course, animals accidentally poison themselves much more often than human beings poison themselves or one another. Anyway, there were four dense paragraphs about sodium fluoroacetate, which came across as the answer to a poisoner's prayers. It barely sounded real:

no color, no odor, no taste, soluble in water, and ultradeadly—the victim dying an agonizing death from either convulsions or heart failure. This incredibly dangerous stuff was banned for use on federal land and available only to certified, insured exterminators. The law required that it be mixed with black dye. According to the *Manual*, the dye was for identification, meaning, I guessed, that poisoners couldn't go around insinuating it into lemonade or beer, but had to stick to drinks that were black already. Coffee, for instance.

Feeling slightly nauseated, I emptied my coffee cup into the sink, went to the bathroom and brushed my teeth, changed into my heavy boots, and pulled on an old jacket and pigskin gloves. After checking the fenced yard for signs of anything even remotely suggestive of rodents, I let the dogs out. Then I went through the gate to the driveway, carefully closed the gate, and set to work on my wood.

The afternoon was, if anything, grayer, colder, windier, and nastier than the morning had been. The unsplit logs seemed to have propagated in my absence. Every piece resisted my wedge. In my effort to split one especially recalcitrant piece, I slammed my sledgehammer against the wedge, pounded my left index finger, and cursed. When Randall Carey showed up to offer me a book—*Good Wives* by Laurel Thatcher Ulrich—and a couple of photocopied articles about Hannah Duston, I was glad for an excuse to quit.

Remember the comic strip character called Tubby? Well, I'd have been willing to bet that Tubby had been Randall Carey's childhood nickname. Not that Randall was fat—he wasn't—but he was nonetheless round, as if he'd been drawn by an illustrator who preferred circles and curves to angles and straight lines. Today he had on khaki pants and a suede jacket that would be ruined if the dark sky let loose. He didn't wear an ascot or carry a stout walking stick, but he looked as if he might have thought about both. In the fresh air, I caught a whiff of men's cologne or aftershave. Bay rum? Isn't that what English gentlemen pat on? In the movies, they do. The only artificial odors you ever smell on Steve are the manly scents of dog shampoo, Panolog cream, and chlorine bleach.

But Randall Carey knew about Hannah Duston. After stowing my sledgehammer, wedges, and ax under the little porch, I invited Randall in for coffee. When he accepted, I led him through the gate to the yard. As thrilled as ever to welcome a visitor, Rowdy and Kimi came bounding toward him. They know better than to jump on people except by invitation. Randall made the mistake of inadvertently issuing one. By then, I was carrying the book and the articles, and Randall's hands were free. As the dogs happily charged up to him, he raised both arms in what I suppose was an unconscious expression of the wish to take immediate flight and soar far above the yard and the dogs. Rowdy and Kimi, however, recognized the signal even in the absence of the command that goes with it: Up! It's a nifty trick. I raise my arms shoulder-high and tell the dogs "Up!" Rowdy and Kimi leap up and rest their beautiful snowshoe paws on my outstretched arms. Only now, of course, the dogs jumped on Randall Carey. He was not favorably impressed.

"Off!" I ordered. To Randall, I said, "Oh, I'm so sorry. Suede, of all things! I'm very sorry. They don't normally do that. They thought you were giving them a signal. Dogs, down!" The dogs hit the ground.

Randall certainly noticed that the dogs were no longer depositing dirt on his jacket and digging their nails into the suede, and although he probably observed that the huge, sharp teeth and smiling jaws were no longer within immediate striking range of his throat, I somehow had the sense that he didn't fully appreciate the perfection of those sphinxlike downs. He was busy brushing off the sleeves of the jacket.

"They haven't torn the suede, have they?" I asked.

Eyeing the dogs, he shook his head. "It's nothing."

"They misunderstood," I explained. Raising my arms, I said, "Up!" And the dogs sprang to their feet, rose on their hind legs, and placed their paws on my arms. Malamutes look especially athletic when their bodies are stretched up like that. Rowdy and Kimi's white tails were wagging. "Good dogs. Okay! Off." To Randall, I said, "You see? It was a misunderstanding. But I'm really very sorry. Come in and we'll have some coffee."

To prevent any additional miscommunication, I put the dogs in my bedroom. Then I made a pot of French roast, offered to pay to have the jacket cleaned (he refused), and, as I'd done on my visit to Randall, assured him that I was the strong alpha leader of my little pack and that Rowdy and Kimi were friendly and gentle. "I train dogs," I explained, gesturing to the dozens of leashes that hung on hooks on the kitchen door. He eyed the leashes with curiosity. I really own more than I need. Maybe he suspected me of having a few dozen additional dogs stashed somewhere, ready to do a real job on his jacket.

"I'm not *afraid* of dogs," Randall informed me.

"Of course not."

"Far from it."

"Of course." After pouring coffee and offering cream and sugar, I took a seat opposite Randall at the kitchen table and thanked him for the material about Hannah Duston.

He inquired about the progress I was making with my research and asked what had aroused my interest in Hannah.

"My car broke down in the center of Haverhill, and I saw the statue." I did not, of course, mention Rita's five-hundred-dollar bet. Rather, I pulled out my folder of notes and photocopied material, and, succumbing to the low impulse to name-drop, casually mentioned that I was having tea with Professor Foley on Friday.

Randall rested a well-groomed hand on the Laurel Thatcher Ulrich book. He smiled. "Read this before you see him," he advised.

I smiled back. "Oh, I always do my homework on time."

"There's a surprise buried in here." He stroked the copy of *Good Wives* as if caressing a fat, sedate cat. "Let me know what you think of it. It's always interesting to see how matters appear to the untutored eye."

The untutored eye! Both of mine blinked. Soon thereafter Randall Carey left. He didn't thank me for the coffee. As soon as he departed, I let the dogs loose. "If that man ever shows up again," I told them, "dig your nails into his damned suede jacket. In fact, have it for lunch."

I was, however, chagrined to discover that Randall Carey was right about *Good Wives*. The book revealed an unsettling connection that Laurel Thatcher Ulrich had made. As I'd known, Cotton Mather preached a sermon about Hannah Duston, who was in the church when he proclaimed her a savior of New England. Four years earlier, Mather had preached a sermon of condemnation about a woman named Elizabeth Emerson. The unmarried mother of one child, Elizabeth Emerson had given surreptitious birth to twins and promptly killed them. In 1693, she was convicted of murdering her newborn babies. Hannah Duston's maiden name was Emerson. Hannah Duston and Elizabeth Emerson were sisters.

Sixteen

The next morning, I put both dogs in the Bronco and set out for Haverhill. Before leaving Cambridge, I stopped to mail a small package to Oscar Fisch. Then I headed north. This time I got off at a different exit from the one I'd taken the day I'd met Hannah Duston. Just off the highway was a nursing home named in honor of Haverhill's colonial heroine. Somehow, the name didn't connote tender loving care.

By now, of course, I knew more about Hannah than I had at our first encounter, yet I felt almost eager to see her again. I'd also learned a bit about Haverhill and now saw it through what I insist on calling tutored eyes. The main drag was a wide thoroughfare lined with municipal and medical buildings in new brick that suggested old mills. I hoped that what the architects had had in mind was an appearance of uncompromising functionality. At the bottom of the hill, the street became a battered concrete bridge that spanned the Merrimack

River. At one corner of the bridge was a defunct Woolworth's, its bleak storefront windows barren except for a scanty display of red, white, and blue banners that weren't quite flags. At the corner opposite the bygone five-and-dime was a small memorial to citizens of Haverhill who had died in Vietnam. Uphill was the G.A.R. Park, which, of course, memorialized the Civil War and also, as you know, Hannah Duston, who had lived a few hundred years too early to serve in the War Between the States and wouldn't have been allowed to enlist, anyway, on the grounds that women were the weaker sex.

During the drive, I'd cultivated a romantic vision of myself addressing a series of profound questions to the mute, memorialized Hannah. I'd also had in mind the practical plan of getting some good photographs to accompany whatever it was I was supposed to be writing. I had no trouble parking. Most of the spaces in a vast blacktopped lot near the G.A.R. Park were empty, and next to the park itself stretched a city block of vacant spots with expired meters. I pulled the Bronco to the curb, fed the meter, and got the dogs out, but soon returned them to their crates. There was at least as much broken glass underfoot as there was grass. A raw-concrete grandstand clearly intended for summer concerts and Fourth of July speeches had evidently served instead as the focal point for a spree of bottle-breaking. Its walls were spray-painted with initials and obscenities. Pigeons poked at the ground as if feeding on shards of glass. Rats with wings.

The weathered-bronze Hannah was still gripping the hatchet in her right hand. Her left index finger still pointed in permanent accusation that now had an obvious cause. Beneath her left arm, above the bas-relief of Thomas Duston's defense of his children, someone had scrawled in big purple letters BURN BITCH. On the opposite side of the monument, above the depiction of Hannah's return, immense block capitals in what looked like thick crayon spelled out INDIAN KILLER. Below the picture of the two women and the boy in the canoe, like verbal fingers pointing back at Hannah, were more graffiti: A.I.M. RED POWER and INDIAN MUR-DERER.

The counteraccusations, no matter how justified, made it difficult for me to get the photographs I'd wanted. The best shot shows only Hannah and excludes the monument on which she stands. On the right of the picture, an American flag waves from a white flagpole. Hannah aims her finger directly at the flag. What I like about the view is that you can read it as you please: Hannah Duston, colonial heroine, savior of New England, points with pride to her role in shaping the country's future. Alternatively, Hannah Duston, Indian killer, directs the blaming eye to national shame.

After I'd taken close-ups of the reliefs, including a few that showed the graffiti, I checked on the dogs and then went across the street to the public library in hope of finding a copy of the old privately printed biography of Hannah that Professor Foley had mentioned. The library was a modern building with lots of levels and lots of glass. As it turned out, the library did not have the book I was after. I did, however, learn its title: *And One Fought Back.* The author was adventurously named Lewis Clark. My effort to find the book itself caused a mildly unpleasant scene. When I inquired at the desk, an important-acting man angrily informed me that the volume had disappeared from the library's special collection. If I'd stolen it, I'd hardly have been making an open inquiry, and I suffer from an honest, wholesome countenance. Still, the man seemed convinced that I was a book thief engaged in a paradoxical scheme to cover up my guilt. I left.

On a street that ran along the river, I found a big seafood restaurant and decided to stop for lunch, but when I pulled into the parking lot, I discovered that the place had gone out of business. Farther along the same street, I located the headquarters of the Haverhill Historical Society, which, according to the article in *Yankee* I'd read at the Newton Free Library, housed tedious exhibits in a shabby old building. To my eye, the museum, Buttonwoods, showed none of the disrepair I'd expected. A modern wing blended smoothly into a handsome old colonial house. The entrance hall was a bright, cheerful room with freshly painted white walls and attractive displays about the Native Americans who'd inhabited what later became Haverhill. So much for trusting the printed word.

The *Yankee* article had made the museum guides sound bored and unhelpful. It seemed to me that they tried their best to assist me despite overwhelmingly adverse circumstances, specifically, two thousand drippy-nosed schoolchildren. Actually, there were only forty or fifty kids, but their noses exuded the nasal discharge of a multitude, and when they opened their mouths to cough, the historic house resembled a gigantic nest of greedy baby birds. Insinuating myself into the group, I piped up to ask about the tribe or clan who'd captured Hannah Duston. Before the guide could answer, a teacher accosted me to explain that the Hannah Duston part came later. And which school was I from, anyway?

Eventually, when the competition among the hackers and drippers had reached a virulent fever pitch, the guide led us into an exhibition hall in the old part of the museum and showed us, among zillions of other objects displayed on the walls and in glass cases, the Hannah

Duston artifacts. The *Yankee* article had suggested that the Duston items were few, dull, and of doubtful provenance: a teapot, some buttons, and what were believed to be the hatchet and the scalping knife that Hannah Duston had used on her abductors.

The artifact I'd come to see, Hannah's "Confession of Faith," was framed in glass. Until 1929, the document had rested, unrecognized for what it was, in the Haverhill Center Congregational Church. One account claimed that it lay in a vault; another, that it was discovered behind a gallery pew. Since it was of no interest to the children, I had the chance to study it. "I am Thankful for my Captivity," Hannah had professed; " 'twas the Comfortablest time that ever I had: In my Affliction God made his Word Comfortable to me." In one of the books I'd consulted, I'd seen an old document that Hannah Duston had signed only with a scrawled *X*. I wondered whether she'd dictated this statement or learned to write at an advanced age. She'd made the "Confession of Faith" at the age of sixty-seven, when she finally applied for full church membership: "I desire the Church to receive me tho' it be at the Eleventh hour." I later read somewhere that she'd dictated the confession to her minister. At the time of her captivity, she'd been almost forty. After her return, she and Thomas had yet another baby, a girl, Lydia. Hannah and Thomas Duston were buried in an old cemetery in Haverhill. The graves hadn't been marked, the guide said, because of the fear that Indians would steal the bodies. The age of sixty-seven was not, after all, Hannah Duston's eleventh hour. She was born in 1657 and lived for nearly eighty years. Only the good die young?

When the tour ended, I asked the guide whether the historical society owned a copy of *And One Fought Back*. Like the man at the library, she got her hackles up. The guide, however, knew an honest face when she saw one. The volume, she informed me, had been stolen. Its author, Lewis Clark, I learned, had taught at Haverhill High School, written the biography in the thirties, and perished in the Battle of the Bulge. No, the guide said, his widow had died years ago. They'd had no children.

The museum, too, was finally childless, so I poked around examining a lot of objects that the *Yankee* article hadn't mentioned and acquiring bits of information I'd missed elsewhere. The boy captive, Samuel, had been stolen in 1695 at the age of twelve; at the time of the massacre, he'd been fourteen, old enough to swing a hatchet. And speaking of hatchets, the blade of the one on display looked as dull as the purported scalping knife. The knife was worn and chipped; it had no sharp edge at all. Could Hannah possibly have brought it home and gone on using it to slaughter pigs and peel vegetables? Or had she dulled and nicked it in a single night?

In mint condition were a collection of pewter plates presented to Hannah by Governor Sir Francis Nicholson of Maryland and a large pewter tankard offered as a tribute by the Great and General Court of Massachusetts on the grounds, I guess, that after all Hannah had been through, what she needed was a good drink. The tankard was engraved with delicate decorations. Its shiny pewter could almost have passed for silver. The tankard looked like the kind of trophy I'd be proud to take home from a dog show.

The truly freakish object on display was, however— and I swear to God I am not making this up; go to Buttonwoods and see for yourself—the third in a series of historical bottles sponsored by the New Hampshire State Liquor Commission and produced by Jim Beam Distillers. The bottle stood more than a foot high and took the form of the Hannah shown in the Boscawen statue, but with her nose and hatchet intact. Also, the bottle was in gaudy color. Hannah's skin was pale. The scalps were red. The bottle looked as if it had never been opened. Hannah's cold-bloodedness had been pretty obvious all along. It had never occurred to me that what coursed through her veins was actually Jim Beam.

After I left Buttonwoods, I took a back route across the Merrimack to a rural section of Bradford, where I stopped in at Janet Switzer's. When I arrived, Janet was in the kennel area just in back of her tiny blue Cape Cod house. Parked in the driveway were her tan RV, tan house trailer, and tan Chevy wagon. The rear ends of all three vehicles were plastered with bumper stickers, including a new one: Monotheism: The Belief in One Dog, the Alaskan Malamute.

A few years earlier, when Janet had had breast cancer, she'd taken a break from breeding. Her face had looked a little haggard, and she'd lost some weight. Today, I noticed, her weathered face had regained its former fullness. Through her short mass of gray-streaked brown waves you could see her scalp.

To avoid causing a commotion, I left Kimi and Rowdy in the car. At a minimum, Janet would've said hello to them and shaken their paws. Without greeting me, she announced, "I might want to use Rowdy at stud."

"I thought you weren't breeding anymore," I said. The statement was as close as I'd ever come to asking about her health.

"I've got a bitch here that ought to be bred. Victoria. She's finished"—AKC champion—"and she's OFA excellent." OFA: Orthopedic Foundation for Animals, an organization that examines and rates hip X rays to determine whether dogs are clear of hip dysplasia. Buying a puppy of *any* medium, large, or giant breed? Oh no you're not. Not until you see proof in writing that both parents are OFA good or excellent, or that they've both cleared something called PennHip.

Walking over to Victoria's kennel, I said, "She's nice. She has a beautiful head."

Victoria, who knew we were discussing her, licked my fingers through the chain link. She had lovely dark eyes, good pigment, decent bone, and small ears. Color and markings aren't all that important in malamutes, but Victoria was Rowdy's color, dark wolf gray, with shadows under her eyes and a trace of a bar down her muzzle. I opened the kennel door and entered. You can't do that at just any kennel, but Janet's dogs have excellent temperaments. I ran my hands over Victoria and checked her mouth. Her bite was good, and she wasn't missing any teeth. "She's out of . . . ?"

"Denny and Lucy. His eyes have been checked?" Janet demanded.

I nodded. "Clear."

"Run a brucellosis test," Janet ordered me. Before you can get a marriage license, you need a syphilis test. Before you breed dogs, you check for brucellosis. Except that no one had yet accepted the proposal. As you'll have gathered, Janet's idea of tactful negotiation was to state outright what she was going to do.

I cleared my throat and asked Janet for a cup of coffee. Seated in her kitchen amid forty-pound bags of premium dog food, water buckets, chew toys, and stacks of dog magazines, I raised no questions about whether the breeding should take place. With anyone else, I'd have put up an argument. I'd have wanted my opinion solicited. I wouldn't have followed orders. With Janet, all I did was ask when she expected Victoria to come in season. It seemed to me that I was playing Mary Neff to

Janet's Hannah Duston, except, of course, that we'd be bringing life into the world, not taking it away. Spurred by the thought, I told Janet all about what I'd been doing in Haverhill. Janet knew who Hannah was; I didn't have to explain. "The book I wanted is missing from the library and from Buttonwoods, too," I said. "It's a privately printed book about Hannah: *And One Fought Back.* The author taught at Haverhill High School. Lewis Clark. He died in World War Two." With no pun intended, I said, "For the moment, I seem to have hit a dead end."

Janet promised to ask around to see whether she could locate a copy.

On the way back to Cambridge, I belatedly realized that Janet and I hadn't discussed a stud fee. Rather, I hadn't raised the matter, but had assumed that, as usual, I'd go along with whatever Janet decreed. I knew the pedigrees of Janet's dogs all the way back to Rowdy of Nome, the first AKC-registered Alaskan malamute. For the first time, I wondered about Janet's own ancestry. I knew as little about her family tree as I'd ever known or cared about my own. Switzer was Janet's married name. I didn't know her maiden name. She grew up in Haverhill. So did her parents. Her grandparents? Great-grandparents? And on back? Hannah and Thomas Duston had had thirteen children. If I recalled correctly, nine had survived to adulthood and married. In the gift shop at Buttonwoods, I'd seen numerous pamphlets about the genealogy of the Duston family. I'd paid no attention. Only now did it cross my mind that Janet might well be one of Hannah's descendants. In certain respects, she was, I thought, exactly the type.

Seventeen

I'm seldom invited to tea by anyone at all, never mind by a Harvard professor emeritus. Although I felt certain that the unpretentious Professor Foley wouldn't object to my usual garb—T-shirt, sweatshirt, jeans, running shoes—I felt compelled to costume myself for the occasion. At the back of my closet, I located a blue corduroy Laura Ashley pinafore and a simple white blouse with ruffles at the neck and sleeves. I wore dark stockings and flats. For the first time since last winter, I removed my good navy wool coat from its dry cleaner's bag. Just before leaving the house, I went over myself with one of those red velvet clothes brushes that actually do a half-decent job of removing dog hair. With a steno pad and pens stashed in my purse, I set off on foot down Appleton, turned right onto Huron, and then made my way against the cold December wind up Fayerweather Street toward Governor Weld's house. The route was familiar. The ladylike attire was not. Slapping the sidewalk, my

leather-soled flats sounded like someone else's shoes. I
may have paused here and there at Rowdy's and Kimi's
favorite trees and utility poles to wait for invisible dogs.

Professor Foley's house proved to be an immense Victorian I'd admired on previous walks. It was painted a
soft, inviting shade of yellow, with shutters and trim in
rich cream. A row of solar-powered lamps illuminated
the path from the sidewalk to the house. The grass had
been cut short for the winter, and the wide flower beds
that ran up to the sidewalk and circled the property in
gentle curves had been put to bed under cozy-looking
blankets of salt-marsh hay. Along the front of the house,
little wooden structures protected the foundation evergreens from snow and ice that would cascade from the
steep roof. The massive front door was deep green. The
electric light mounted above it was on. On the brick
stoop by the door, a big pot of pale pink chrysanthe-
mums had toppled over in the wind. Still encased in
plastic, the *New York Times* and the *Boston Globe* lay on a
long, wide jute mat. A sheaf of magazines, letters, and
junk mail protruded from the brass mail slot. The windows at the front of the house were dark.

I pushed the doorbell and heard distant chimes. No
lights came on. No footsteps approached. No voice
called out. I rang the bell again. This *was* Friday, I reminded myself. I checked my watch: ten after four. To
avoid seeming gauche, I'd tried to arrive a few minutes
late. Mounted on the door was an old-fashioned door
knocker, a brass lion's head that I'd assumed to be
mainly decorative. I pounded hard. Then I again rang
the bell.

Elderly people who live alone, I reflected, sometimes
establish a sort of home-within-a-home at the back of the
house. Perhaps Professor Foley didn't use the front
rooms of this gigantic place, but denned up in the

kitchen or a breakfast room, and took it for granted that visitors would seek him out in the part of the house where he really lived. The explanation felt far-fetched. I pursued it nonetheless. I couldn't believe that Professor Foley had forgotten his gracious invitation.

To avoid trampling the lovingly winterized flower beds or shoving my way through the shrubbery to get to the back door, I returned to the sidewalk and made my way down a narrow gravel driveway that led to a two-car garage and the rear of the house. Lights were on in what I guessed was the kitchen, but when I rang the bell at the back door, no one answered. Reluctant to conclude that Professor Foley had stood me up, I fished for ways to excuse him. I was a stranger in the world of those who routinely took tea: To habitual sippers, four o'clock might be universally understood to mean four-thirty or even five. Perhaps Professor Foley intended to serve a real English tea and was now hurrying home from one of the fancy shops on Huron Avenue where he'd bought fresh scones, little cakes, and out-of-season giant strawberries to be served with Devon cream. If so, I didn't want to be caught lurking around his back door.

Returning to the front of the house, I felt obliged to explain my presence there to onlookers who were, in fact, nonexistent. I again rang the bell, listened to the chimes, and pounded the lion's head door knocker. Eager, I suppose, to set something right, I put the over-turned pot of mums back on its base by the door. At four thirty-five, I came to my senses. The mail might not have arrived until the afternoon, but the newspapers had been delivered in the early morning. Professor Foley was elderly, but he'd shown no sign whatsoever of forgetfulness and every sign of gentlemanly manners. And, no, my own memory wasn't slipping, either. I'd been invited for four o'clock on Friday. If Professor Foley wasn't here to welcome me, something was wrong.

In my own immediate neighborhood or another like it, I'd have marched up to one of the nearby houses to ask whether anyone had seen my inexplicably absent host. Here, I hesitated, mainly, I guess, because I was afraid that any of the grand doors to these imposing arks might be opened by a uniformed maid. It's not that I'm exactly phobic about maids. I'm just not used to them, and on the rare occasions when I encounter them, they make me nervous. There's something about maids that seems so . . . judgmental. Before I open my mouth, I always feel as if I'd already said the wrong thing. But maybe I confuse them with nuns. All that black and white. Anyway, steeling myself against the fearsome prospect of encountering a maid, or maybe just a neighbor who'd make me feel small, I went to the house closest to Professor Foley's—not, I might mention, Governor Weld's—and boldly rang the bell. The person who promptly came to the door was a plump, apple-cheeked woman with thick brown hair piled in a loose knot on her head. She wore a brown wool skirt and what I thought was called a "twin set," a cardigan over a pullover, in the medium brown of her skirt and hair. That's a cardigan sweater, of course, not a Welsh corgi; there was no sign of the comforting presence of any kind of dog. Faltering only a little, I introduced myself and stated my dilemma. "The mail is in the mail slot," I went on to explain. "The newspapers haven't been taken in. I couldn't help worrying. But maybe Professor Foley just forgot. I wondered whether anyone had seen him today. Or maybe he's gone away?"

The woman shook her head and frowned. "No, he'd have told me. I have a key. Let me get it and grab a jacket, and we'll run over."

A few minutes later, after dutifully ringing the bell by the front door and waiting while no one answered, she inserted the key in the lock and opened the door. "He has an alarm system," she informed me, flicking on the lights and stepping over the pile of mail that had fallen from the slot, "but it's never turned on." Even so, as I followed her, she opened the front-hall closet and examined the digital display on a little plastic box.

"George!" she called out. "George? It's Lydia! George? Are you all right?" Ignoring me, she swiftly moved to a huge dining room with a fireplace at one end, an immense sideboard laden with china platters and tureens, and a mahogany dinner table with twelve chairs neatly grouped around it, and not crowded in, either. At the head of the table, one place was set. A solitary lace place mat held a flower-painted plate, polished silverware, and a wineglass. In front of it stood a small book stand. I glanced at the book it held open: *The Unredeemed Captive* by John Demos, the story of Eunice Williams. As a young girl in Deerfield, Massachusetts, Eunice had been captured in a raid in 1704 and taken to a settlement near Montreal, probably the same one, I guessed, where Hannah Duston and Mary Neff would have ended up if Hannah had accepted her captivity. Eunice Williams had more than accepted hers: She'd horrified her family and, in fact, all colonial New England by refusing to cooperate in efforts to release her and, indeed, by marrying within what she must have considered her own tribe.

"George! George!" the neighbor persisted. Swinging open a door that led to the kitchen, she came to an abrupt halt. Veering around, she accidentally slammed into me. Her apple cheeks were suddenly white. "Dear God," she breathed. "Dear God."

I brushed past her. Sprawled facedown on the shiny,

speckled linoleum of the kitchen floor was the body of a man I barely recognized as Professor Foley. Everything about the scene—the awkward twist of the legs, the strange angle of the neck, the hand outstretched toward the spilled coffee mug, the little puddle of liquid by the mug, the glare of the harsh lights—was a duplicate of what I'd seen in the police photo Claudia had given me of Jack Andrews's dead body. Professor Foley's most distinctive feature was hidden: His blue eyes had glinted with the charm and curiosity of a bright toddler's. Now his head faced away from me. I approached slowly and tiptoed around the remains. The eyes were open. They were still, of course, blue. In all other respects, they were no longer George Foley's. The stench was strong and vile, like the reek of a dirty nursing home that somehow housed a filthy dog kennel. I felt sickeningly relieved that I didn't have to touch the corpse. Death was all too apparent; there was no need for me to verify it.

"His heart, I suppose," said the neighbor, Lydia. Suddenly losing control, she bent over, covered her mouth with her hand, and gagged.

"Go outside," I told her. "I'll call for help."

The outdated kitchen had the kind of old gas stove that's coming back in fashion as an antique. A few clean dishes rested in a rack by an empty soapstone sink. The new white refrigerator looked out of place. The walls were the ubiquitous lime green of the 1950s. I couldn't find a phone. Even if there'd been one, the stench would have driven me out. I don't know why we hadn't smelled it the second we'd entered the house. We hadn't been expecting it, I guess. And the walls were thick, the rooms immense. Obeying my instruction, Lydia headed back through the dining room and out through the front door. In the hallway near the door stood a small desk that served as a telephone table. Sucking air from the outdoors, I picked up an old beige Princess phone, called 911, gave Professor Foley's address, and said that I was certain he was dead. Hanging up, I spotted among the scraps of paper by the phone one that bore my own name and number. *Friday,* Professor Foley had written on the slip of paper. *Tea.* Next to the telephone was a neatly trimmed newspaper clipping that I recognized as the *Globe*'s article about the Cambridge rat invasion. I wondered why the article was by the phone. Had Professor Foley placed a call about the rats?

Just outside the door, Lydia was sobbing and retching. Although I didn't know her at all, I put a hand on her shoulder. "I'm so sorry," I said. "They'll be here soon," I added, without specifying who *they* were. "I'll wait. Do you want to go home?"

Pulling herself upright, she said, "No, no. I'll stay here."

"He was a close friend?" I asked.

Before she could reply, something moved in a nearby flower bed. Although it was dark out, the light mounted over the front door illuminated a wide area. A clump of salt-marsh hay rose and fell. A dark shape appeared and vanished.

"A rat!" Lydia cried. "Damn, damn those things!"

"I'm not sure it was—"

"Oh yes it was! That hay is attracting them! I've told George—" Breaking off, she took a rattling breath that suggested asthma. She reached into a jacket pocket, groped, and removed an inhaler. "Pardon me," she said. As she dosed herself, I asked whether she needed a doctor.

"No, I'm used to it. This does the trick. What doesn't help is all that hay."

"It's what serious gardeners always use," I said. "I suppose it provides an ideal nesting spot for—"

"Rats! And the foolish thing is that George was as upset about them as anyone else! He called the city. I did, too! But the little man I talked to was far less responsive than one might have wished. It really is ridiculous! We're asked to believe what is patently false! If you listen to the city, these rats are barely the size of a mouse. And George himself saw one that he swore was the size of a full-grown woodchuck!"

"He didn't try to poison them, did he?"

Still laboring for breath, Lydia said, "Well, the truth is, we did discuss it, but—"

The sirens drowned out the rest of her sentence. The first official vehicle to arrive was a cruiser. Almost as soon as the uniformed officer reached the front door, a big emergency medical van pulled up, and a second cruiser followed.

"In the kitchen," I said to the first officer, a handsome blond guy with blue eyes and pale New England skin. I gestured to the open front door. "Through the dining room, then through the swinging door."

Tearing past Lydia and me, the cops and the EMTs rushed to save a life far beyond earthly salvation. In almost no time, the first officer returned. "Relatives?" he asked.

I shook my head.

"I'm a neighbor," Lydia said, "and a friend."

"I was supposed to have tea with Professor Foley," I reported, forgetting that we hadn't even said who the dead man was. "When I got here, the newspapers were lying here"—I pointed to them—"and the mail was in the mail slot. I kept ringing the bell, and I didn't get an answer. Then I tried the back door. Finally, I got worried, and I went next door and asked—"

"Lydia Berenson," the woman said. "I had George's key. We went in and found him."

Pulling out a notebook, the young cop took down information: Professor Foley's name, mine, Lydia's, our addresses. Professor Foley's next of kin, Lydia reported, was a son who taught economics at Berkeley. "I have his number," she said. "Shall I call him?"

"We'll take care of that, ma'am," the cop replied. "We'd appreciate the number."

It is not in my nature to keep my mouth shut. "Kevin Dennehy is my next-door neighbor," I announced. "Is he going to be . . . ?"

"I don't have that information at this time, ma'am." The cop sounded as if he were reciting a line he'd memorized at the police academy, where, I have concluded, students are drilled in uttering the phrase "at this time" and flunk out if a simple "now" passes their lips.

"Are you assuming that this is a natural death?" I asked.

"Ma'am, at this time we're not assuming anything."

Eighteen

Lieutenant Kevin Dennehy's name carried less clout than I'd imagined. Or maybe his colleagues suspected me of exaggerating the extent of our friendship. "Kevin keeps his beer in *my* refrigerator!" I testified. That's true. His mother is a Seventh-Day Adventist. She won't allow alcohol in her house. Meat, either. I was about to say so, but censored myself. Kevin might be ever so slightly irked at me if I tattled in detail to his brothers and sisters on the force about all the things Mommy wouldn't allow. Anyway, I got stuck hanging around George Foley's house, first in the cold outdoors, then in a warm cruiser that stank of stale fast food and fresh bodily fluids.

Official vehicles arrived in great number, as did neighbors, joggers, fitness walkers, dog walkers, and ghouls attracted by a hullabaloo. The crowd on foot and on wheels grew so dense that the police blocked the street and tried to disperse the onlookers. The barricades, of course, aroused new curiosity and attracted yet more passersby. Waiting around, I learned frustratingly little about Professor Foley's death. He'd been seen alive late yesterday afternoon; Lydia Berenson had exchanged a few words with him. He'd seemed in his usual good health and excellent spirits. Since Lydia had said something about his heart, I asked her whether he'd had a history of cardiac problems. On the contrary, she replied. He'd had a physical a month earlier and had been elated to find himself suffering from nothing worse than minor arthritis.

If I'd felt useful, I wouldn't have minded waiting around. My uselessness was, however, my own fault. When questioned, I limited myself to factual replies and reserved for Kevin my speculations about the correspondence between this fatality and the murder of Jack Andrews. It must have been almost seven o'clock when I was finally free to leave. A cop gave me a ride home.

Steve and I were supposed to be going out to dinner at Rialto, which is in the Charles Hotel and is by far the fanciest and best restaurant in Cambridge. The decor is what I guess would be called a warm version of Art Deco, voguish enough to please the celebrities and the rich out-of-towners who stay at the hotel, but stopping short of the New York trendiness that would scare away the Cambridge clientele. The food is so good that it always makes me wish I were the kind of person who can send compliments to the chef while keeping a straight face. In brief, a romantic dinner at Rialto is my idea of the perfect cure for the emotional wounds that fester when, for example, he refuses to spend Thanksgiving with her father, and she refuses to spend it with his mother.

Until I found Steve at my kitchen table studying an issue of the *Journal of the American Veterinary Medical Asso-*

ciation and idly stroking the heads of my dogs, I'd forgotten that we were supposed to go out. Instead of greeting either him or the dogs, I stood rigid and silent. As Steve rose, I said, "He died."

Steve wrapped his arms around me. "Your professor?"

"My professor."

Without permission, the dogs leaped up to nuzzle our faces. I didn't correct them.

"You're shaking," Steve said.

"Have the dogs eaten?" I asked.

"No. I thought you'd fed them before you left."

"No. Could you feed them? And take them out?"

Steve is not the kind of insensitive clod who, in these circumstances, says something dense like "Never mind about the damn dogs! What about you?"

"Tie them up before you feed them," I said stupidly.

Instead of saying "I know," he spoke quietly to the dogs as he hitched them at opposite ends of the kitchen, measured correct portions of defrosted Bil Jac, sprinkled on dry kibble from the bag in the closet, and added water. As always, Rowdy and Kimi yelped, shrieked, bounced, and whirled in circles until their dishes hit the floor.

"I love to listen to them eat," I said. "Before Rita got her hearing aids, she thought that dogs ate silently. Did you know that? And she couldn't hear them when they drank water."

"She told me." He went to the cabinet where I keep my small supply of liquor and poured me a glass of cognac. When he handed me the drink, he kissed the top of my head.

I took two big sips and swallowed. "I need to call Kevin." My voice sounded loud. I lowered it. "I think Professor Foley was murdered. I need to talk, but the dogs have to go out. Steve, I don't want them loose in the yard. I keep worrying that they'll kill a rat that's been poisoned. Could you just take them for a little walk?"

While Steve walked Rowdy and Kimi, I took a hot shower. When he and the dogs returned, Rita was with them. I was in the kitchen wearing wool socks, flannel-lined jeans, a turtleneck, and a heavy fleece pullover, not exactly an outfit meant for Rialto.

"So what's this about murder?" Rita demanded.

"I need to call Kevin," I said.

"Have you eaten?" Rita asked.

"We're going to Rialto," Steve told her.

"We're not," I said. "I can't. And I need to talk to Kevin."

"He's away for a week," Rita said. "He left today."

"Kevin? He's never away. He never goes anywhere. Where is he?"

"I'm sworn to secrecy." Rita was serious.

"Where is he?"

She didn't really reply, but asked, "Do you have any food in the house? And I don't mean dog food." She can be very bossy.

"Eggs," Steve said. "Potatoes. And beer."

"Oh, for God's sake, Holly! You wouldn't treat an animal like this. If Steve didn't feed you, you'd die of malnutrition."

"I'm not hungry. Steve, you'd better cancel the reservation."

Instead of using the phone in the kitchen, he headed in the direction of my study.

The second he left, Rita said, "You listen to blues, Holly. Haven't you heard? A good man is hard to find."

"I don't know what you're talking about."

"Didn't you see his face?"

"Rita, the face on my mind right now is Professor Foley's."

"There you have it. You think that he doesn't notice that he always comes last?"

"Steve? He does not come last."

"When have you ever put his needs before your dogs, your work, or your interests? You praise your dogs every time they look at you, and you take him for granted. You aren't hungry, so he doesn't need to eat. He's waiting to take you to Rialto, and—"

"This is none of your business," I said coldly.

"Right. It isn't my business. It's merely my profession. I deal with it all day long. Do you at least have any wine in the house? Crackers and cheese?"

"There's a bottle of white burgundy in the refrigerator. And some cheddar. And I do have crackers." Rita's words bit into me. The wine was a present from Steve. The cheese was what I used to train the dogs.

When Steve returned, he uncorked the bottle. Rita put the cheese and some crackers on a plate. All three of us drank the wine, but only Rita nibbled on the cheese and crackers.

"So what's going on?" Steve asked.

Feeling selfish and guilty, I outlined everything I knew about Professor Foley's death and most of what I suspected about its tie to Jack Andrews's murder.

"The police *are* treating it as a homicide?" he asked.

"Well," I said, "they're at least treating it as an unexplained death. They didn't really tell me anything, though. *That,*" I said, glaring at Rita, "is why I need to talk to Kevin."

With a cool little smile, she said, "He'll be back in a week."

"There's enough gruesome mystery already about

this whole business," I snapped. "There's no need for you to go around deliberately mystifying—"

"I beg your pardon! I am merely respecting a confidence."

"Kevin is having an affair with someone! And he doesn't want his mother to find out. Who? And how did he happen to tell you?"

Rita's face was blank.

"With a woman of color! His mother will have a fit! Or is she Jewish? She's not Christian, she's older than he is, she drinks, and she eats meat! I've got it! He's fallen in love with an elderly alcoholic kosher butcher! Mrs. Dennehy will—"

Rita remained impassive. "Have you ever considered writing novels? It sometimes strikes me that fiction is your strong suit."

"If you recall, I'm a colonial historian."

Steve refilled Rita's wineglass. To me he said, "Let me get a few things straight. The position of the body."

"Exactly like in that crime-scene shot of Jack Andrews's body. Facedown. Twisted. Arm stretched out. All the rest. And, of course, the cup of coffee."

Steve was skeptical. "There are only so many ways to fall down."

"True," I conceded.

"The coffee could be incidental. It might have nothing to do with—"

"It wasn't incidental in Jack Andrews's death. It was laced with sodium fluoroacetate. And that's not exactly what I call—"

"Where have I just heard of that?" Rita asked. "Or maybe read about it?"

"I might have mentioned it," I said. "It's what killed Jack Andrews. Or what was used to kill him. It's rat poison. Well, it's not ordinary rat poison. It's a banned substance now because it's so dangerous. It's colorless, odorless—"

Rita raised her wineglass. "Got it! It's in the book I'm reading. *Midnight in the Garden of Good and Evil.* It's about Savannah. It's full of strange characters, but one of them has a bottle or whatever of sodium fluoroacetate. What he talks about is putting it in the water supply and wiping out the entire populace."

"And does he do it?" I asked.

"Obviously not," Rita said. "Savannah is still there."

"I thought you were talking about a novel," I said. "The book is nonfiction?"

"Well, the names have been changed, but the story is supposed to be true. I keep wondering how much really is, though. A lot of it is so bizarre that it's a little hard to believe. I wondered whether this bit about the poison could possibly be true."

Steve spoken authoritatively. "If it's sodium fluoroacetate, almost none goes a long, long way."

Rita drank some wine. "A bottleful could poison a city?"

Steve smiled. "Depends on the size of the bottle."

Rita emptied her glass. "Mr. Science strikes again."

He really had, too. My direct tactics had entirely failed to persuade Rita to divulge Kevin's whereabouts. Steve had just kept refilling Rita's wineglass. Before she revealed Kevin's true whereabouts, she swore us to secrecy. "If either of you so much as whispers a word to Kevin about this—"

"Never," Steve promised.

"Not a word," I vowed. "Who is she?"

"*She,*" Rita whispered, as if Kevin might overhear, "is something I've been trying to talk him into for a long time." Rita, for once, put her elbows on the table and leaned forward. "He has finally decided to do some-thing about his chronic occupational stress."

"Sex therapy!" I exclaimed.

Rita looked put out. "Don't be ridiculous!"

"What makes you think he needs sex therapy?" Steve demanded of me.

"Damn it, Rita! Where *is* he?"

For the sake of drama, I am sure, she let a few mo-ments of silence fall before she spoke. Her voice was low and intense. "Kevin Dennehy," she announced, "is spending the week at a stress reduction workshop in the Berkshires. He is at this very moment at a retreat in the hills of western Massachusetts communing with Nature, and I forbid both of you to utter a single word to him about it or you'll destroy all my hard work. This is some-thing that's crucial to his physical and mental well-being, and it has taken me more than a year to talk him into it."

"She *has* been trying," I informed Steve. "That's true. I can't believe he's really done it. Is this the place where you go around tracking raccoon spoor?"

"It's an ashram," Rita replied defensively. "It com-bines meditation and breathing exercises with seminars about lifestyle changes. As I understand it, it does in-volve hikes in the woods."

"Rita," I said, "Kevin is a city kid. He's afraid of trees."

Steve agreed. "He sees a tree, he sees a mugger lurk-ing behind it."

"Precisely why he needs this week," Rita said smugly. "He'll return a new man. Now if you'll excuse me, I'm going back upstairs."

After she left, Steve said, "I'm going to Rialto. You coming or not?"

"You canceled the reservation."

"I'm going to sit in the bar and drink. Alone."

"Give me two minutes to change my clothes." I hesitated. "If you want company."

He did.

Nineteen

On Saturday morning, after Steve had left for his clinic
and I'd finished such daily chores as vacuuming up dog
hair and washing my own, I made a fresh pot of coffee
and covered my kitchen table with every bit of material
I'd gathered about Jack Andrews's murder: Jack's obituary, Shaun McGrath's, the photographs Claudia had
given me, the notes I'd made about my conversation
with Brat Andrews, the Violet Wish portrait of Chip,
Randall Carey's book with the chapter about the murder, and the list of people I'd phoned to inquire about
the mysterious Tracy—that tall girl, as everyone called
her—who'd handled Jack's show dogs. On the kind of
yellow legal pad to which every real writer is addicted, I
jotted notes about Gareth Andrews's mad rambling:
rats, dead and alive, their sharp teeth, the stench of
death, Claudia, Oscar Fisch, the recovery movement,
"Uncle" George Foley, and John Winter Andrews, who,

in his son's deranged mind, now and forever drank rat poison, yet did not die.

The surviving members of Jack's family, I thought, had told me all they were willing or, in Gareth's case, able to relate: Even if I ignored Oscar Fisch's plea to stop "harassing" Claudia (and her child, too, of course), I'd probably learn nothing new. Had Claudia, in fact, stolen the library copies of *Mass. Mayhem*? Breaking into her house on Francis Avenue, I decided, wasn't worth the risk. There was probably an elaborate alarm system, and I was a dog writer, not a cat burglar; I'd certainly get caught. Brat, I felt convinced, had said everything she intended to say. As to Gareth, I had no illusion that I could distinguish between his delusions and whatever more-or-less accurate memories he retained. It occurred to me, however, that if Gareth had been on Fayerweather Street near the time of Professor Foley's death, whenever that was, his purple parka and aqua backpack—never mind his behavior—would've made him memorable. As one more odd duck paddling and quacking in Harvard Square, Gareth might be easy to overlook; near Governor Weld's house, however, there'd be watchers on guard for just such rare birds. Oscar Fisch clearly didn't want to talk to me. Randall Carey claimed to remember no more than he'd written in a book ten years earlier. Despite extensive efforts, I'd had no luck in tracing the untraceable tall Tracy, whose short brown hair might now be long and gray, and who might have switched from golden retrievers to black-and-tan coonhounds, Kerry blue terriers, or no dogs at all.

I again phoned the McGraths, who still hadn't returned my call. This time, I got an answer. The voice was a woman's.

"Shirley McGrath?" I asked.

"Yes."

The names in the phone directory, I reminded my-self, corresponded to the names given for Shaun's parents in his obituary. Eighteen years ago, Shaun's parents had lived in Arlington. This Shirley McGrath lived there, too. She *must* be Shaun's mother. If not, I was about to make a real fool of myself. "My name is Holly Winter. I'm a writer. I'm doing a story about the murder of Jack Andrews." I heard a sharp intake of breath. I went on. "I believe that Shaun was innocent."

I listened to about ten seconds of silence. Then the woman said, "We never discuss Shaun." She tried to be polite: She said good-bye before she hung up.

"Damn!" I told the dogs. "And damn Kevin Dennehy and his stupid ashram!" I still found it hard to believe that Kevin had, as he'd have phrased it, fallen into the clutches of the Eastern brain snatchers. Kevin's idea of meditation, for heaven's sake, was to contemplate the depths of a can of Budweiser. Not that his work was exactly relaxing. I mean, you can see how the prospect of getting shot would fray someone's nerves after a while. But if Kevin needed to reconnect himself to Nature, why had he listened to Rita instead of me? I could just picture beefy Kevin out in the Berkshires eating brown rice and kelp with a bunch of turban-wearing om-chanters or trailing through the icy forest after some beatifically smiling back-to-the-woods fanatic in quest of inner peace in the hoofprints and dung of a white-tailed deer. Not that I object to Nature. Well, admittedly, I hate brown rice, I'd just as soon eat clamshells as sea-weed, and you won't catch me swathing my head in bed-sheets, but there's nothing wrong with inner peace. And as for animals both wild and domestic—rats excepted—my unbridled looniness speaks for itself, doesn't it? The mere sight of Rowdy and Kimi brings a beatific smile to my face, and, more to the point, to Kevin Dennehy's. So why did he have to go and listen to Rita? Why, oh why, didn't he just get a dog?

Turning to a fresh sheet of yellow legal pad, I went through the chapter in Randall Carey's book in search of the names of people I might have overlooked. I came up with only two: Ursula Pappas, Jack's secretary, who'd been in Greece when he'd been murdered, and Estelle Grant, described as a typist who had overheard a quarrel between Shaun McGrath and Jack Andrews. *Secretary. Typist.* Eighteen years had passed since Jack's murder. Now, Ms. Pappas would be called an administrative assistant. By now, she could be the CEO of a publishing house in Athens. In the years since Jack's murder, Ms. Grant had probably forgotten how to shift the carriage of a typewriter. Her name could be changed or, Cambridge being Cambridge, hyphenated. She could be anywhere. Both women could be as elusive as "that tall girl."

I never found out where Ursula Pappas ended up. According to the ever-useful phone book, however, Estelle Grant lived in Cambridgeport. Yes, she informed me, she was the same Estelle Grant who'd worked at Damned Yankee Press. She'd been temping there when Shaun McGrath poisoned Jack Andrews. She'd been filling in for someone who'd been on vacation in Greece. Temp work, Estelle volunteered, was still her day job. Now, she was polishing the novel she'd been drafting eighteen years ago. As a matter of fact, she'd incorporated Jack's murder in the plot. I told her that I, too, was a writer. She offered to let me read her book.

Like every other professional writer, I don't have time to read my own unpublished manuscripts, never mind other people's. Furthermore, other people's unpublished fiction is usually even worse than mine. The characters are often flat. Worse, most of them are human. And when they're canine? If you love dogs, even under the best of published circumstances, you hardly dare to turn a page because, in book after book, your favorite characters are always getting disemboweled, drowned, or run over, often by the end of the third chapter, and there you are brokenhearted with a few hundred pages still to go with nothing but people, people, people. Anyway, in Estelle Grant's case I made an exception. I'd love to read her manuscript, I said. I didn't ask whether there were any dogs in her book. If so, I could always skip to the end to make sure they were still alive.

I invited Estelle to have lunch with me in the Square, but she pulled what I now see as a fast one on me. She claimed to be busy, but offered to let me pick up the manuscript. Cambridge has at least as many unpublished writers as it does psychotherapists, perhaps more. There's a connection there: The would-be writers who aren't published because they can't get the words out go into treatment for writer's block, and the prolifically unpublished get driven mad in a whole variety of different ways. Some find themselves stuck in the neurotic dilemma of being so terrified of rejection that they won't let anyone read their work. Others overcome the fear, only to discover that, contrary to what their therapists promised, it was all too realistic after all. They get rejections from agents that consist of nothing but their own query letters with "No!" scrawled in the margin. Self-esteem plummets. Prozac time! Back to the shrink!

Meanwhile, the poor shrink has succumbed to an occupational hazard almost as dire as getting shot: Sooner or later, the therapist, too, decides to write a book, and, being a Cambridge therapist, starts off not by sitting at a desk or keyboard but by consulting another Cambridge therapist about fears of self-revelation and inadequacy, and ends up hiring a writing tutor, who turns out to be another therapist's patient, in other words, an unpublished writer frantic to earn a living.

Expert that I am on this subject, I quickly diagnosed Estelle Grant as having reached the stage of conniving desperation that writers attain when they discover that even their own mothers can't be persuaded to read their books. Until I plowed through Estelle Grant's manuscript, she wouldn't tell me a damned thing about Damned Yankee Press. I could hear the deal in Estelle's voice. I agreed to fetch the book.

She lived on a narrow, car-lined street of rickety asbestos-shingled three-family houses a few blocks from the river. Even before the year's first snowstorm, two of her neighbors had staked their claims to on-street parking. One spot was marked by three official-looking orange traffic cones selected, I thought, to create the impression that a parking-spot thief would be placed under immediate citizen's arrest. The other was occupied by two battered and bent aluminum folding lawn chairs that effectively suggested a history of having been smashed over the heads of unwise drivers who'd failed to respect the significance of the resident snow-shoveler's territorial claim. No fool, I double-parked, dashed up the tumbledown stairs to Estelle's shaky little front porch, and rang a bell labeled with four names, one of which was hers. The door was opened immediately by a woman wearing black tights and what I assumed was a formerly tunic-length blue-patterned wool sweater that had been misguidedly washed in hot water and consequently made its wearer look as if she'd absentmindedly forgotten to put on a skirt. Even if Estelle hadn't introduced herself, I'd have known who she was: She answered the door with a thick manuscript in hand. Purring on Estelle's shoulder was a tricolor kitten that chewed on her long, thin, wavy brown hair while kneading the shrunken sweater with its paws. The kitten was adorable. Estelle was scrawny and had the kind of pale, sickly-looking skin that I associate with people who work in health food stores and subsist on mung beans, strips of dried seaweed, and other foreign objects that would make a dog throw up.

"I'm double-parked," I told Estelle.

She handed me reams of would-be blockbuster. As if to confirm my supposition about the deal she'd offered me, she said sweetly, "We'll talk after you've read it."

"I can hardly wait."

"The chaos is deliberate," she advised me. "Damned Yankee Press was the most disorganized place I've ever worked." With pride in her voice, she confided, "My novel is drawn from life."

Twenty

Estelle Grant's novel was called *Multitudes in the Valley of Decision.* Although I traced the phrase to the Old Testament, I never did figure out the meaning of the title. *Multitudes* seemed to refer to the book's thousands of adverbs, most of which were unpronounceable, pedantic, or both: "sillily," "inchoately," "hermeneutically." *Valley,* I deduced, alluded to the depths to which prose can sink. As for *Decision,* mine would've been to burn the manuscript.

Instead of saying or asking like normal people, the characters were always interjecting, interpolating, querying, or essaying. The women were forever crying out. The men kept ejaculating. The creative process, I should explain, had transformed the real publishing house into a fictional house of prostitution. Maybe the novel was supposed to be an allegory. The narrator was one Stellina Brandt. Jack Andrews appeared, I thought, as a lovable client named Mack Sanders. Shaun Mc-

Grath, in contrast, was cast in the role of a sadistic pimp called Seamus McPhee. Especially considering the book's theme, I was, for once, happy to discover a complete absence of dogs. The only animals, other than most of the human characters, were rats. Poison figured in the story. Leather abounded. Characters of both sexes were always getting their bottoms slapped. A rabbi kept suffering flashbacks about a homosexual encounter on a submarine. The brothel was raided by the police, most of whom were regular customers of the establishment. In crucial scenes, Stellina repeatedly gasped, shrieked, sighed, moaned, sobbed, wailed, groaned, whimpered, or giggled sillily, inchoately, or even hermeneutically, as the mood took her, "More! Yet more!"

"If you'd had to read this book," I told Steve late that same Saturday night, "you wouldn't want to have sex, either."

I finished the manuscript the next afternoon. At a loss as to what to say to Estelle about a work she was still polishing after eighteen years, I decided to describe the novel as "complex." My judgment of writing is merciless, but when it comes to writers, I'm all sympathy. Estelle's eager voice on the phone inspired me. "Complex!" I cried out, sighed, or perhaps gasped before shrieking in triumph, "Hermeneutic!"

By then, I'd looked up "hermeneutic" in the dictionary. I didn't really understand the definition—something about principles of interpretation—but at least I knew how to pronounce the word. Estelle was so pleased that she invited me to her house for herbal tea.

An hour later, having managed to park in a spot unoccupied by traffic cones, lawn chairs, or, of all things, another car, I was seated at Estelle's kitchen table choking down sips of the true explanation for her prose. I came close to advising her that the way to get published was to switch to coffee. The kitchen walls had been painted white sometime around 1965, I guessed. The psychedelic-orange trim on the windows probably memorialized someone's bad trip a few years thereafter. The old white gas stove reminded me of the one at Professor Foley's. The refrigerator dated to the same era as the stove. The chipped white sink was clean and empty. Arrayed neatly on open shelves were a great many bottles of food supplements, together with boxes and jars of seeds, beans, and whole-grain cereals. Between the kitchen and the living room, in place of a door, hung numerous long strings threaded with ziti and elbow macaroni. The kitten was having fun batting at the pasta. The liquid in my mug looked and smelled like samples that cat owners deliver to Steve in specimen cups.

"The rats in the cellar were typical," Estelle said in disgust. "So was the irresponsibility about the poison." Today, she was fully dressed in a sort of sari or toga that seemed to have been fashioned from an Indian bedspread. Her eyes were a beautiful shade of bright blue, but the whites were shot with red, and the pouches underneath were yellow and puffy. "Jack was really a sweet, charming man, but in a lot of ways his mind was off in space somewhere. The place was always in chaos. The doorbell was broken—it was gone, missing—and there were a couple of wires dangling out that you had to put together to make it ring! Fortunately, most of the time, the door was open, unlocked, and people just walked in. The files were a mess. The supply cabinet had a million beat-up manila folders you were supposed to reuse, and no pens except green, and then maybe three or four five-pound bags of sugar and a few dozen cans of coffee! And that was where Jack was storing the poison!"

"*With* the food?"

Estelle nodded. "And the cellar! The first day I was there . . . I was there a week. I started the Monday before Shaun murdered him. I was there the whole week. And the following Monday, too, the day Jack was murdered. So, the first day, Jack sent me down there to look for a box of books, which was ridiculous to begin with, because I was supposed to be typing, for God's sake, not hauling cartons around, but I made the mistake of going down there, and Jesus! I've never seen such a mess in my life. There was old office equipment, electric staplers, collating machines, all this trash, and moldy manuscripts piled on the cement floor, and cardboard cartons, all this junk everywhere. I mean, any books that'd been stored there would've been all mildewed, anyway, but, hey, what did I care? It was a day job, right?"

I murmured agreement. Actually, I was glad to have something to do with my mouth besides drink that kitty-cat tea. "I tried temp work myself a couple of times," I told Estelle. "I wasn't much of a success at it. Now, I manage to scrape by doing a column and freelance articles, but I still haven't published a book."

"What's your column about?"

"Dogs," I said.

Estelle blinked.

When I'd explained about how Chip had assisted mankind in a new and publishable way, Estelle understood perfectly. Then she went on about the cellar of Damned Yankee Press: "And this rat went running across the floor and right over my foot! And, I mean, I don't get hysterical about mice or anything, but this was a really big rat, and I went hightailing it up the stairs, and I never went down there again."

"Of course not. Estelle, how many people worked there?"

She licked her lips. There was nothing even remotely sensual about the act. Stellina Brandt would have enticingly flicked her pink and hungry tongue. "Jack," Estelle said. "Shaun. This secretary who was away. I forget her name. She was the one I was filling in for. Then there was a woman who basically worked for Shaun. She used the computers. Really, she just keyboarded, but back then, it was a big deal. Computers! There was a part-time bookkeeper, but she quit while I was there. Shaun told her she was fucking everything up, in those words, and Jack tried to get her to stay, but she stormed out. And there was an older woman, Elsie, who did most of the practical stuff about orders for books. There were a few other part-time people. I don't remember them. It really was a *small* press."

"Do you ever see any of the people from there?"

"I used to run into Elsie now and then, but she died a few years ago. No one else."

The chaos of *Multitudes in the Valley of Decision* had made me wonder whether Estelle could produce a cogent account of anything, but she managed to give me a blessedly clear and simple outline of the daily routine at the press, at least to the extent that there had been one. Regular office workers arrived at nine and left at five. Part-time people, she thought, came and went at will. Some, she had suspected, handed in time sheets that vastly overstated the hours they'd worked. Shaun McGrath had challenged someone on the subject, but Jack had intervened. Shaun himself worked nine to five. Jack arrived when he felt like it, Estelle thought, sometimes at nine, sometimes at ten or so, and he came and went during the day. He walked his dog. But he always remained at his desk after everyone else had left. "Jack always stayed from five to seven. Everyone who worked there knew that. He did some editing then, and he wrote letters." She remembered perfectly: The police had been interested, and she'd gone over Jack's schedule many times with them.

"Did you type any letters for him? Or did the person who used the computers?"

"The police asked about that, too. I did a few, but they were just business letters, like to Delta Dental and Harvard Community Health Plan, a couple of bookstores, that kind of thing. He did his own letters to his published authors and to people who sent in manuscripts. That was one of the really sweet things about Jack. When he rejected books, he didn't just send out form letters. He sent everyone a personal note. We talked about it. That's sort of in *Multitudes*, right? Mack is sort of based on Jack."

"I wondered," I said.

"And that's important for his character: that he never really wanted to *reject* anyone."

"Yes, I remember. Estelle, did Jack usually keep Chip on leash? In the building?"

"Sort of. Jack used a leash when he took him in and out."

"Did you used to go into Jack's office?"

"Not a lot. The office where I worked, the main office, was on the first floor, naturally, and Jack's office was on the third floor, so most of the time, if I had to ask him something or whatever, I just used the phone. Mostly what I was there for was to tell people that their checks were in the mail! But, no, Jack wasn't one of the ones who want you running in and out all the time."

"When you went to his office, did he tie Chip to his desk?"

"No. I like dogs." She reached down and scooped up

the kitten, which had abandoned the dangling pasta. "I like cats better, though."

"What about Shaun McGrath?"

Estelle's face clouded. "Let me tell you about Shaun McGrath. First of all, we were supposed to call him Mr. McGrath. Do you believe it? In this pigpen of an office? In Cambridge? And not just on the phone, to people who called, but to his face!"

"And he called you Estelle."

We shared a smile.

"Naturally. Even back then, Jack didn't go in for any of that kind of bullshit. And it wasn't like it was an insurance company or something. Even if it had been halfway organized, it would still have been pretty informal."

"What about that Monday? The day he was murdered."

"I went over that a million times. With the police. Really, there was nothing special. What I do remember is Friday, the Friday before, because that was the day when Jack got rid of the poison. That wasn't just Shaun. I mean, it wasn't just Shaun who told him not to keep it around. Everyone did. It really was dangerous. Obviously."

"And what did Jack do with it?"

"Typical." Estelle shook her head. "I didn't see him do it, but apparently he just took the bottle outside and threw it in the trash. Elsie told me, I think, or someone else in the office. I remember we talked about it, but it was crazy, and it was just like everything else that went on there. Anyway, nothing special happened on Monday, not that I can remember, and not that I could remember back then, either. Jack and Shaun had a fight about something, but they had a fight about something practically every day."

"*Fist*fights?"

"No, sometimes they didn't even raise their voices. Shaun would just go around sulking, and you'd know that Jack had told him to quit bothering people or whatever."

"Did they ever argue about the dog?"

"Not that I heard."

"Do you ever remember hearing that Shaun forged Jack's signature on an insurance policy?"

Estelle raised the kitten to her shoulder. It started chewing her hair. "No, but it would've been just like him. He always struck me as a very calculating person. No one could stand him. I don't know why Jack ever got hooked up with him, except that Jack was such a nice man—he was ready to like everyone."

"And on Tuesday? The day after the murder?"

"I showed up for work. The police were there. I spent a long time answering questions. Then I went home. I never went back. The press is still in business, you know. They still hire temps, but not me! No way am I ever setting foot in there again! Of course, I've thought about the place a lot. Like the police? In *Multitudes*? I think it's always really vital to start with what you know."

Twenty-one

If I substituted the electric zap of a shock collar for my smiles, praise, and treats, neither of my dogs would throw a rivalrous fit of shrieking when it was the other dog's turn to train for obedience. Rowdy's pad cut had heightened the competition. Although we could work on attention, heeling, and retrieving, he was still forbidden to jump. Furthermore, he was starved for the vigorous exercise that's the best cure for destructiveness in the house. When I trained Kimi in the yard, his keen ears picked up whispered commands, and when I put Kimi and our portable PVC jumps in the car and headed for a park or a tennis court, I'd return to find signs of Rowdy's regression: damp remnants of chewed magazines, and unanswered and now unanswerable letters from strangers whose return addresses resided in Rowdy's stomach. If I crated him, he battered the wire-mesh door so violently that I was afraid he'd reopen the wound. As I've said, training with punishment would've killed the rivalry and solved my problem by teaching both dogs to associate obedience work with a nonlethal version of capital punishment. Not for anything, however, would I electrocute my bond with my dogs.

In the midafternoon on Monday, my cousin Leah's arrival offered a temporary solution. Although Kimi is definitely mine and although I work with her, it's mainly Leah who trains and shows her. Unfortunately, in the past few weeks, Leah's studies at the ivy-infested place down the street had been interfering with Kimi's education. The time-grabber was chemistry. Leah wants to become a vet. Anyway, on Monday afternoon while Leah was working with Kimi, I removed Rowdy from the audible evidence that Kimi was having fun while he wasn't by taking him for the kind of long walk he needed. Purely by coincidence, our route on that sunny, chilly day just so happened to take us onto Cambridge Street and down a little side street where we just so happened to pass Damned Yankee Press.

In truth, I'd noticed the address in one of the Damned Yankee guides. I'd borrowed the book from Rita, who relishes what I consider to be the gross discomforts of B&Bs and country inns—afterthought bathrooms, no privacy—and who, on arrival in heaven, will pose polite questions about local museums and historic buildings, and will expect to rent a tape recorder with a headset to wear while she takes a self-guided tour. Even to my critical Maine-bred eye, *The Damned Yankee in Maine* was surprisingly accurate. Portland *does* have a lot of good microbreweries. The Union Fair *is* well worth a visit. Helen's Restaurant in Machias *does* serve the best fresh strawberry (or, better yet, raspberry) pie in the state. There really *are* snowy egrets in the wildlife refuge in back of the cement plant on Route 1 in Rockland. The listings had been updated since Jack Andrews's murder. Eighteen years ago, there'd been no microbreweries, and Helen's had been in the center of Machias, not on the way out of town. Still, I felt convinced that it was Jack Andrews who'd shared my love for the taste of Helen's pie and my fondness for the long-legged, golden-slippered birds that improbably inhabit a marsh in back of a factory in Rockland, a community that happens to be right near my own hometown.

I intended only to stroll by the press. Well, naturally, if Rowdy was seized by the impulse to mark a tree, fire hydrant, or utility pole, I might glance up at the third-floor windows and imagine the face of Jack Andrews on the other side of the panes. But I never meant to go inside. What impelled me to mount the steps was my startled realization that, after eighteen years, the doorbell still consisted of wires protruding from a small hole next to the front door. The press, I should mention, occupied a wood-frame building—once someone's house, I suspected—with a small porch. Wide stairs ran almost to the sidewalk. The front lawn, such as it was, consisted of two little patches of dirt on either side of the steps. Dying dandelions poked through matted leaves. On the sign fastened by the door, the central letters had faded almost completely. Or maybe a disgruntled employee or neighborhood kid had scraped the paint. For whatever reason, the business now proclaimed itself:

DAMN   PRESS.

Because I do most of the maintenance and repair on my own house, I knew that the loose doorbell wires didn't carry enough current to hurt anyone, but instead of making the contact, I tried the door, found it unlocked, and walked in. Piled in a tiny foyer were two pairs of old-fashioned galoshes, a broken ski pole, three unmatched cross-country skis, and a stack of telephone directories still in the plastic bags in which they'd been delivered. Grasping the knob on the inner door, I scratched my hand on a loose screw. When I pushed the door open, escorted Rowdy in, and glanced around, it hit me that a loose screw was, indeed, the perfect introduction to the place.

A wide hallway lay ahead of me. To my left, an archway opened into a big front office that must have combined the original living room and parlor of the house. Everywhere, and I mean *everywhere,* were the greatest number and variety of objects I'd seen piled, heaped, stacked, and just plain dumped since my last visit to my hometown sanitary landfill. Antique IBM PC system units with gaps in place of floppy drives supported ancient dot-matrix printers on which teetered fat old monitors with dirty screens. A gooseneck lamp with a broken neck perched lifelessly on a radiator that was shedding dandrufflike chips of aluminum paint. What else? Rolled-up carpets; snakelike lengths of cable; overstuffed trash bags; a framed print displaying Notre Dame Cathedral through cracked glass; six or eight four-drawer file cabinets in different colors—green, brown, tan—with what looked like twenty years of unfiled letters, invoices, and folders mounded on top; scarred oak schoolteacher's desks covered with thick manuscripts and loose sheets of paper; unplugged answering machines wrapped in their own cords; and cartons stamped with book titles, for instance, *The Damned Yankee in Vermont, The Damned Yankee in Connecticut, The Damned Yankee on Nantucket, What She had Done: The Legend of Lizzie Borden, Perennials for the Maine Seacoast Garden, Viking Visitors to Precolonial Cape Cod.* Dozens of copies of Damned Yankee books in every condition from mint to battered squatted atop one another as if en-

gaged in prolonged efforts to breed yet more Damned
Yankee books; Estelle Grant's transformation of the
small press to a brothel finally made sense. Here and
there, fast-submerging islets of order testified to
doomed efforts to conquer the chaos. A column of
neatly aligned boxes bore labels in block capitals. Above
a dusty rectangle on a wall hung a plastic-covered sheet
of instructions for a photocopier that wasn't there.

From somewhere behind the folders, books, mailing
envelopes, telephones, and "While You Were Out" slips
clustered around a modern computer on what I supposed was a desk, a melodious feminine voice with a
trace of an accent announced, "I don't work here! I'm
just a temp! It's only my third day! But may I help
you?" Before I could respond, a phone rang. "Damned
Yankee Press!" the voice said pleasantly. After a pause, I
heard, "I'm so terribly sorry. The check is definitely in
the mail. It was sent yesterday." Arising from behind the
barricade, a pretty young Asian woman with fine bones
and immense glasses smiled at me and said, "Sorry
about that! I really don't know what's going on here."

Taking another look at the multitudes—ah, yes, multitudes!—of boxes, trash bags, and assorted rubbish, I
asked, reasonably enough: "Is the press moving? Or
maybe . . . ?" I left unspoken the thought that it was
going out of business.

"I wondered the same thing!" the woman replied.
Her articulation was precise. Raising a hand above the
pile of stuff that separated us, she made a gesture that I
took as a invitation to approach. I got within a yard.
Rowdy did his agile best to follow. The woman smiled
puckishly and whispered, as if eager to share a heretofore secret delight, "Don't ask me! I'm only a temp!"

Returning her smile, I asked whether anyone else was
around.

"Heaven knows!" she exclaimed gleefully. "I feel like Alice in Wonderland: 'People come and go so quickly here.'"

What inspired Rowdy to push past me was perhaps the happy tone of the word *here*. Or maybe he mistook the various obstacles in his path as a novel sort of agility course for dogs. For whatever reason, he wove and squeezed by me to present himself to the woman, who gave his head a tentative pat and announced as if conveying great news to both Rowdy and me, "In my country, dog meat is a very popular food!" To my mixed relief, she added, "Among the poorer classes. Savages! Barbarians! Here, everything is much better: Burger King, McDonald's. At night, I go to school, and in the daytime, I answer telephones and—"

"Jack Andrews!" I blurted out. "On the list on the wall!" In the same block capitals I'd noticed on the cartons, some unknown calligrapher had long ago printed a list of names and telephone extensions. Like the instructions for the vanished photocopier, the list was covered in protective plastic. Shaun McGrath's name was there, too.

"An old list!" the woman pronounced. "At Harvard Extension School, I take courses in philosophy. Here, I ponder archaeology! Dig, dig, and who knows? At the bottom perhaps are artifacts of prehistoric cultures."

"Jack Andrews," I said, "died eighteen years ago."

Lowering her voice, tilting her head downward, and peering rather ominously over her huge glasses, she said in weirdly dire tones, "In the cellar is a box with his name: 'Jack Andrews. Contents of desk.'"

So thoroughly unaccustomed am I to uttering even the most innocent and innocuous of white lies that on the rare occasions when I deviate from the truth, I veer wildly from veracity by venting all my pent-up mendacity at once. Bursting into what I am chagrined to admit were real, or at least wet, tears, I let out a cry of ecstasy: "Uncle Jack's desk! The picture of Aunt Claudia! The special pen set! Oh, my cousins will be thrilled!" Regaining genuine control, I asked timidly and solemnly whether it might be possible for me to take a peek at the box that bore the name of my beloved Uncle Jack.

In response to my inquiry, the young woman disclosed yet another respect in which Damned Yankee Press had, in the eighteen years since Jack Andrews's murder, retained what I took to be its original character: The cellar, she informed me, had rats! On her first day here, the coffee machine had broken. Instead of following the admirable American course of sending her to buy a new one, someone called Leo—her employer, I gathered—had insisted that there was a perfectly good percolator on a shelf in the basement and, with no warning about the rats, had dispatched her in search of it. The dirty, dented percolator and its frayed electric cord had rested on the box labeled with Jack Andrews's name.

"Did you actually *see* a rat?" I asked.

She nodded.

"It couldn't have been a mouse?"

Playfully wagging a finger at Rowdy, who wagged his tail in return, she shook her head and replied with the confidence of true expertise, "In my country, you too could be food." As before, she amended the statement: "Among the poorer classes."

"Well," I said, suppressing a shudder of nausea, "family pictures are priceless, and what's the worst thing a rat can do?"

"Bite you," she informed me promptly. "Transmit diseases."

What drove me into that cellar was not really, I think,

the hope of finding anything relevant either to Jack's murder or to Professor Foley's. Rita subsequently made much of the nature of my lies about "Uncle" Jack: In claiming kinship with Jack, she insisted, I had told the psychological truth. At the time, I felt only the impulse to touch objects that had been Jack's: pens, pencils, paper clips, the debris of the life he'd lived in the office where he'd been poisoned.

After extracting herself from behind the computer and the other components of the barricade, the smiling young woman led me to a door, unlatched and opened it, reached in to flick on bright fluorescent lights, and provided clear, detailed directions to the shelf where she'd found the percolator. I was embarrassed to speak my mind to Rowdy in a stranger's presence. I therefore fell back on an effort at thought transmission: "You go first, pal, because I'm sc-sc-sc-scared!" After he'd compliantly barged ahead and gone halfway down the steep flight of dirty stairs, I had second thoughts, not about my cherished position as the alpha figure in his life, but about the possibility that where there were rats, there might also be poison.

"Rowdy, wait!" Gathering his leash in my hands, I hurried down after him. To make mortally certain that I had full control and could prevent him from gobbling up whatever deadly snacks he might encounter, I grabbed his collar, raised his head, and kept him tucked next to me.

The basement turned out to be a damp, musty-smelling version of the upstairs, but with dozens of freestanding, or in some cases free-falling, shelf units. Following the precise directions I'd been given, I turned right at a Xerox machine that had probably started to acquire value as an antique. Making my way down a sort of alleyway between shelves, I passed several eye-level landmarks the young woman had mentioned: a greasy-looking toaster oven and a box that had once contained Gordon's Gin. A few steps past the Gordon's, I came to a set of shelves with boxes boldly labeled with red marker. As I'd been told, on my left I found one about twice the size of a shoe box that read:

JACK ANDREWS
CONTENTS OF DESK

It was sealed with heavy brown tape. Scattered on the strip of tape across the top of the box were what I hoped were coffee grounds deposited by the old percolator. After checking for anything that could possibly be rat poison, I released my grip on Rowdy's collar, looped his leash around my left wrist, and reached for the box with both hands.

Just as I was getting the filthy box settled on my right hipbone, where I could support it with my arm, Rowdy, with no warning whatsoever, hit the end of his leash. With the reflexes of a real dog person, instead of sensibly letting him bolt, I did exactly what I'd been schooled from birth to do. As I tightened my grip on the leash, tripped, and got dragged across that grimy, gritty concrete floor, I could practically hear my mother's injunction: *Never, under any circumstances whatsoever, Holly, do you ever let go of the dog's lead! Never, never! Is that crystal clear? Never!*

The warning had been a standard feature of her lecture on my behavior at dog shows. What's more, she'd been talking about golden retrievers, not Alaskan malamutes. She was, however, an obedience trainer of the old school—dentists drill with less fervor than hers—and it never even crossed my mind to obey common sense. Ahead of me, Rowdy had his head lowered in the classic, correct pose of a sledge dog hauling weight, but the force that drove him was far deeper than the urge to pull. Not a yard beyond Rowdy's jaws, a rat scuttled across the floor. Like a separate animal, its tail slithered behind it. Don't ever let anyone tell you that rats are creatures of God. This one was fat with evil, and greasy-coated and nasty-looking, as if it had just come from filthy places where it had committed vile acts of repugnant ratness.

Hitting the concrete floor, I'd landed on my left elbow. Pain ran up through my shoulder and down my back. As I struggled to raise myself, I could feel the blood drain from my head. Through the pain and the rising nausea, I fought off the fear that, within seconds, that loathsome rodent would be locked in Rowdy's predatory jaws and that I—the dog-obedience pooh-bah, the alpha figure in Rowdy's life—would be powerless to make him drop his mauled and bloody and probably poison-infested prey.

After what felt like several hours—five seconds?—I managed to crawl from my knees to a firm sitting position. Finding myself near the ancient Xerox copier, I braced my feet against it, gave Rowdy's leash the kind of neck-wrenching jerk I hadn't administered for years, and finally succeeded in finding my voice and croaking Rowdy's name. As Rowdy briefly turned his head, the rat must have seized its chance to escape. "Rowdy, watch me! Rowdy, here! Good, good boy! Good dog. Good dog." With sweet words and tugs on his leash, I drew him to me. Digging scraped, bleeding hands into my pockets, I found scraps of desiccated cheese. Rowdy licked them off my palms. His eyes were bright. His beautiful white tail was tailing back and forth across his back. The escape of the rat bothered Rowdy not at all. "You disgust me," I told him.

Leaning on Rowdy, I finally got to my feet and retrieved the box I'd dropped, the one marked with Jack Andrews's name. My retreat from Damned Yankee Press was uneventful. The cheerful young woman paid no attention to the box I carried, to the holes in the knees of my jeans, or to what must have been the pallor of my face.

"There really are rats there," I told her.

"Yes," she said with a smile.

An hour later, in my own kitchen, when I'd disinfected and bandaged the wounds on my hands and knees, I drew a kitchen knife across the tape that sealed the box. Rowdy sniffed eagerly. The scent, no doubt, awakened happy memories. Kimi explored my shoes with her nose. I opened the box. Inside were the pens, pencils, and paper clips I'd expected. To my amazement, there actually was a small framed photograph of Claudia, Brat, and Gareth. Among the other odds and ends, I found only one item of interest, a slip of paper on which someone had scrawled four words: *And One Fought Back*.

The privately printed book about Hannah Duston.

Twenty-two

In case you, too, are ever traumatized by a rat, let me give you some advice: Don't expect any sympathy from your vet. Steve's attitude that same Monday evening made me half wish I'd started an affair with an exterminator instead. Steve did, however, insist on examining the physical damage. For strictly medical reasons, he made me take off my jeans. Wearing nothing but panties, socks, and a Big Dog T-shirt he'd given me—YOU CAN MOVE A MOUNTAIN, BUT YOU CAN'T BUDGE A BIG DOG—I sat shivering on a kitchen chair as he gently removed the gauze and tape from my knees.

"What's this grease you've smeared on?" he asked.

"Panolog," I mumbled.

"What?"

"Panolog cream. Prescribed by *you*. It worked just great on Kimi's—"

"Into the bathtub," he ordered. "Soap and hot water.

These abrasions are filled with grit. Don't they teach first aid in Maine?"

"They teach you to go to the dump and shoot rats, only it's a nighttime sport, and you just see the ugly things from a distance in the headlights of your car."

As Steve led me to the bathtub, scrubbed my knees and elbows with soap, and made me rinse the scrapes under hot water, he accused me of maligning some of his favorite patients. "Clean, intelligent pets," he said.

"Cop-out pets! You ever hear of 'a boy and his rat'? 'A girl and her rat'?"

"Some people don't have time for dogs."

"Cats. Cats are *real* pets. They're not disgusting, beady-eyed, humongous *rodents*. This one weighed a minimum of five pounds. Steve, that's rinsed enough. I'm freezing. Can't I get out of here?"

"No, and if it weighed five pounds—"

"Oh, it did! Professor Foley's neighbor, Lydia, said that he told her he saw one the size of a woodchuck, and naturally, I thought that was an exaggeration. But *now* I realize it was probably an underestimate. I am getting out of this tub now!"

"Whoever would've guessed," he said, handing me a clean white towel, "that beneath this feminist exterior—"

"Rats are the enemy of the human race. It's just that women are a lot freer than men to express everyone's true feelings on the subject."

Back in the kitchen, as the dogs assisted Steve by licking my injuries and running off with gauze pads, I said, "Besides, this was a *sick* rat. All the hair had fallen off its tail, and the bare skin was all scaly . . ." I shuddered at the memory.

"Rats have hairless tails. The skin on their tails is supposed to be scaly."

"All the more reason to exterminate the damned things. *Now* I finally understand why Jack Andrews had that sodium fluoroacetate. If what you're dealing with is *rats,* no measure is too strong!"

Steve's Fletcherizing relative must have forced him to chew his thoughts as well as his food. He ruminated for thirty seconds before he said, "The only good rat is a dead . . . ?"

Another half-minute passed in silence.

"Rats are rats," I finally said.

"There is nothing inherently evil about rats."

"Rats *are* rats," I repeated. "The situations are not comparable." I now had a towel wrapped around my waist. I'd left my socks in the bathroom. My legs and feet were an unattractive shade of winter white; by comparison, the fresh bandages had a great tan. I was still wearing the T-shirt, but its sleeves were damp. I went to Steve and held his face between my gauze-encased hands. "But the feelings are."

He stroked my hair.

"The feelings are comparable," I said. "We all have it in us, don't we?"

And then, naturally—it happens all the time—even before the dogs had had a chance to pounce on us, Steve got called away on an emergency caused, as usual, by yet another Cambridge intellectual who hadn't been able to endure the prospect of depriving her dog of his so-called freedom to be a dog—his natural right to savor the ultimate canine experience of being crushed by a car—and now expected Steve to repair the damage that was her own damned fault. In cynical moments, I wonder why these dog-murdering romantics bother to let their dogs run loose. It would be altogether simpler and easier if these people would just get in their cars and run over their dogs themselves. The effect would be the same, really, only the owners would have slightly more control than they do now over which body parts get destroyed and whether the dogs live or die.

After Steve departed, I called Brat Andrews. I did not confess that I'd passed myself off at Damned Yankee Press as her cousin. I told the truth: I said that I was very sorry about Professor Foley's death. Brat's response was terse, but the pitch of her voice was high and she sounded sincere. "Uncle George was a good friend of Daddy's."

I said that I hated to bother her right now, but that I had a few questions. I'd be as brief as possible. "Your father grew up in Haverhill," I said. "I know this may sound off the wall, but the local heroine there is a colonial woman named Hannah Duston, and—"

"Daddy knew all about Hannah Duston. There's a statue of her in the middle of Haverhill. Daddy did a report about her when he was . . . in high school, I think. Maybe when he was younger. I remember because he used to make fun of himself for what he called it: 'Intrepid Heroine.' He got an A on it. I don't think the title is so stupid, but Daddy did."

"There's no chance you still happen to have a copy of . . . ?"

"Of Daddy's paper? That probably got thrown out the day he brought it home from school. I'm sure he didn't have it."

"One other thing. Brat, I'm really sorry to keep raising painful topics, but—"

"You'd rather ask me than Claudia."

I cleared my throat. "Brat, you don't happen to know who adopted Chip? You told me that right after your father died, Shaun McGrath took Chip. But I don't know where Chip went after Shaun—"

Brat's voice was deep and angry: "Is this some kind of joke?"

"Not at all. Your mother said she found him a good home. I wondered—"

"Claudia is a goddamned liar. The night Daddy died, after he didn't come home, she went over there, and she didn't have a key, so she called Shaun McGrath, and she sent Chip home with him. And then that slimy little bastard killed Chip, too."

"He killed *Chip*?"

Brat's voice was high again. "He said Chip was stolen out of his car while he was at Daddy's funeral. I always knew better. He wasn't satisfied with murdering Daddy. He had to go and murder Chip, too."

Twenty-three

It could be worse. When Elizabeth Emerson was eleven years old, her father, Michael Emerson—Hannah's father, too, of course—was convicted of cruelly and excessively beating and kicking Elizabeth. Michael Emerson was fined and released. Fifteen years later, in 1691, when Elizabeth, already the mother of one out-of-wedlock child, was charged with murdering her newborn twins, the law presumed her guilty, and not a single witness stepped forward to defend her. During the nine and a half months that Elizabeth Emerson spent in prison before her execution, not a single person visited her. Not her sister Hannah. Not her mother. Not her father.

So it could be much worse. Still, I sometimes long for the kind of father who calls and announces who he is. "This is Daddy," maybe? Is that what normal fathers say? I wouldn't know. Even when my father phones mere acquaintances, there's no need for the preliminary statement that he is Buck Winter. Whether you hear Buck bellow long distance in your ear or see him close up, the only creature you could possibly mistake him for is a bull moose. Other people's fathers, I believe, say things like "How are you, dear?" The vocalization of the bull moose, in contrast, is usually rendered as a deep *ugghh.* Not that my father is unsolicitous. For example, he almost always begins by asking about my dogs.

Not long after I'd finished my conversation with Brat Andrews, the phone rang and the familiar paternal roar crashed into my left eardrum. The pad cut was healing, I replied. Leah had worked with Kimi this afternoon.

My father then produced a weirdly smug-sounding version of *ugghh* while simultaneously speaking comprehensible English: "Tracy, uuugghhh, Littlefield!"

"How did you find that out?"

"Guess!" he challenged.

"Surfing the Internet." I wasn't kidding. Buck was, in fact, the principal reason I was not yet on-line. Having him embarrass me at dog shows was bad enough. I had no desire to become his roadkill on the Information Superhighway.

"No," he ugghhed.

This time, I got it. My late mother collected dog show catalogs. "Old show catalogs. I should have thought of it myself. You found Jack's name—John Andrews's name—and she was the agent for his dog." In a catalog, *agent* means handler.

As usual, Buck corrected me. "Dogs. Plural. Tracy Littlefield. They co-owned two goldens. Maybe more."

"And you don't remember . . ."

The show catalogs had, indeed, reawakened old memories. Instead of supplying a detailed description of the tall Tracy Littlefield, Jack Andrews, or both, my father launched into a critique of their golden retrievers, which, as I'd assumed from Chip's picture, hadn't come from my mother's lines and which, my father claimed, were sound but not typey. "Not typey" was not a compliment; in Buck's opinion, the golden in question hadn't represented the essence of the breed. My father seldom says anything negative about a dog. I concluded that on at least one occasion under one AKC judge, one of Jack and Tracy's goldens had beaten one of ours.

I was eventually driven to bellow back at him. "Tracy Littlefield's address!"

In an apparent non sequitur, Buck replied in tones of grief-stricken disappointment, "You know, Holly, your mother"—here he paused lugubriously—"was a woman who understood dogs."

I ignored the combined eulogy and lecture that followed. At the back of a show catalog, I should mention, is an index of exhibitors, together with their addresses. "Do you have the catalogs there? Would you please look up Tracy Littlefield's address?"

"Georgetown," he growled, as if it, too, had let him down by failing to understand dogs.

"Georgetown, Maine?"

"Georgetown, Massachusetts," he replied in disgust. "Never heard of the damn place." My father is almost as loyal to the state of Maine as he is to dogs. He takes particular offense at innocent cities like Portland, Oregon, and Augusta, Georgia, which he evidently suspects of an attempt at geographic social climbing that consists of a futile effort to pass themselves off as their betters.

"It's near Haverhill," I said, more to myself than to my father. "It's right next to Bradford." I can never shake the irrational impulse to try to please my father. "Bradford," I reminded him, "is Rowdy's birthplace."

When I finally got Buck off the phone, I called Information. There was no listing in Georgetown for Tracy

Littlefield. Armed with Tracy's last name, I called Janet Switzer, who said, "Oh, Tracy Littlefield! The groomer! Whatever happened to her?"

"I have no idea. That's what I'm trying to find out."

"I used to see her at shows. She lived in Georgetown. She worked at the library."

"I thought you said she was a groomer."

"She was. She had goldens."

"Sound," I said. "But not typey." It takes me a day or two to recover from a conversation with my father. "Ignore that. That's what my father thinks. Actually, I saw a picture of one of her dogs, a head study. Violet Wish did it. He had a very typey head."

Violet, as you know, is the Bachrach of show dogs. I didn't have to explain who she was.

"Violet did that head study of Denny," Janet said. Denali: Rowdy's late sire. Janet knew that I knew which head study she meant.

"I know."

"You ought to have Violet do one of Rowdy."

"And Kimi," I said. "If I ever have the money, I will." Let me point out that it was neither my fault nor Janet's that we'd strayed from the subject of Tracy Littlefield. Dogs possess a magnetic power over the conversation of dog people: No matter how hard we fight to stay on another topic, we get drawn back. Triumphing over the almost overwhelming impulse to discourse at length on the prospect of Violet Wish canine portraits, I said abruptly, before the dogs won out, "So Tracy Littlefield worked at the Georgetown Library?"

"No—Haverhill. The Haverhill Public Library. I used to see her there all the time. She checked books in and out. I don't think she was a professional librarian. When I needed help with interlibrary loans, I had to ask someone else." Like a lot of other people with Northern breeds, Janet had undoubtedly been borrowing arcane books about polar expeditions and the native peoples of the Arctic. Corgi fanciers track down books about Wales. If you love your puli or your Kuvasz, you're bound to get curious about Hungary. Virtually all dog fanciers feel this compulsion to learn about the breed's origins, and even if we have the money to buy the rare books that we increasingly crave, we sometimes can't find them. Consequently, we rely on interlibrary loans.

"Tracy groomed on the side," Janet continued.

"She had a shop?"

"No, she just used her own grooming area at home, in her laundry room. She rented a little house in George-town, not too far from here. The basement had one of those big old set tubs, and she had a grooming table and her own dryers. It was kind of makeshift, but she did a good job. I used her when I didn't feel like grooming. I trusted her with the dogs."

So what's not to trust about a dog groomer? Most of the time, nothing. Almost all groomers become groomers in the first place because they like dogs. When the owners aren't around, however, a few groomers handle the dogs roughly.

"The dogs were crazy about Tracy," Janet added. "She really did love dogs."

"She was friends with a guy named Jack Andrews," I said. "They co-owned some goldens. She handled his dogs. Did you ever meet him?"

"Not that I know of. I might've seen him. Tracy wasn't really a friend of mine. She was kind of quiet. Shy. I just used to see her around. But she was a very nice girl. I wonder whatever happened to her."

"If I find out," I promised, "I'll let you know."

And the next morning, Tuesday, I began to trace the heretofore untraceable Tracy. Even with my extensive network of dog people to tap, even with a last name, the search took a while. Tracy Littlefield did not belong to any of the local dog clubs. When I supplied the name Littlefield, people said, "Oh, yeah! Littlefield! Tracy Littlefield!"

"Tall," I'd add. "Quiet. Shy. But nice."

And the person would say, "Yeah! That's her!"

But Tracy Littlefield did belong to one dog organization. She was a current member of Yankee Golden Retriever Rescue. To avoid any misunderstanding, let me spell it out: The disaster area in breed rescue isn't an earthquake in some distant city, but a local highway where someone's stopped briefly to throw out the family pet or a pound where the owner has turned in the dog with all the regret I'd feel in tossing an empty bottle in a bin for someone else to recycle. Anyway, Yankee Golden Retriever Rescue was (and still is) one of the oldest and most efficient breed-rescue organizations in the country. Tracy Littlefield belonged. According to a friend of mine who had the membership list, Tracy lived in Ellsworth, Maine. I also got her phone number.

A woman answered. "Tracy's Doggone Salon!"

Instead of blurting out questions about Jack Andrews, I calmly asked whether I was speaking to Tracy. When the woman said yes, I made a quick decision. I also made an appointment. Tracy could fit Kimi in the next afternoon. Ellsworth, Maine, is where Down East really begins. It's the coastal town where you turn off Route 1 to get to Bar Harbor and Acadia National Park. Ellsworth is about 250 miles from Cambridge. That's a long way to go to get a dog groomed. The distance seemed like nothing. I had the creepy sense that in meeting Tracy, I'd find myself at long last face to face with Jack Andrews.

Twenty-four

Owls Head, Maine, boasts two principal tourist attractions—the Owls Head lighthouse and the Museum of Transportation—and, in the person of my father, a one-man tourist repellent. When my mother was alive, summer visitors used to pull to the side of the road to take snapshots of her perennial garden. Every once in a while, an out-of-stater would march up to our freshly painted front door, rap the polished brass knocker, and issue a brazen offer to buy the place. My father always responded by making a prompt counteroffer on the bidder's spouse or children. These days when the cars slow down, my father misinterprets the dropped jaws, and when a bargain-hunter condescends to inquire about taking the place off his hands, he continues to propose the kinds of wife-for-barn and child-for-house swaps that weren't funny to begin with and now, I fear, strike the tourists as serious and scary. My own visits home have gradually become less and less frequent. Steve, the most mellow of men, balks at accompanying me.

After I dropped Steve at the airport early on Wednesday morning to catch a flight to Minneapolis for a belated Thanksgiving with his mother, I reminded myself of the many reasons I'd refused to go with him. Let me just report that on my last visit, Steve's mother served green slime with miniature marshmallows and fake mayonnaise at every meal except breakfast for three days in a row. On individual plates. No cheating. At lunch on the fourth day—this is the truth—she left the room and, in desperation, I fed The Blob to her cocker, who waited until his mistress came back to return my gift, which had turned to a slimy semiliquid that looked like pond scum swarming with monster-size maggots and obviously hadn't been safe to ingest to begin with. The rug was white. Originally. Mine was the only clean plate on the table. When a dog betrays me, I know I'm someplace I don't belong.

I headed north, picked up 95, and, staying far west of Owls Head, took the highway to Bangor before cutting over to the coast. In case your image of Maine comes from television and the movies, I should mention that Ellsworth possesses a downtown with small shops, a little river, a bridge, an old-fashioned movie theater, and the mandatory historic house. The de facto center of Ellsworth, however, is a wide strip of heavily mall-lined road that ends where Route 1 makes a sharp left and sprints north toward Washington County and away from the tourists instead of continuing straight ahead on Route 3, which leads through Trenton to Mount Desert Island, and thus to Bar Harbor and Acadia National Park. Acadia, I might mention, in a transparent effort to drum up tourist business for my poverty-stricken home state, not only offers all those justly famous mountains-

meet-the-sea vistas best enjoyed while consuming in-
credible quantities of Maine lobster, but is one national
park that really does welcome dogs.

The only scenery visible from the parking lot of the
motel where I'd made a reservation consisted of a drive-
through fast-drink gourmet-coffee stand, two gigantic
supermarkets, dozens of storefronts that glared com-
petitively at one another across Route 1, and, in the distance, the alluring view of the L.L. Bean outlet. Like the
park, however, the motel welcomed dogs. When I
checked in, the young woman behind the desk merely
glanced at Rowdy and Kimi, smiled blandly, and said,
"Oh, and you have pets." As applied to my obsession,
the word *pet* always strikes me as ludicrous. Then she
asked the routine Maine question about malamutes:
"What percent?"

I told the truth. "None. They're Alaskan malamutes."

Her brother-in-law, she replied, had one just like that,
only bigger. His was eighty-eight percent. "There's a
guy in Owls Head who breeds them," she added.

Hybrids. Wolf hybrids.

"He doesn't actually breed them anymore," I informed her, without admitting that the guy was my father. As you'll have gathered, his hybrids are a topic I
prefer to avoid. "As a matter of fact, he's getting back
into golden retrievers."

An hour later, at three-thirty, I parked my Bronco on
a narrow, mainly residential side street off Route 1
around the corner from a shop that, according to a fad-
ing sign, had once sold fresh-cut flowers and fresh-
caught fish. By then, the juxtaposition didn't seem
strange. I was beginning to reorient myself to life in
Maine. Here, economic survival depends on the kind of
diversity evident in roadside signs that offer guns,
ammo, live lobsters, worms, crawlers, ceramics, acu-

puncture, lawn ornaments, pick-your-own organic raspberries in season, and specials on permanent waves—all at the same establishment. In a copy of *The Ellsworth American* that I'd bought in the motel lobby, I'd noticed that on the following Saturday, a local club was sponsoring an event advertised as a "family fun shoot." ("Sorry, Junior," announces Dad, loading his target pistol, "I'm afraid you drew the short straw today, son.") If you didn't feel like practicing a radical and shockingly delayed form of family planning, you could attend what was billed as a "fire-walking seminar" at what was rather outrageously described as an "alternative wellness facility." Truly! I quote: ". . . a fire-walking seminar on Saturday from 1:00 to 6:30 P.M. The seminar will facilitate a positive relationship with terror. Active participation in walking on coals is strictly voluntary." The fee was fifty dollars. Preregistration was encouraged—why, I couldn't imagine. You'd think it would have been better not to leave time for second thoughts. I prayed to Almighty Dog that Kevin Dennehy's ashram in the Berkshires didn't supply hot coals. Fire-walking was the kind of macho challenge that Kevin would never be able to resist.

Anyway, Tracy's Doggone Salon was housed in a converted single-car garage attached to a small, neat lime-green bungalow. On the dormant grass in front of the house, the December wind inflated the bodies of two artificial Canada geese and sent a wooden Sylvester chasing after a fleeing Tweety. Tracy's sign swung from a little wrought-iron post. Parked in the driveway was a dark van with white letters on the side that read JAMES W. LITTLEFIELD. PLUMBING & HEATING. Stacked against the side of the converted garage were a few dozen lobster traps. Leaving Rowdy crated in the Bronco, I got Kimi out. As I led her up the path to the door of the shop, a gust fresh from the pile of lobster traps washed me in the rank, salty reek of rotten fish. From Manhattan, are you? Well, remarkably enough, these cutesy coffee tables *are*, now and then, also used to catch lobsters. Hence the bait.

"And now," I said brightly to Kimi, "you get to have a lovely bath." I'd chosen her because Rowdy's pad cut was temporarily sparing him what he perceives as his frequent ordeals-by-water.

My plan, such as it was, fell apart the second I opened the shop door. The plan was this: Catching sight of Tracy, I was to appear momentarily puzzled. "You look familiar," I was supposed to remark. "Didn't I used to see you at shows with Jack Andrews?"

But I've leaped ahead of myself. The interior of the shop, I should first note, contained more equipment than I'd expected: a pair of waist-high tubs with wall-mounted force dryers nearby, two grooming tables equipped with arms and grooming nooses, three or four tall stand dryers, a row of empty wire-mesh crates, a crate dryer, a fat trash barrel overflowing with dog hair, scads of brushes. The setup was professional. The tubs had been built into the tiled wall, the grooming tables were hydraulic, and lined up on the floor were the same gallon-size brown plastic bottles of Eqyss Bio-Tek shampoo and grooming spray that I swear by and special-order myself. Near the door was a little waiting area for human clients: two plastic-covered chairs and a low Formica-topped table that held a coffee maker, mugs, sugar, powdered creamer, and a stack of dog magazines, including, I was happy to see, the latest issue of *Dog's Life*.

Her back to me, a tall, thin woman with short brown hair—Tracy, at last!—stood at one of the grooming tables and vigorously brushed the coat of a handsome little short-haired dog that, at a guess, was half Jack Russell terrier. Energetically sweeping up from the floor what looked like the shorn coat of a black standard poodle was a young man who wore jeans and a University of Maine sweatshirt. What immediately wrecked my plan was the kid's uncanny resemblance to the affable face I'd studied in Jack Andrews's college graduation photo: the cleft chin, the pleasant expression, even the oddly expectant suggestion of features on which character hadn't yet been written.

So exact and so startling was the likeness that I jumped when the boy spoke. "Hi. Mom'll be right with you."

I nodded stupidly.

Taking in Kimi, he asked, "What percent?"

"She's an Alaskan malamute."

His grin was identical to the one that Jack Andrews had flashed to Brat in the family snapshot. "If you say so."

Swiveling her head around, Tracy—she *had* to be—ran her eyes over Kimi, smiled at me, and said softly to the kid, "She's not putting you on, Drew." Catching my eye, she asked shyly, "Show dog?"

As I was bobbing my head, Kimi suddenly emitted a prolonged peal of *woo-woo-woo*s punctuated here and there with *ah-roo* and culminating in what was obviously a friendly question that demanded an immediate response.

As Tracy listened to Kimi, her face lit up. An impish smile appeared. When Kimi had finished, Tracy replied, "Relax! I won't strip out your show coat. I'm an old hand."

I liked her gentle voice. Just as everyone had remembered, she was very tall, probably five ten, and her hair was still short and brown, cut in a cap that framed an

ordinary face, neither pretty nor homely, with forgetta-
ble features. But how could everyone have recalled her
height and forgotten that quirky, elflike smile?

"Drew," Tracy said, "could you take Lucky home?
Owner lives down the street," she explained to me. "Elderly lady."

"Aw, Mom—" the boy started to protest.

"And if she offers you a Coke, you say yes, and you say
please and thank you, and then you sit there for a minimum of ten minutes, because . . ."

". . . you are going to be old yourself some day,"
Drew continued, mimicking his mother, "and it won't
hurt you to take ten minutes to cheer up an old . . ."

". . . lady who really *has* been very nice to you,"
Tracy concluded cheerfully.

At the end of the ritual, Tracy picked up the Jack
Russell mix and handed him to Drew. As the dog
changed hands, the mother and son exchanged smiles.
A photograph taken at that second would, I knew, have
shown the kind of capture-this-moment family snapshot
you see in ads for film and cameras. In reality, the pho-
togenic little family dog belonged to someone else.
And—sorry, I know it's corny, but there's no other way
to say it—the father was permanently out of the picture.

Twenty-five

As soon as Drew left, Tracy took Kimi's lead and walked her to one of the grooming tables. "You don't have to wait," she told me. "Really, I know what I'm doing. I won't ruin her coat. What's her name?"

"Kimi."

"Kimi, up on the table! *Woo-woo-woo!*" Tracy, you see, really did speak dog. Kimi replied by hopping up. "Good girl! Anything I ought to know? Any issues about grooming?" She sounded oddly like Rita: *issues!*

"Not really."

Tracy slowly and gently picked up one of Kimi's front feet.

"Drew," I said abruptly. "Andrew?"

Holding Kimi's foot, Tracy deftly clipped nails. "Yeah."

"I thought it might be *Andrews.*" I dragged out the *s.*

"Nice kid." As soon as the clippers were safely away from Kimi's foot, I added, "He looks exactly like Jack."

Tracy dropped the clippers into an open drawer attached to the table. Resting one hand on Kimi's back, as if claiming ownership, she growled, "Who the hell sent you here?" If I'd suddenly punched Tracy in the stomach, she wouldn't have looked more angry or sounded more menacing than she did now.

"No one sent me. I'm all on my own. I started to write a story about Jack Andrews. I'm a dog writer. I heard about his murder and the connection with his dog."

"There was no connection," Tracy snapped.

"Yes, there was. When Jack's body was found, Chip was tethered to his desk."

"Why?"

"Because Jack wasn't alone. Therefore, murder. Not suicide."

Speaking more to herself than to me, Tracy said vehemently, "Jack would never have killed himself. Never."

"I didn't know him. I wish I had. I feel . . . Tracy, I'm not here to make trouble. I write for *Dog's Life*. I started working on what was supposed to be a little story, and then . . . Tracy, among other things, I grew up with goldens. I used to show them. My mother was a breeder. I did a lot of competition obedience."

Tracy's eyes darted to Kimi. A hint of the elfin smile appeared. Her voice, however, carried a note of hostility. "But you weren't happy with your scores, so you switched to malamutes?"

Among the top obedience handlers these days, it's fashionable to show off by switching from the so-called traditional obedience breeds, meaning the *good* ones—the golden retriever, the Border collie—to what are supposed to be the challenges of whippets or Afghan hounds. Hah! I am not impressed. Admittedly, whippets and the Afghan hounds are terrible *obedience* dogs, but for unparalleled thumb-your-nose-at-the-handler *disobedience*, the Alaskan malamute can't be beat.

"On the contrary," I said. "My last golden was so perfect that . . . Anyway, I never meant to get a malamute. I ended up with one. Rowdy. I kept him. He has his C.D.X. He's working in Utility. I have no complaints."

"I know who you are." Tracy spoke in approximately the tone I'd use if I suddenly realized I was confronting Charles Manson. "I read your column. You write about your dogs."

"Yes," I admitted. "That was the other reason I, uh, got involved in the story about Jack. Because of *Winter*. His middle name."

"Are you . . . ?"

"No relation. It's a common name. But goldens, the name, some other, uh, coincidences. I also happened to be working on a story about Hannah Duston. Jack Andrews came from Haverhill. My other dog, Rowdy, was born there. In Bradford. You used to groom for his breeder. Janet Switzer?"

In the manner of a real dog person, instead of saying what a nice person Janet was or "Oh, I remember Janet. How is she?" or something else normal, Tracy said, "Beautiful dogs. Good temperaments."

You can probably guess the rest. Having driven all the way from Cambridge to Ellsworth to find the truth about Jack's secret life as well as his murder, and having unexpectedly discovered that his hidden life in what I'd assumed to be show dogs had produced a human son, I naturally had to go out to the car to get Rowdy so that Tracy could see the descendant of the dogs she'd once groomed for Janet. As will be obvious to anyone in dogs, Tracy then had to drag out her old brag books and show me pictures of the champions she'd finished years ago.

About thirty minutes into the uninterrupted dog talk, she suddenly asked, "Do you really want Kimi groomed?"

"Sure," I said. "Why not?"

As promised, Tracy did an excellent job, and while she brushed and lathered and rinsed and dried and brushed, we kept chatting and hollering over the rush of water and the roar of the dryer about Janet Switzer, Violet Wish, my late mother, my infamous father, dozens of people in goldens she'd known years before, and, of course, dogs and more dogs. When Kimi's coat was finally dry and stood off her body just the way it's supposed to, I at last said, "You know, Tracy, I really didn't come here to cause trouble. I honestly didn't. Even before I saw Drew. I didn't know about him, you know."

"No one did. Not even Jack."

The door to the shop abruptly burst open. Drew stuck his head in. "Mom?"

"Dinner! Is Jim . . . ?" To me, she said, "Jim's my brother. We share the house."

"He's gone to volleyball," Drew said. "He's going to grab a sub. Can I—?"

"When you took Lucky back, did you stay for a visit?"

"Yeah."

"For how long?"

"Fifteen minutes."

"Good kid."

Drew had to be seventeen. His mother, I thought, treated him like a twelve-year-old. With remarkably good cheer, he rolled his eyes. "Mom, I'm—"

"What time'll you be home?"

"I finish at eleven." Turning to me, he said, "Nice to meet you."

When he'd left, Tracy said, "Drew's a hard worker. He works with my brother, Jim—plumbing and heating—and he's got a night job, and he helps me out here. He's a smart kid. Good grades. He wants to go to college, but he's got to take a year off first to save up."

"It's not a bad idea, anyway." But all I thought of were Jack Andrews's other two children, who'd dreaded the catastrophe of switching from private to public school. To this day, Brat resented the threat. Meanwhile, the unknown brother who looked exactly like her deified Daddy was working three jobs to save for college, and doing it with apparent good spirits, too.

Changing the subject, Tracy asked, "You hungry?"

Instead of accepting her offer of dinner, I persuaded her to eat out with me.

An hour later, after I'd fed and walked the dogs, Tracy and I were sitting at a booth in what I'd been happy to learn was a branch of Helen's Restaurant that had opened in Ellsworth. Like the original in Machias, this Helen's was a year-round eatery favored by the locals, not just a tourist place. At five or five-thirty, there'd probably been quite a few patrons. Now, at seven-thirty on a Wednesday evening in December, there were a lot of empty tables.

Looking up from the menu, I said, "Lobster. My treat." I lied: "I can charge it to *Dog's Life.*" Have I mentioned that I train with food? Tracy ordered baked stuffed. I had what may seem like an odd choice for the time of year, lobster salad, but I prevailed on the waitress to serve it the way the Helen's in Machias sometimes does, with the mayo on the side and the salad consisting of a mound of lobster meat.

"So how did you meet Jack Andrews?" I asked Tracy.

"By accident. Outside a motel in Stowe, Vermont. I was there for a show. I had three dogs with me, two of my own and one I was handling for someone else. And one of them got loose. Maybe the crate wasn't latched right. Anyway, I had my van pulled up by the motel room, and I was unloading, and one second the dog was in his crate in the back of the van, and the next second he was loose. Jack helped me catch him. We started talking. He helped me walk the dogs. The next day, he came to the show with me."

"He was in Vermont selling books?"

"Visiting bookstores. Promoting the guides. You know about those?" She cracked a lobster claw, extracted the meat, and dipped it in butter.

"Yes. Tracy, when was this?"

She finished swallowing. "Four years before he died. We clicked right away. Well, not exactly right away. The show was really what did it. He discovered this wonderful thing that had been missing from his life."

"Dogs," I said.

She gave that quirky smile. "Wrong," she said. "Fun."

She proceeded to tell me, now with a straight face, that Jack's wife hadn't understood him. I almost choked on a piece of tail meat.

Without the slightest show of emotion, Tracy added, "I've always thought she killed him. She always sounded to me like a perfect bitch. Her or Gareth. That was their son. From what Jack said, I thought she and Gareth had a really sick relationship. Gareth was glued to his mother. He always took her side against Jack." *Her, she, his mother.* Never *Claudia.* I couldn't help thinking of what had struck me as Brat's deliberate insistence on referring only to *Claudia,* never to *my mother.*

"Did you ever meet Jack's children?"

"Not when he was alive."

I was amazed. "Afterward?"

"At his funeral. I didn't meet them. I just saw them. That was the only time I ever saw them. Her. Gareth. Brat."

"Jack called her Brat?"

Tracy's eyes flashed. "Not in a mean way. It was his pet name for her. When she was little, I guess, she had a hard time getting out 'Bronwyn Andrews'—it was sort of a mouthful—and the way she said it, it sounded like 'Brat.' "

"Tracy, how did you end up going to Jack's funeral? It seems . . ."

She put down her fork and licked her lips. "I read about Jack's death in the paper. No one told me. Who would've? And of course, I never called him. Not even at work. He'd call me now and then from there. And he wrote to me. It seems funny, but he did. Jack had a sort of old-fashioned streak. He'd send notes. Not love letters, nothing like that. Just about what he was doing, shows we'd been to, judges, dogs, where we'd meet, that kind of thing. He died—he was murdered—on a Monday night. Monday, November fourth. I didn't find out until I read the obituary." Her voice broke. She reached into her purse, fished around, found a tissue, and blew her nose.

"I'm so sorry," I said. "I didn't mean to . . ."

"It's okay. I'm all right. It's just that . . . I never talk about him. My brother, Jim, knows, but he doesn't want to hear about him."

"What does Drew . . . ?"

Tracy's narrow shoulders moved almost imperceptibly back. Instead of giving me an immediate, direct answer, she said, "I'm not the only single parent around."

"Far from it. Besides, it's none of my business."

"Drew knows his father died. He knows I've never been married. But Jim had lost his wife only a few months before Jack died, so Drew more or less grew up thinking that, uh, parents died, I guess. That it was normal. Marguerite, my sister-in-law, died of leukemia, and

Jim needed help raising their kids. So, right after the funeral, I quit my job and moved up here."

"Tracy, where did you hear the suggestion that Jack might have killed himself? Unless I missed something, it wasn't in the paper." For some reason, I felt as if she wouldn't want me to look at her while she answered. I fiddled around with what remained of my lobster meat, dunked a piece in the mayonnaise, and ate it.

Eventually, she said, "Like I told you, I went to Jack's funeral. I was scared shitless. I don't know what I expected. That someone would come up to me and . . . ? I don't know. Anyway, no one did."

"You went all alone?"

"I didn't have anyone to go with," she said. "Unless you count Drew. I was two months' pregnant. As soon as I . . ." She broke off. "I must've read Jack's obituary a hundred times. It was like, if I read it enough, it'd be someone else. I wasn't in my right mind. So, the funeral was the next day. I didn't have a lot of time to think it over. And I just went. Maybe it sounds crazy, but I couldn't just let Jack die and do nothing. And I had this weird sense that he was . . . This is nuts, but I had this sensation that he was still alive, that the whole thing was made up. Or if it wasn't, he'd want me to be there. Or maybe both: that if I didn't go, he'd be hurt that I'd stayed away. It's crazy, but that's how I felt."

"It doesn't sound crazy to me. It sounds like grief."

"Well, it sure was. You know, I never expected him to leave her. It wasn't one of those deals. Jack never made any false promises."

"I didn't think he had."

"Well, he didn't. And I never pressured him. I was going to have an abortion. I wasn't going to tell him. Jack was never going to know. Then . . . This is going to sound even crazier, but I guess what made me change my mind was finding Chip."

"You've lost me."

The smile was back again, mischievous and capricious.

"*You* found Chip?" I asked.

"Not exactly. Well, yes and no. I mean, I co-owned Chip, so you couldn't really say I stole him."

"Tracy, Brat Andrews told me that Shaun McGrath killed Chip. You know who Shaun was?"

"Jack's partner. But he didn't—"

"Tracy, it is widely assumed that Shaun murdered Jack."

The news seemed to hit her as a total surprise. At Jack's funeral, she said, everyone had been whispering about suicide, about how he'd poisoned himself. To the best of her knowledge, the suspicion of murder had been hers alone. She'd kept her eye on the newspapers for anything to do with Jack's death. Newspapers had been her only source of information. She'd evidently never heard of *Mass. Mayhem.* I didn't mention it.

"I saw that Shaun McGrath was killed," she said. "He died in a car crash. Was that . . . ?"

"It wasn't murder. It really was an accident." I outlined as briefly and neutrally as possible what I'd learned about Jack's death, the police investigation, and the assumption that Shaun McGrath had committed the murder. Tracy's portrayal of the relationship between Jack and Shaun was different from the others I'd heard. According to Tracy, there hadn't been any real bitterness or enmity. Jack's complaints about Shaun had focused on trouble between Shaun and the other employees. Tracy seemed to have no idea that Jack had ever had any serious financial troubles at home or at work. ("In case you wondered," she said, "I always paid my own way.") No, the police had never questioned her. No one had. Dog people might have asked about Jack, she guessed, but she hadn't been to a show since Jack died. Every once in a while, she ran into someone who remembered her, but she'd been shy back then, and no one was ever surprised when she said almost nothing. She'd never considered going to the police. What would she have told them?

The truth, I thought. "Tracy, about Chip?" I asked.

Again, the elfin smile. "Did I steal Chip?"

"Jack's wife didn't want him."

"Well, we did co-own him, but I've never been sure of the legalities. I wasn't showing anymore, and I didn't want to breed, so it didn't really matter. You want to know what happened?"

"Yes."

"Like I told you, I went to Jack's funeral. You know that she never cried? I watched. I was curious. I was probably staring at her. I sat up near the front, toward the side. I was so shy then, I don't know how I had the guts. But I did. I watched her. She didn't shed a tear. There were a lot of people there, a lot more than I expected, which was good, because no one asked who I was or what I was doing there. Jack had a lot of friends. So, from the obituary, all I knew was that he was dead. It was only there, at the funeral, that I overheard all this talk about suicide. And of course, I'd never seen her or the kids before. And the whole thing really threw me. I left the second the service was over."

"Of course."

"And then the weirdest thing happened. I was walking to where I'd left my car, in a parking garage, and I passed this convertible parked on the street. The top was up. One window was half down. And there was Chip. Sticking his head out. I didn't think about what I was doing. It didn't occur to me to do anything else. I reached in and unlocked the door, just like it was my car. I got Chip, and I walked off with him."

"And?"

"And nothing. Chip lived to thirteen. End of story."

I left for Cambridge early the next morning. When Rita stopped in during a free hour in the afternoon, I told her all about my long conversation with Tracy. "I understand perfectly," Rita said. "The woman groomed Rowdy's ancestors and uses the same esoteric brand of dog shampoo you do. Consequently, it makes complete sense for you to suspend your critical faculties and un-conditionally accept every word she said. Do I have that right?"

"Yes," I told Rita. "You do."

Twenty-six

"This Tracy person was pregnant," Rita said. "Her lover was married. At a minimum, she might've expected some financial support from him. Do you have any decaf?"

"Would you not call her 'this Tracy person'?" I said. "And, no, all I have is the real thing. You want tea? You want a drink?"

"No. I still have clients. Tea would be nice." As I filled the kettle and dug out tea bags, Rita exercised her imagination. "For all you know, this Tracy expected him to leave his wife and marry her, and when he refused—"

"I told you. Jack never made any false promises."

"This story she's told you is unverified," Rita pointed out.

"There's no reason to assume she's lying. Presumed innocent?"

"Let's set aside guilt and innocence for the moment and simply consider a rather different scenario."

"Fine. Claudia isn't so oblivious to Jack's secret life after all. She knows about Tracy. Maybe she even knows Tracy is pregnant. Anyway, from Claudia's point of view, Jack is a terrible husband. He throws money away. She hates him. She hates his dog. Chip would definitely have been tied up if Claudia had been in Jack's office that night. And look at the consequences. Where would Claudia be now if Jack had lived? She's far better off with him dead! Jack's life insurance is what got the family through. Oscar Fisch told me that. Shaun wasn't the only one due to benefit. Because of that insurance, Claudia has her doctorate, she lives on Francis Avenue, and she's an associate professor at Harvard."

Rita dresses like Manhattan, but her attitude is pure Cambridge. "Still doesn't have tenure," she remarked snootily.

Unjust, isn't it? Only the full professors have tenure, and hardly any of them are women. And exactly what song is sung at commencement each year? *"Fair* Harvard." The nerve!

"Just the same, Rita, Claudia is a lot better off than she'd be if Jack had lived. Furthermore, Claudia knew Professor Foley very well. Tracy Littlefield doesn't even know he existed."

"Did you ask her?"

"No. Why would I?"

"Jack Andrews never mentioned Professor Foley to her?"

"Why would he?"

"Because Foley was an old, dear *friend* of his, my friend. Foley was the kind of person she could subsequently have gone to for help in rearing Jack's second son."

"She raised Drew herself."

"College tuition? She shows up on Professor Foley's

doorstep with pictures of a boy who looks, according to you, exactly like Foley's esteemed late friend? And Professor Foley puts the pieces together: the boy's age, Jack's murder, her need for money, any doubts he might have harbored about Shaun McGrath's guilt."

"We don't know that he had any doubts. We don't even know that he'd ever heard of Tracy's existence, let alone Drew's. What do you think Jack did? Went to Professor Foley and said, 'Oh, by the way, George, I'm leading a double life'?"

"Why not? And even if Foley learned the story last week from this Tracy person, he might have worked it out then and there, and simply confronted her and accused her of murdering Jack."

"Damn! I'll tell you something, Rita. George Foley really could have answered a lot of questions. I don't understand much else, but I really am sure that the reason to get rid of him was to shut him up. When I talked to him on the phone, all I asked him about was Hannah Duston. I should've asked him about Jack Andrews."

"Holly, it's also possible, you know, that your professor died a natural death."

The kettle whistled. I made tea-bag tea, which Rita doesn't really like, in mugs that Rita frowns on because they're not tea cups and also because they're decorated with pictures of Alaskan malamutes and not covered with hand-painted roses, violets, and stupid gilt squiggles. I missed Kevin. He'll happily drink any beer out of anything. I resentfully handed Rita her cup.

"What are you saying, Rita? Purely by coincidence, Professor Foley picked that time to die of a heart attack? The police didn't assume that. I don't know why *you* should. Speaking of which, if Kevin would only get back here, I could find out what's going on in the Foley investigation. I never thought he'd stick it out this long."

"He isn't due back until tomorrow."

"In theory. In fact, I've been expecting him to show up since Saturday morning. I don't know why he didn't at least leave me the phone number."

Rita examined her mug with distaste. "So you couldn't call him."

I took a big sip. "He'd probably love a call. He'd be a lot happier at a homicide investigation than he is out there in the Berkshires chewing seaweed and burning his feet on—"

"Your capacity for stereotyping astounds me."

"I am not stereotyping Kevin. He's a Cambridge cop, he eats meat, he drinks beer, he's obsessed with his job, and I have never once heard him do anything but make fun of any of this 'Eastern alternative body-mind holistic fitness crap.' That's a direct quote."

"As it happens, I was referring more to—"

My doorbell interrupted her. The dogs, as usual, leaped to the defense of their pet biped by flying silently to the front door, where they stood wagging their tails ready to welcome whatever robber, rapist, or Jehovah's Witness was trying to spring an attack on me. Mail-order dog-supply companies unwittingly reward this malamute version of guard-dog behavior by including free bonus dog biscuits with every order. The positive-reinforcement history is so strong that Rowdy and Kimi are convinced that the sound of a van outside followed by the presence of a person at the door signals a UPS driver bearing an edible treat.

As usual, the dogs were right. Except this time the UPS package wasn't from Cherrybrook and didn't contain anything to eat, unless you count paper, which Rowdy and Kimi prefer when it's spiced with a condiment such as the glue in the spines of books and on the flaps of envelopes. In extremis, the dogs will, however, devour paper unseasoned, especially if it bears the scent of other people's dogs, as does almost all my mail, of course, including the large padded mailing envelope that had just arrived. It came from Janet Switzer and contained a photocopy of the privately printed book about Hannah Duston. Janet had promised to look for it. She'd come through.

"And One Fought Back!" I exclaimed. "Really, Rita, you know that old saw—'If you want something done, ask a busy person'? What it really ought to be is, 'If you want something done, ask a dog person.' "

Muttering about violations of copyright law, Rita emptied her mug in the sink and left for her office. After brewing a cup of strong coffee, I settled myself at the kitchen table and eagerly prepared to learn the full, true story of Hannah Duston, including what I hoped would be a wealth of detail about the parents who had produced Hannah and her baby-murdering sister, Elizabeth Emerson.

According to Laurel Thatcher Ulrich's book, *Good Wives*, contemporaries of Hannah and Elizabeth had had no interest in exactly what grabbed me: the streak of violence the two sisters shared. Rather, Elizabeth had been a condemned murderer, a sinner, whereas Hannah had been a shining symbol of God's sustenance in the wilderness, a heroine. What accounted for Hannah's guts—my word, of course, not the scholar's—applied to hundreds of men and women who'd passively endured Indian captivity until they were "redeemed"—ransomed for goods or traded for hostages—or who, like Eunice Williams, had become permanent members of Indian communities through adoption or marriage. Hannah Duston wasn't the only woman who'd slaughtered pigs; virtually everyone had. Other women had stood up to their neighbors and served as what Ulrich

called "deputy husbands." Furthermore, plenty of unmarried women undoubtedly had had babies without
promptly committing infanticide. Elizabeth Emerson
herself had already been an unmarried mother when
she'd given birth to the twins she killed. According to
Ulrich, the colonists hadn't seen any connection between the two acts of violence, hadn't even viewed them
as such, hadn't sought a pattern handed down from
parents to children in the Emerson family, hadn't suspected the lurking presence of a sinister family secret.

But I did! Among other things, although Hannah had
supposedly been inspired by God to deliver herself,
Mary Neff, and the boy Samuel from the clutches of the
so-called savages, she'd not only scalped ten human beings, but had waited twenty-two years after doing so before finally becoming a full member of her church. In
1697, when Cotton Mather preached a sermon lauding
Hannah Duston as the defender of Zion, he also took
her to task: "You continue Unhumbled in Your sins,"
he'd said. Hannah had been baptized as a child. Not
until 1724, when at the age of sixty-seven she dictated
the "Confession" I'd read at the Haverhill Historical Society, did she offer the proof of conversion needed for
full membership in the church. I had no illusion that in
chastising Hannah Duston, Cotton Mather had shared
my doubts about the goodness of her character or harbored my suspicions about her family. Even so, I wondered whether in squeezing her into the mold of New
England's heroine, Mather, who'd heard Hannah's tale
firsthand, hadn't found her a tight fit.

What I hoped for in the obscure old book, *And One
Fought Back,* was not a Rita-style analysis of the dynamics
of a radically dysfunctional family, nor did I expect
from the author, Lewis Clark, the kind of conclusion
that Oscar Fisch would probably have reached: that if

Hannah and Elizabeth had only joined the recovery movement and found solidarity with other survivors of parental abuse, Hannah would've ended up waiting to be traded for a hostage or contracted a bigamous marriage with one of her captors, and Elizabeth would've spared the babies and founded a proto–support group for unwed mothers. All I wanted was additional confirmation that as music ran in the Bach family, as dogs ran in mine, so violence ran in Hannah and Elizabeth's.

In the book, I found facts I'd read elsewhere: Hannah was almost forty years old when taken captive. By then, she'd borne twelve children. The oldest, a daughter of about eighteen, was also named Hannah. A son, Timothy, was two and a half. After Hannah's release, she and her husband, Thomas, had a thirteenth child. Her parents were Hannah and Michael Emerson. She was their oldest daughter.

I encountered a few oddities and discrepancies that had now become familiar to me. Was the newborn Martha Duston included in the count of Hannah and Thomas's children? According to Clark, she was. When the assailants slew the baby, did they smash her head against a tree, as most accounts claimed, or, as a few said, against a rock? A rock, Clark said. Some inconsistencies I'd learned to ignore. *Duston,* as Clark explained, was variously spelled *Dustin* and *Dustan;* inconsistent spelling, it seems, was common in that day. As Clark realized, Cotton Mather had inadvertently misled generations of scholars by giving the date of the massacre and scalping as April 30; Mather had meant March. The boy captive who joined Hannah and Mary Neff in the killing was Samuel Leonardson, Lennardson, or Lenorson; Clark used *Lenorson.*

As to facts, I learned nothing new. Like his predecessors, Lewis Clark had missed the connection that Laura

Thatcher Ulrich had made in her book: He clearly hadn't known that Hannah and Elizabeth were sisters. I felt disappointed. Elizabeth had identified the father of Dorothie, her first child, as a man named Timothy Swan. She'd brazenly called the baby after his mother. So far as I knew, she hadn't named the father of her twins, but had denied her second pregnancy and, when charged with infanticide, utterly denied her guilt: "I never murdered any child in my life," she'd testified. Clark, however, didn't even mention Elizabeth.

Like me, Clark had tried and failed to discover the name of the tribe or clan that had captured Hannah. What surprised me was both the thoroughness of the scholarly account and the engaging style of the writing. Lewis Clark cited his sources. Better yet, like *Good Wives* and like *The Unredeemed Captive,* his little privately printed account brought life to Hannah's era. Of Thomas Duston's decision to save his older children instead of his wife and baby, Clark wrote with neither Dwight's undisguised admiration nor my own skepticism. Hannah herself emerged as neither heroine nor fiend. From the little book, I learned no facts. From Lewis Clark, who died in the Battle of the Bulge, I learned a lesson in shunning moral judgment.

Twenty-seven

That same Thursday evening at dog training, instead of emptying my mind of worldly thoughts to contemplate the Infinite in Kimi's deep brown eyes, I found myself preoccupied with violence. Not that I practiced it! Not since my most recent religious conversion, which took place at a revival-tent obedience seminar led by Patty Ruzzo, who preached the gospel of the ears-up, eyes-bright, correction-free method so passionately that I was vaguely disappointed when Patty didn't ask us to approach the high jump, cast off our dogs' choke collars, and vow to go forth and jerk no more. Even without actually impelling me to speak in tongues, Patty got across the Good News that I could train with nothing but positive reinforcement and really didn't have to hurt my dogs.

I suspect that all converts have the same experience I did: Doing good proved comparatively easy. The hard part was *not* sinning. I'd been training with food and smiles for years; I had no trouble dishing out yet more treats and sweet talk. The malingerers were my left wrist and my big mouth. All on its own, my hand would jerk the collar, or I'd say something negative. Then I'd beg Kimi not to tell Patty.

Because of my current preoccupation with violence, dog training that night was a little less relaxing than usual. Also, I felt guilty about Rowdy, who knew that Kimi had gone with me to have fun while he'd been left out. Consequently, when Kimi and I got home, I fought my fatigue and set out for a little compensatory walk with Rowdy. To avoid offering him false hope, I decided not to take Concord Avenue toward the armory, where the Cambridge Dog Training Club meets, but followed Appleton to Huron and turned left.

The night was bitterly cold and dry, frigid, with no promise of snow. I wore my down parka and heavy fleece mittens. In his permanent double-layered coat, Rowdy pranced along with a smile on his face, enjoying a temperature reminiscent of the ten below that he relishes. In the manner of all real dog people everywhere, I talked nonsense to him about his mending paw and Leah's chemistry course, and otherwise gave him a full explanation of why he'd had to stay home and miss his treats, his praise, and the pleasure of my company. In the manner of all male dogs everywhere, he concentrated on marking every hydrant, hedge, and utility pole we passed. The construction on Huron Avenue that had presumably caused our rat invasion had been a boon to Rowdy, producing as it had a sudden proliferation of traffic cones, big orange barrels, and stacks of black pipe that he'd welcomed as a kind of manna sent by God to relieve his starvation for fresh objects on which to leave his scent. Now, in December, the work had ended. "It's very unfair that they took your orange barrels," I was babbling in empathic outrage. "The Lord giveth, Rowdy, and the Lord taketh away."

"Bullshit!" The deep, hoarse voice cut through the rumble of a passing truck.

"Bullshit yourself!" I muttered, thinking that if fools chose to eavesdrop on private, privileged, and sacred communions, they had only themselves to blame for what they overheard. Then I realized that the voice emanated from a half-block ahead of us and that in any case the white noise of the traffic had masked the words I'd meant for no one's ears but Rowdy's. Glancing ahead, I saw parked near the minimart at the corner of Huron and Concord a dark panel truck. As Rowdy and I approached, the lights from a streetlamp and the store let me read the gold letters inscribed on its rear doors:

MUSIC HAUL
HARMONIOUS PIANO TRANSPORT
KEYED TO YOUR RANGE

Leaning sullenly against the open passenger door of the truck, Brat Andrews kicked the curb with one of her combat boots and repeated loudly, "Bullshit!"

"Bronwyn!" The voice was a woman's. "Who brought you up? Now, stop cursing and come and help! Gareth is not feeling well, and—"

Brat, who stood in the gutter, replied, evidently to herself, "Gareth is psychotic! Gareth is out of his fucking mind! And so am I to have—" What made her break off was the sight of Rowdy, who, abruptly shifting to his ferocious guard-dog mode, pulled on his leash, wagged his way to Brat, sized her up, dropped to the pavement, and rolled onto his back in the hope of a tummy rub. Ignoring me, Brat bent over and scratched his white chest.

"Holly Winter," I reminded her. "Johann isn't with

you?" The question was perfunctory. Rowdy wouldn't have missed the presence of a male Rottweiler.

"I'm very protective of Johann," Brat informed me. "I never expose him to noxious substances." With a jerk of her thumb, she gestured beyond the door of the truck to three people clustered around a trash barrel at the corner of Concord Avenue. "Claudia, for example. Also, Oscar and Gareth. The Toxic Trio."

Oscar, who wore a dapper-looking overcoat and one of those fur hats you see on TV on the heads of Kremlin officials, stood a little apart from Claudia. Swathed in a bulky quilted coat, she hovered over Gareth, who, in turn, hovered over the barrel. With the deliberation of a connoisseur, he slowly fished through its contents. To-night, he still wore the aqua backpack, but in place of the purple parka, he had on a long, formal-looking coat that I mistook for the jacket of a man's evening suit. Claudia was chastising him in tones too low for me to hear. Oscar had his arms folded across his chest. I had the impression that he was trying to look bored.

"He's got the apron, too," Brat informed me. She stretched her arms out to flex the muscles hidden under a heavy pea jacket.

"What?"

"On the coldest night of the year, my psychotic brother chose to dump his parka somewhere. What he's wearing is the ceremonial regalia of a Freemason. Apron and all. One of Claudia's neighbors saw him and called her, and when she got here, she called me from a pay phone, and I should've stayed the fuck where I was." She thumped her hands together, presumably to keep them warm.

"He'll freeze to death," I said.

"He'll go to a shelter, where they'll keep him for the night and send him away in the morning with a parka that Claudia'll be embarrassed to have him seen in. Ergo, her presence here. Ergo, his dumping his parka. He wants attention, he ditches something she's bought him, he hangs around where one of her friends'll see him, the friend calls her, she shows up, she makes a fuss, he gets what he wants."

"He really could freeze."

"That's his leverage. Claudia doesn't actually give a shit whether he does, but she's up for tenure, and if her son freezes to death in walking distance of her office, there goes her image as the maven of child care." In a fashion characteristic of Cambridge children of important people, Brat assumed that I knew what her mother did. She was, of course, right.

"As it is," I said, "Gareth doesn't exactly boost her image."

"Bullshit," Brat growled. "He elicits sympathy. Poor Claudia, gallantly struggling with blah-blah-blah. This isn't one of Gareth's better scenes. He usually pulls them in the Square, where there's a bigger audience." On his feet again, Rowdy was fixing Brat with that big-brown-eyes look designed to convince her that he'd discerned in her a special and wonderful quality of character that every other creature she'd ever met had somehow missed. She was compliantly resting a hand on his head. "Good-looking dog," she said. "You show him? In breed?"

"Yes."

"Conformation's a lot of bullshit," she said.

With unpardonable disloyalty to a sport I love, I said, "Sometimes." Hey, if what you want is loyalty, get a dog.

"What are doing here, anyway?"

"I live here." Claiming the neighborhood as my own, I felt like Rowdy with one of the orange barrels. "I live down the street. And you? What's your role in—"

The heretofore silent Gareth suddenly burst forth with the kind of ranting he'd directed at me days earlier in the Square. This time, his object was Oscar Fisch, his mother's second husband. "Son of a bitch! Son of a fucking bitch! Poisoner! Poi—son—er!" Wildly addressing a startled couple who were passing by, Gareth, in the manner of the Hannah Duston statue, pointed a finger of accusation at Oscar and announced, "This man, Oscar Fisch, murdered my father and married my mother!"

The couple twittered nervously. "And I suppose your name is Oedipus," the man murmured before scurrying off.

Brat was still leaning against the door of the panel truck and resting her hand on Rowdy. "The interesting feature of Gareth's delusions," she remarked, "is that, in one way or another, they're always grounded in reality. Claudia *was* cheating on Daddy. She married Oscar less than a year after Daddy died."

"Why are you telling me this?" I started to say, then bit my tongue. The exchange we were having reminded me of an experience Rita once had after a vacation in the Bahamas. Returning to Cambridge, she'd gone to her office to see her first patient, a distressed woman who poured out sordid details of sexual adventures and fantasies to poor Rita, who hadn't yet reoriented herself to what she did for a living and wanted to say, "I'm a total stranger to you! Don't you realize that it's inappropriate to tell me these intimate details of your personal life?" Rita, however, actually was a shrink. Why confide in a dog writer about your mother's love affair? Because, I realized a bit belatedly, your brother is cracking up, you're scared, you're angry, and you don't want your pain to show. "Your father had a lover, too," I longed to say. "You have a teenage brother named Drew. He's sane, friendly, and hardworking. He looks just like your precious Daddy."

Gareth, meanwhile, still raving at top volume, had switched from the blatantly Oedipal theme to the topic of Uncle George—George Foley—who, according to Gareth, kept drinking poison but still refused to die. When I'd encountered Gareth in the Square, hadn't he said the same thing about his father? *Claudia was cheating on Daddy*, Brat had just informed me. *She married Oscar less than a year after Daddy died.* I'd assumed a connection: Claudia's affair had been with Oscar, whom she'd married after Jack died. Had I misinterpreted Brat? Had Brat herself been wrong about the identity of Claudia's lover? The elderly George Foley had been a handsome, charming man. Forty years his junior, I'd certainly felt the attraction. Eighteen years ago, he must have been even more boyish and vigorous than when I'd met him. Claudia had *married* Oscar Fisch. Had George Foley been her lover? Gareth's delusions, his sister claimed, were always somehow grounded in reality. *This man, Oscar Fisch, murdered my father and married my mother!* Gareth had raved. Was it possible that a lover of Claudia's really had murdered her husband?

By now, Gareth had abandoned his interest in the contents of the trash barrel. He was pacing and circling widely and wildly around it, shaking his fist at Oscar, accosting passersby, and haranguing Claudia with disjointed tirades about Harvard, electric wires, and experiments with rats. As Gareth's steps brought him close to us, Rowdy's tail stopped wagging and his beautiful eyes moved from Brat to Gareth to me. With no display of anything at all—no growling, no raised hackles, not the slightest flattening of his ears—Rowdy took a few casual steps that placed him firmly between Gareth and me.

Eyeing Rowdy, Brat asked, "This doesn't bother him?"

"Not much bothers him," I said. "On the rare occasions that something does, he has it for dinner."

Gareth's resonant, educated voice now sounded feverish. Pacing and circling, he reminded me of an animal in a zoo, a polar bear, maybe, exhibiting stereotypical behavior that worried his keepers. Trailing after him, his mother kept plucking at the sleeve of his Masonic coat. As one of his long strides brought him within a few yards of Rowdy, I heard Claudia quietly demand to know where he'd left his new parka. "Gareth, this will not do!" she scolded, as if taking her little boy to task for showing up after Little League practice without his new baseball glove. "Now, Gareth, listen to me! We bought that parka at Eddie Bauer only a few weeks ago. You picked it out yourself. Don't you remember? We had such a nice time shopping for it. Now will you please stop and think where you've left it?"

Gareth produced a monumental roar: "RATS! RATS AND POISON!"

With a sort of placid toughness, Brat said, "Good. Once Gareth seriously locks on to rats, the end is in sight."

"What is the end?" I asked, intrigued.

"I pin his arms behind him and haul him into the back of the truck. Oscar drives." As if to illustrate, she nodded to Oscar, who'd distanced himself from the action and now stood by the curb as if he had no idea who these people were and was merely waiting for the next bus.

Reaching into his pocket, Oscar pulled out a set of keys and took calm, efficient steps toward the van.

"When we get to the hospital," Brat continued, "with luck, Gareth's still nuts enough so they admit him." She gave me a wry smile. "Timing is crucial. If he's merely deluded, they won't take him. The trick is to get him there the second he's ready to turn violent."

"He does get violent?"

"Yes," Brat said, "but usually just with psychiatrists."

Oscar was now in the driver's seat. As he started the engine, Brat asked me casually, "You ever find a copy of the book?"

"Yes," I said. "I found it in a used-book store."

"Claudia must've missed that one."

"When you told me she had dozens of copies, you meant library copies."

Brat finally moved from the panel truck and headed toward Gareth. Over her shoulder, she said, loudly enough for Claudia to overhear, " 'The portrayal is felt to be unflattering and unfair.' Her very words."

It seemed best to remove Rowdy from the events that would follow. Watching for traffic, I led him across Huron Avenue. When we reached the sidewalk, I stopped briefly to glance back. As she'd foretold, Brat had her brother's arms pinned behind him. She was so strong that even the big aqua backpack didn't impede her. As if Gareth were a sort of semihuman piano, she was hauling him to the back of the truck. I felt inexpressibly sad. Rowdy eyed the proceedings with detached curiosity. Bizarre behavior is of great interest to dogs.

When Brat finished heaving Gareth into the truck, she slammed the doors. Cupping her hands around her mouth, she called to me across Huron Avenue. "Hey, he's not heavy," she hollered sourly, "he's my brother."

Twenty-eight

When I got home, I couldn't sleep. I paced restlessly until I realized that I was unwittingly mimicking Gareth. My body, I decided, was making a freakish effort to understand behavior that had baffled my supposedly higher faculties. Reluctant to awaken Rita by going upstairs and knocking on her door, I went outside, stared up at her windows, and found them dark. If I tried to reach Steve in Minneapolis, his mother might answer, and I didn't feel like talking to her. I contemplated trying to find out whether Gareth had acted violent enough to earn himself a hospital bed, but had no idea which hospital to call. McLean? Mount Auburn? The Cambridge Hospital? Some small private facility I'd never heard of? For all I knew, part of the family routine might consist of driving from one emergency room to another in search of the right—or wrong—match between Gareth's rage and the sight of some poor psychiatrist's face.

Eventually, I found peace in what would strike a lot of people as a ridiculous activity: I wrote a belated letter of condolence about the death of a dog, an Alaskan malamute named Attla, who'd belonged, and always would, really, to David and Shilon Bedford, who started out as sledding enthusiasts, got carried away, so to speak, and now run a sled dog outfitting company, Black Ice, in New Germany, Minnesota. The name Attla was a tribute to the famous Athabascan musher George Attla. The canine Attla lived up to the legend. He was a big dog—a hundred and five pounds—and a little old-fashioned-looking for the U.S. show ring, but he earned his Canadian championship. Attla's great strength, however, was just that: brute force. On a team, he drove so hard that his phenomenal power set the pace for the other dogs. Even running uphill, even with extra weight to haul, he wouldn't break pace or change gears. With tears in her voice, Shilon Bedford had told me, "Attla had no mental wall! He was such an honest dog! He never gave anything but his best." Attla had retired from his racing career a few years ago to lead an easy life in an honorable position in the Bedfords' first kennel. Last spring, he'd shown the first signs of congestive heart failure. The disease progressed fast. In August, Attla had refused his food. "And when a malamute stops eating," Shilon had said, "you know the end is near." I'd learned of his death only a month ago.

Attla died at the age of ten and a half. My letter to Shilon and David was little more than a note to say how much I'd admired Attla and how sorry I was for their loss. What assailed me as I wrote was a depressing sense of the painful overcomplications of human lives: Brat's fury at her mother, Claudia's crazy effort to impose normality on Gareth's madness, the apparent hopelessness of his condition, the complex questions of Claudia's love life and Tracy Littlefield's truthfulness, the murders of Jack Andrews and Professor Foley, the death of Shaun McGrath, the chaotic mess of Estelle's dreadful novel and her pitiful faith in its merits, the sad pretensions of Randall Carey, Jack's seeming reincarnation in his post-humous child, the violence of Hannah Duston and her captors, the death by hanging of Elizabeth Emerson, Steve's refusal to spend Thanksgiving with my father, mine to spend it with his mother . . . The list seemed endless.

What finally brought me comfort was the rediscovery of my eternal refuge: My friends had loved Attla as intensely as I loved my dogs. How often is it possible to love so purely? How often is it possible to know exactly how other people feel? So if a letter of condolence about the death of a dog sounds foolish, go ahead and smile. But if you do, hope that you never love a dog.

When I awoke on Friday morning, even before I opened my eyes, I could tell that Kimi had taken advantage of Steve's absence and my unconsciousness to pursue a campaign she'd been patiently waging for months, a crusade based on her conviction that wherever people slept must be the prime spot. Her goal was to insinuate herself under the covers and between the sheets. Like a skilled dog trainer, she'd set out to teach me this new routine by breaking the exercise into its component parts and working on it one small step at a time. Months ago, she'd started by worming her way almost imperceptibly up toward the headboard. Once I'd mastered the head-on-the-pillow phase, she'd proceeded to the next step by waiting until I was asleep to slip one front foot under the top sheet. It is, I suppose, remotely possible that she whispered subliminal messages in my ear: *You will let Kimi under the covers! Nothing will make you happier than to have a big, hairy dog nestled next to you between the sheets!* At first, she removed the paw the second I awoke. Today, she gave me a few moments to learn to tolerate its presence. Before my religious conversion, I'd have grabbed Kimi's paw, removed it, and told her to forget the doomed crusade, thus unintentionally reinforcing the behavior by paying attention to it. Now, I emerged from sleep trying to plan a positive behavior-shaping strategy to achieve my goal.

To say that I woke up thinking about dog training is to say that I woke up happy. My dogs and I were alive and healthy. I was blessed with the incomparable friendship of dog people and the love of an excellent vet. Compared with Gareth Andrews, my father was barely eccentric, even if Steve thought otherwise. Once I got really clever at applying positive reinforcement to dog behavior, I could switch species and shape his mother right up, preferably by conditioning her to move to Fiji. Kevin Dennehy was due back from his ashram today. I'd leave the murders in his beefy, competent hands. The construction in my neighborhood was almost finished: The vile rats would retreat. And for all the complications I'd encountered in accepting Rita's bet, I actually had learned a lot about Hannah Duston and would certainly be able to write something that had nothing whatsoever to do with dogs.

The optimism stayed with me throughout the morning. In response to a tactful complaint from my third-floor tenants, I cleaned the accumulated bits of freeze-dried liver, solidified cheese, and miscellaneous other transmogrified dog treats out of the coin-operated washer and dryer in the basement. Although the sky remained clear and the air dry, I surveyed my snow shovels and went out to stock up on sand and ice-melting crystals. When I returned, the machine had a message from my cousin Leah, who announced that she had a ton of stuff for me about Hannah Duston. Confident that the world would shape itself around her plans, she said she'd arrive for lunch at twelve-fifteen.

The intellectual nourishment Harvard provides for its freshmen is undoubtedly rich and varied. According to Leah, however, Harvard has worked out a deal to buy up the beef, poultry, meat by-products, animal liver, and fish meal that fail to meet the standards of Bil Jac for inclusion in its fresh-frozen dog chow. No other theory, she maintains, can fully account for the hamburger patties served to undergraduates. Until I'd tasted Harvard's food myself, I dismissed my cousin's complaints as the usual college-kid gripes about mystery meat. I'm still not convinced that she's absolutely correct. The appearance of the brownish-colored layer in the middle of my lasagna, for example, strongly suggested Pro Plan Turkey and Barley Formula, and the lamb and rice in my Greek casserole could have been Iams or Pedigree.

Since the contents of my cupboards, refrigerator, and freezer consisted mainly of what would have been more of the same, I ran to the row of gourmet shops on Huron and arrived home with an assortment of salads and cheeses just as Leah's bicycle rounded the corner from Concord. A few years earlier, when she'd habitually been costumed in cycling shorts, leotards, rugby shirts, running shoes, and other such athletic gear, her idea of strenuous exercise had been to train for marathon long-distance phone conversations by working up a sweat placing a series of short local calls. Now that she'd cast aside the bright aerobic colors of the body, she pedaled around Cambridge dressed exclusively in the hue of the mind: existential black. Her only concession to the spurned style of her youth was a shiny ebony helmet. Her red-gold hair streamed out beneath it, and her face was flushed from the cold and the exercise. Imagine a medieval damsel as painted by Dante Gabriel Rossetti on Prozac. Perch her on a bike, replace her tubercular pallor with the glow of health, and there you have Leah, who greeted me by scanning the bags in my arms and caroling, "Free food!"

But Leah is graced with infinite forgivableness. From the saddlebags on her bike, she produced numerous volumes, photocopies, and lists of references about Hannah Duston.

Five minutes later, when she'd hugged the dogs and I'd set the kitchen table and spread out our little feast, we sat down to lunch, and I said, "Leah, you've really brought me a ton of stuff. Thank you."

"When my parents called, it gave me something to talk about. Some of it's just background. Colonial New England. Indians. But this isn't all. Some things weren't in the stacks. I've put in requests." She picked a mussel out of her pasta salad and ate it. "Widener really does have almost everything. It's a good thing that Harry Elkins didn't make it to a lifeboat."

Harvard's main library is a memorial to Harry Elkins Widener, who went down on the *Titanic*.

"It was hardly a good thing for *him*," I said. "Wasn't he a young man?"

"No. I think he was in his twenties. Anyway, now he's immortal. What more could one desire?"

"Life. And if we're going to get philosophical, what I'd like to discuss is ethics." I summarized everything I knew and wondered about the whole history of Jack Andrews, Claudia, Brat, Gareth, Professor Foley, Oscar Fisch, Tracy Littlefield and her son, Drew.

"You don't *know* that Claudia had an affair with anyone," Leah pointed out. "What you know is that her daughter says she did. And that her daughter hates her."

"That's true."

"And that madness runs in the family."

"Leah, so far as I know, it isn't genetic. Besides, the only certifiable person in the family is Gareth. Jack seems to have been perfectly sane, Brat is unconventional, and Claudia is . . . Well, she stole a lot of library copies of the book with the chapter about Jack's murder, but I'm sure she doesn't consider herself a thief."

"Kleptomaniacs don't, do they?"

"I don't know. Apparently, her rationalization is that she was portrayed unfairly in the book. Mostly what she is, is erratic. She'll be melodramatic, and then kind of vague, and then, with Gareth—" I broke off. "But Gareth doesn't count. It's hard to imagine how you'd act normal when Gareth's around."

"Maybe *he* killed his father so he could marry his mother." Leah paused to devote herself to chicken salad. "Symbolically, one assumes."

"One certainly does!"

"How old was Gareth?"

"When Jack was murdered? Sixteen."

"Oedipus might not've been any older than that. I don't think Sophocles says. You want me to look it up?"

"Not really. Rita would say that Freud would say that—"

"So what's Gareth's alibi?"

"For his father's murder? I don't think anyone's ever asked. Jack died sometime after five o'clock on a Monday night. He used to work alone in the building between five and seven. Gareth and Brat were presumably doing their homework or something. I have no idea. They must've known about the rats, and they probably knew about the poison. They both used to hang around Damned Yankee Press. I don't know where Gareth was when Professor Foley died, either. I should ask Kevin to find out. Gareth has delusions about Professor Foley, but then he has delusions about everyone else, too."

"What about Brat?"

"Oh, I'm sure Gareth probably has crazy ideas about her. I don't remember if he mentioned her, but—"

"No, I mean maybe *she* murdered her father."

"Brat? She worshipped him. She still does."

"How old was she?"

"Eleven. But it's really impossible. For one thing, she loved Chip. He wouldn't have been tied up if she'd been there."

"Maybe to keep him from drinking the poison?"

"That's an idea. Possibly. But, Leah, Brat venerates Jack's memory. She adored her father."

"So if she found out about Tracy Littlefield? You know, Holly, a lot of parents act as if little kids can't hear. And she was Daddy's little girl. Maybe he didn't quite get it that she could understand, and he let something slip. And then, of course, there's always Electra."

"Who?"

"She hated her mother for murdering her father."

"Brat *does* hate Claudia, or at least she's chronically furious at her. But Brat doesn't think that her mother killed her father. She really does believe that Shaun Mc-Grath murdered Jack."

"Deep in her heart," Leah persisted, "maybe she knows that it was really her mother."

"Claudia is at least a plausible suspect."

"Is she outrageously gorgeous?"

"Who, Claudia? No. She's attractive enough in a Cambridge sort of way. Her husband, Oscar, looks at her as if he thinks she's gorgeous. Exotic, maybe. He's very protective. He's decided that she was the victim of Jack's financial abuse. And eighteen years ago, she was probably more fetching than she is now. Maybe men think she's beautiful. Maybe Professor Foley did. It's always hard to predict. Steve will tell me about some woman he says is a nice person but who is really dumpy and homely, and then, to me, she'll look like the cover of *Vogue*. Or he'll think that someone is a knockout when I think she looks like a million other people."

"So what's the ethical dilemma?"

"Do I tell Kevin about Tracy Littlefield? Also, do I tell Brat about Drew? Or, maybe, do I tell Tracy about Brat and let her decide?"

"No to all three," said Leah firmly.

"Thank you. It's so comforting to have a Harvard student in the family."

"Think nothing of it. Speaking of which, I have to get back. Oh, there's one more Hannah thing you're going to want to take a look at. It's all about her. I'm getting it for you. It's an old dissertation."

"Widener didn't have it?"

"Widener doesn't have dissertations. The new ones are in Pusey, but after nine years, they get moved to the depository. I put in a request on Tuesday, I think it was. They probably have it for me by now. I just couldn't carry any more today."

"Are you allowed to check it out?"

"I don't know, but if it looks good, I can Xerox it for you."

"It's a whole dissertation about Hannah?"

"That's what it sounds like. It's called . . . It's on the list I brought." She got up and fished through the stack of books and articles she'd left on the counter. "My reference list is here somewhere. Here it is. 'An Analysis of Interpretations of a Unique Captivity Experience: A Contextually Based History of Evaluative Approaches to the Legend of Hannah Duston.' "

Leah handed me the list. I scanned it. My eyes locked

on to the title of the dissertation. And then on to the name of the doctoral candidate who'd written it.

"I'll be damned," I said. "How unlike him. He never told me he wrote his thesis on Hannah Duston. No wonder he knows all about her."

"Who?"

"Randall Carey. The guy who wrote the chapter about Jack's murder."

Twenty-nine

I rented my third-floor apartment to its present tenants under the misapprehension that in installing the wife, Cecily, in my building, I'd pulled off a major coup in the world of dogs. Imagine my shock when I found out that Cecily wasn't a real judge. In fact, she has no connection at all with the American Kennel Club; all she does is sit on some circuit court. She doesn't even own a dog. She and her husband do, however, dote on their two immense smoke-colored Persian cats, Learned and Billings, who spend their lives sunning themselves on the carpeted window perches that enable them to peer safely and disdainfully down at the side yard.

As befits a judge even of the non-AKC variety, Cecily is a person of tremendous poise and dignity. Today, although she was home with a ferocious sinus infection that blotched her cinnamon skin and painted dark shadows under her reddened eyes, her hair was still in its usual neat cornrows, and when I stopped in before running my errands to ask whether I could do anything for her, she was wearing her quilted red plaid housecoat with the authority of a judge's robes. She didn't need anything, she assured me, but thanks. Her husband was away for a week on business; she had no domestic or social obligations. She'd spend the day drinking ginger ale and catching up on her paperwork. She gestured to a chair that, like the cats' perches, overlooked the side yard.

My initial disappointment about Cecily's true judicial position had quickly turned to the same irrational fear I had about Rita: that unless I kept the property up, my perfect tenants would move elsewhere. Today, mindful of Cecily's presence, I was especially eager to maintain the tony tone appropriate to the rents I charge. Consequently, as soon as Leah left, I turned to the task of splitting and stacking the remaining wood. Besides, as I've suggested, although training dogs is my first-choice form of meditation, splitting wood runs a close second, and I wanted to let the matter of Randall Carey and his doctoral dissertation rattle around in my head more or less on its own. The temperature outside had warmed to the mid-thirties, but a warning breeze blew from the north, and the sky looked like one immense blue eye of a Siberian husky the size of the cosmos. Whenever a car approached on Appleton, I'd glance down the street to see whether Kevin was finally returning, but after an hour, only a single small birch log remained to be split, and Kevin still hadn't shown up.

Just as I was about to slam my ax through the last log, a male voice made me jump. Although my hand didn't slip, the ax fell closer to my toes than I liked, and I was glad that I'd taken the precaution of wearing my heavy leather boots. Randall Carey, I thought, hadn't meant to startle me. I felt annoyed at him nonetheless. Even a bookish city dweller, it seemed to me, should have had the sense to avoid suddenly distracting me as my sharp, heavy ax was about to pound down near my left foot. Gripping the ax in my right hand, I kicked the pieces of just-split wood toward the small pile I hadn't stacked, and said a curt hello.

Randall Carey was, as far as I could tell, as oblivious to my annoyance as he was to its cause. "Hello, there," he said, rounding and prolonging the *o* in *hello* to achieve what I thought was supposed to be the tone of an Oxford don greeting a rival who has just made a laughingstock of himself by publishing an academic paper containing a misplaced comma in a quotation from Flaubert. Randall wore the same suede jacket the dogs had jumped on. On his head was a gray tweed hat suitable for a movie actor in the role of an elderly Scottish doctor who plays a lot of golf.

Instead of stowing the ax on top of the woodpile under the stairs, I let it swing lightly from my hand. There was no need to invite Randall to visit, I reminded myself. I certainly wouldn't invite him in for coffee.

"The modern-day Hannah rests from her labors," Randall said.

"Indeed she does." I reminded myself that I held the ax.

In his usual supercilious fashion, he said, "I've brought you something."

For the first time, I noticed that slung over his shoulder was one of those green book bags that I remembered from trips to Harvard Square with my mother when I was a kid. Was it possible that The Coop still stocked them? Or maybe Dr. Randall Carey, the historian, had preserved this symbol of Cambridge from the days before green book bags were displaced by backpacks. I had, however, no doubt about the contents of his academic artifact. A book bag? Books. Articles. Maybe, belatedly, his own dissertation.

I contemplated raising my eyebrows and looking down my nose. "Thank you," I said flatly. "I hate to spoil the surprise, but if it's a copy of Lewis Clark's book, I already have one."

My first hint that something was amiss came when Randall failed to take the book bag off his shoulder, open it, and pull out whatever he'd brought. From the way he kept looking around at the woodpile, Kevin's house, mine, the driveway, and the two cars parked in it, Cecily's Volvo and my Bronco, I had the sense that he found the surroundings unacceptable for some kind of big-deal presentation. Mildly paranoid as I'd become about the rat invasion, I'd stopped leaving the dogs unsupervised in the side yard. They were in the house, and the wooden gate stood open. Uninvited, Randall Carey headed toward the yard. I again noticed that roly-poly, little-boy walk. As if the property were his rather than mine, he gestured to me to follow. Still carrying the ax, I did. I was armed. What risk was I taking? Hannah Duston had killed women and children. With the same hatchet, however, she'd also killed grown men.

As Randall Carey pulled the gate closed behind us, my eyes darted to the third floor of the house. From behind the window with the cat perch, Billings and Learned peered comfortingly down at me, and I caught sight of Cecily, who was enjoying the company of her cats and probably taking advantage of the natural light to study a law journal or a brief or whatever it was that judges perused. In the person of Cecily, Law and Justice were at hand.

When Randall Carey turned to me, his face looked weirdly happy and smug, as if he were about to spring some wonderful surprise. I found his silence disquieting.

"What's all this about?" I asked bluntly.

"You'll see." By now, he was smiling. He took a seat on my park bench. I remained standing. Finally removing the green book bag from his shoulder, he rested it next to him, eased it open, and reached inside. "Close your eyes," he said.

"You must be joking."

"Indulge me," he said. "Close your eyes."

I cheated, probably not convincingly, but Randall was busy with the book bag and seemed not to notice. In fact, there wasn't anything for me to see except Randall's wide back. The cloth of the bag rustled lightly. Paranoia! With sudden, irrational terror, I listened for the slosh of liquid. An apparently benign surprise? Cappuccino? A thermos of latte? A milky, sweet surprise. The special of the day: half Vienna roast, half espresso, with just the merest colorless, odorless, flavorless soupçon of sodium fluoroacetate. Randall Carey, who held a Harvard Ph.D. in history, had earned his doctorate eighteen years ago, the year Jack Andrews died. Jack was from Haverhill, the city of Hannah Duston. As a boy, Jack had written a report about the local heroine. As a man, a student in Professor Foley's own department, Randall Carey had written a dissertation. His topic had been Hannah Duston. Later, he'd written a book about murder in Massachusetts, a book with a chapter about the killing of Jack Andrews. And like Claudia, like Oscar Fisch—like Gareth?—Randall Carey didn't like dogs. My right hand squeezed the ax handle. Until a few minutes ago, I'd been splitting wood. Now, in my panic, I was struggling to reassemble a pile of ragged, splintery pieces that fit together only here and there. The whole, however, eluded me. I couldn't begin to see its shape.

Squinting, I watched Randall turn. When he spoke, the depth of his voice jarred and frightened me. "You can look now," he said.

Opening my eyes, I must simultaneously have opened my mouth in a giant *O*. The limp book bag lay on the bench. Positioned directly in front of me, about a yard away, Randall proffered the last two objects I expected to see: a collar and a leash. I must have gasped. Perhaps he assumed that I was pleased with his gift. The matched pair were of heavy leather. The collar was a flat band about a half-inch thick and a good two inches wide. How could anyone imagine that I would want or need such a thing? The correct collar for an Alaskan malamute is the kind that Randall had seen on my dogs, a rolled-leather collar that won't flatten the coat around the neck. The leash was equally inappropriate. A good leather training lead is strong but not bulky; it's narrow and thin enough to let you fold or crumple it in the palm of your hand. This leash was as thick and wide as the collar. Randall Carey had been in my kitchen, where he'd seen the leads that hung on the inside of the back door: show leads, retractable leads, leather leashes in four-foot and six-foot lengths, nylon leashes in bright colors, and not one that looked even remotely like this.

"I've been a very bad boy," Randall said meekly. His voice was odd: soft, husky, and childish.

I didn't catch on. Tactfully ignoring what seemed to me his peculiarly ill-chosen presents, I clutched for meaning. *A very bad boy?* His dissertation on Hannah Duston? He really should have told me about it.

"You certainly have," I informed him.

In my own defense, let me say outright what must be obvious: that the world of purebred dogs and dog training is a remarkably wholesome place and that Holly Winter is one of its most wholesome denizens.

To my amazement, Randall Carey dropped to his knees before me. In remarkably doglike fashion, he was actually panting. Extending the heavy leather objects upward in his hands, he caught his breath and growled softly. "Dominate me!" he pleaded. "Dominate me just the way you do those big, bad dogs!"

Raising my eyes in what I suppose would've been a plea to that giant blue Siberian eye overhead, I caught sight of Cecily, who happened to be glancing out the window. My perfect tenant! I should never have filled the deep pits that Kimi had dug in the yard. In her wisdom, Kimi had tried to provide me with a choice of holes to crawl into.

"Randall, for God's sake," I ordered in my best alpha-leader voice, "get the hell up!"

Mistake!

Falsely encouraged, Randall moaned, "I love it! I love it! I love your boots, I love your ax, I love your—"

"Stop!" I commanded.

His head wobbling, his mouth hanging open, his breath coming faster and faster, he groaned, "You are Hannah! I prostrate myself at your feet! I am your first victim. It is dark midnight. We are in the wigwam. The fire burns low. I lie helpless. Asleep. Above me, you raise your hatchet! I—"

Words came to me from the Bible, words about Jael and Sisera: *At her feet he bowed, he fell, he lay down.* With the little dignity I could muster, I said in what I hoped were sexless tones, "Dr. Carey, you are suffering from a profound misunderstanding."

Still on his knees, he groaned, "More!"

"You are making a fool of yourself," I said gently.

"Yes!" he sighed.

I spoke very calmly. "There has been a profound mis-understanding here. I have been very naive. I thought you meant your dissertation on Hannah Duston." Almost whispering, I told him that the best thing would be if he'd stand up and leave. "And take these, uh, things with you," I added. "They are of no interest to me at all."

I turned my back on him. Still carrying the ax, I walked to the gate, opened it, and left him alone in the yard. Then I went into the house. Peering through the blinds of my study, I watched him make his dejected roly-poly way down the drive.

My talk about myself as the alpha leader. My ax, my leather boots, my prominent display of leashes. My big, tough dogs. Combined with my interest in Hannah Duston? Carey had seen me as the modern-day Hannah: the ultimate dominatrix.

Thirty

I tried to extend to Randall Carey my fragile view of
Hannah Duston, Mary Neff, Samuel Leonardson, and
their Indian captors as desperate people in circumstances too desperate for me to understand. I had never
had a child, never mind stood helplessly by as armed
men grabbed my six-day-old baby girl and crushed her
head against a tree. Hannah and her companions had
not had the benefit of the books I'd consulted. Hannah
hadn't even known how to read. When she'd finally
acted on what she'd called "a great Desire to come to the
Ordinance of the Lords Supper," she'd dictated those
words and her entire "Confession of Faith" to her minister. *I* knew that Thomas had rescued the Duston children left behind. Until her return, Hannah did not. If I,
too, had believed that the bondage would culminate
when, still recuperating from childbirth, I was stripped
naked and forced to run the gauntlet, what would I
have done?

Of the circumstances of her captors, I knew so little that I had only an educated guess about their tribe: Abenaki. I knew who Hannah's captors were not: the original inhabitants of the area that became Haverhill, whose stone axes were displayed at Buttonwoods, where, in my pursuit of the Duston artifacts, I'd barely glanced at drawings of dugout canoes that had carried men, women, and children soon exterminated by a "great plague," as it was called, a European disease, smallpox, perhaps, or the plague itself. Three hundred years after Hannah's violent escape, the rage of today's Native Americans was scrawled in new graffiti on her statue in Haverhill. Yet Hannah's captors, survivors themselves, had adopted the young Samuel Leonardson; they had not held his fair skin against him, but had eagerly sought human beings, regardless of origin, to replenish their own vastly diminished numbers.

In trying to imagine myself the hostage of impulses like Randall Carey's, I failed completely. His urge felt as distant as the three centuries that separated me from Hannah and her captors alike, as deeply beyond me as the murder of a newborn infant or the slaying and scalping of child victims, as outlandish as the Native Americans and the English colonists had seemed to one another. For the grisly acts committed by both sides, I could recite explanations I'd read: In immediately killing their captives, Indians had dispatched the young, the old, and the infirm, those who wouldn't survive the trek to French territory. The prisoners had had practical value as replacements in families destroyed by dislocation, starvation, and disease; monetary value as goods to be traded for the necessities of survival; political value as barter for French hostages held by the English colonials; and psychological value in a war of fear. In returning to the bloodied wigwam to scalp her victims,

Hannah, too, had had practical motives. She'd been convinced that in the absence of irrefutable proof, no one would believe what she and Mary and Samuel had done. She'd hoped for money. She'd received it.

Randall Carey, in contrast, had attempted nothing grisly. The ax had remained in my hand. He had humiliated me; I'd felt like a fool. Dear God! What, if anything, was I going to say to Cecily? The whole scene, however, had been utterly unlike my silly fantasy of poisoned latte.

Feeling sullied by the episode, I took a long hot shower. Letting the water run through my hair, I reminded myself that I was blameless. It wasn't as if I'd paraded around half-naked in a garter belt. I wore heavy boots to split wood because I'd once seen my father drive the blade of an ax through his foot. Rita, I remembered, had once worked herself into a frenzy trying to track down the source of a quotation she'd heard attributed to Freud. "Sometimes," Freud was supposed to have said, "a cigar is just a cigar." I couldn't remember whether Rita had succeeded in her quest, but I knew that in my case an ax was just an ax, and boots were just boots, no matter how Randall Carey might view them. Excluding a couple of sets of lace underwear, the only thing I owned that could possibly be construed as sexual paraphernalia was a cream-colored silk bed jacket that Steve had bought for me at Victoria's Secret.

As for Hannah Duston, almost from the moment she returned to Haverhill, she had become a symbol of everything from Motherhood Revenged to the triumph of Puritan Christianity over popish heathenism to the European devastation of Native Americans. But a *sexual* symbol? The prospect of running the gauntlet naked had obviously been a sexual threat. In 1821, Timothy Dwight had described Hannah Duston as "threatened

with torture and indecency more painful than torture."
The Boscawen statue—both the original and the gaudy
reproduction on the Jim Beam bottle—had, I realized
for the first time, a weirdly erotic element. The clinging
drapery revealed Hannah's buxom body and drooped
low over her right breast. But the drapery was a conven-
tion of the times, wasn't it? And the breast an allusion to
motherhood?

Dogs were obviously a symbol, too, but, for me, a symbol of the redeeming power of simple love in a world of
violent complexity. All dogs and especially all malamutes were like Attla: strength and honesty made mani-
fest. My own dogs were my dispellers of demons and my
shelter from the maelstrom of human enigma: In times
of overwhelming pain and chaos, there is no greater
comfort than the rediscovery that sometimes a dog is
just a dog.

Scrubbing my feet with a loofah, I told myself that
flowing down the drain with the soap and the water and
the sweat I'd worked up splitting wood was whatever
irrational sense of responsibility I'd felt for Randall
Carey's aberrant misreading of me and everything
about me. Only then did I let myself feel deep relief that
I'd been foolishly and wonderfully wrong about Randall
Carey's surprise gift.

When I'd finished drying my hair and getting
dressed, I took Rowdy and Kimi for a quick walk, during which, I might add, we encountered neither rats nor
madmen—nor anything or anyone else to upset or
worry me. When we returned home, Kevin Dennehy's
car was still missing from his driveway. Where was he?
He'd left for the stress-reduction and lifestyle-change
workshop, or whatever it was, last Friday, a week ago
today. In my experience, which admittedly was limited
to obedience-training seminars, summer camp for dogs

and owners, and other such canine-centered events, a
week meant that you arrived on the first day and left on
the seventh. Even if Kevin's week at this retreat in the
Berkshires ran from Friday to Friday, shouldn't it have
ended early this morning? Didn't its organizers need to
prepare for the next week's group? The trip from the
Berkshires to Cambridge should have taken Kevin two
or three hours. If, as I suspected, he'd broken the jour-
ney home from this rice-and-tofu haven by stopping for
a roast beef sandwich or ham and eggs with home fries,
English muffins, and a side of caffeine, he should still
have been here by now. Was it possible that the soles of
Kevin's feet were too charred and sore to let him drive?
Worse yet, had he done a beer-to-Buddha about-face in
his outlook on life, donned a turban, quit the force, and
decided to stay?

The blinking light on my answering machine signaled
what proved not to be a message from Kevin proclaiming his permanent retreat from the Cambridge PD.
Rather, the message was from Leah. She announced
that she had Randall Carey's dissertation on Hannah
Duston. She was calling from a pay phone in the library
and would call back in a few minutes.

As I waited, a connection came to me, one I'd missed
in my panicked effort to piece together a meaningful
whole from pieces that had fit together here and there,
but refused to lock in place. The material Leah had
brought still lay on the counter. I quickly double-
checked her list of references. As I'd remembered, Randall Carey's dissertation was dated eighteen years ago.
The connection: As my scabbed hands and knees reminded me, among the odds and ends found in and on
Jack Andrews's desk eighteen years ago, after his murder, had been that tantalizing slip of paper that bore the
title *And One Fought Back.* A privately printed book. A

dissertation. Both about Hannah Duston. Jack's interest in her. Randall's.

With photographic recall, I could see the heading of Jack's obituary: JOHN W. ANDREWS, PUBLISHER. His profession: publisher. In pursuing his lives, public and private, open and secret, I'd viewed Damned Yankee Press mainly as the scene of his murder. In tracking down his wife, his lover, his dog, and his children, legitimate and otherwise, I'd treated the Damned Yankee guides as Jack's excuse to make business-as-pleasure trips to bookstores in towns and cities where and when there just so happened to be dog shows. Jack's profession, however, had been more than a cover for his hidden life in dogs. John W. Andrews, publisher, had also published books: the guides, of course, and books of regional interest, books like the ones still stacked everywhere at the press, including, for instance, a book about Lizzie Borden. It had even briefly crossed my mind that Jack might have thought about reissuing *And One Fought Back.*

The phone rang. Before Leah had a chance to say more than a few words, I said, "Hang on!" Returning with the photocopy of the privately printed book, I asked, "Leah, do you have that dissertation right there with you?"

"Yes. You want me to copy it?"

"Yes. No. I want you to read me parts of it. Do you have a lot of change with you? Never mind. Give me the number, and I'll call you right back." I hung up and dialed. When Leah answered, I said, "First, would you open to the beginning? Does it say who his thesis advisor was? Or the members of his committee?"

"Uh, yes. Oh, you know who it was? Carey's advisor was George Foley. That makes sense. Colonial historian."

"I know. Leah, flip through, would you? See if you

can find the section where he actually describes what
Hannah did. Somewhere, there's got to be a . . . No! I
just thought of something better. See if you can find
where he talks about Timothy Dwight. Dwight was the
president of Yale. He wrote a book called *Travels in New
England and New York*. He discusses Hannah. And
Thomas. Is there an index?"

"No, of course not."

Rapidly leafing through my photocopy of Lewis
Clark's obscure book, I came to a chapter called "In
Every View Honorable: The Conduct of Thomas Dus-
ton."

"Leah," I commanded, "look in the table of contents.
There is one, isn't there?"

"Of course. Hang on. Here we are."

"Does there happen to be chapter called anything like
'In Every View Honorable'?"

"Yes," she said. " 'In Every View Honorable: The
Conduct of Thomas Duston.' "

"Turn to it. Read me the beginning."

"Uh, here we go. *'Beneath the pointing finger of Hannah
Duston on the Haverhill statue, a relief depicts Thomas Duston
on horseback, his gun aimed at an Indian, his children—' "*

I interrupted her. " *'—his children clustered behind. The
inscription reads: HER HUSBAND'S DEFENSE OF THEIR CHIL-
DREN.' "*

"How did you . . . ?"

"Because I'm reading the same words."

Together, we cross-checked other sections. Some pas-
sages in Carey's dissertation were obviously his own. We
found references in the dissertation that didn't appear
in Lewis Clark's book. Many phrases, sentences, and
paragraphs from *And One Fought Back* had, however,
been rewritten, paraphrased, or lifted in their entirety.

Leah was aghast. "He *plagiarized* it? Well, when Harvard finds out—"

I did tell you, didn't I, that in the eyes of Harvard, nearly all serious crimes are, in one way or another, abuses of the printed word? And in Cambridge, the eyes of Harvard are the eyes of God.

"Leah, would they really . . . What do you call it? Expunge him? After all this time?"

"I think so. At a minimum, they'd strip him of his degree."

Dr. Randall Carey: the name in the phone book, the name on that shabby mailbox, the name by the doorbell. Doctor no more. The back window of my kitchen gave me a view of Kevin's driveway. It was dark out now, and his mother had put on the outside lights. Her car was in its usual spot. Kevin still wasn't home.

"Look," I told Leah. "This is really important. Say *nothing* to anyone about this. Not a word. Don't even photocopy that dissertation, okay? Just give it back. Turn it in. I want it out of your hands *right now.* Until I tell you otherwise, you've never seen the thing in your life."

"Holly—"

"Do it! I am not joking! Leah, Jack Andrews read Clark's book when he was a kid. It was in the Haverhill Public Library. He must've used it for his report. For whatever reason, he also read Carey's dissertation. He made the connection. But he didn't tell Professor Foley. Maybe he didn't have a chance. He was murdered first. Professor Foley didn't make the connection, either. And when he finally did . . . ?"

"I get the picture. And you can sort of see why Professor Foley missed it to begin with, because advisors aren't necessarily all that expert in whatever esoteric topics their students are doing research on. But how did Foley find out now? Why all of a sudden, after all these years?"

"For one thing, one reason he missed it back then and for a long time is what you said yourself: 'Widener has everything.' That was probably his mentality, too."

"Correctly so."

"Almost. And that attitude is what Randall Carey took into account. He plagiarized a book that *wasn't* in Widener and that academic types didn't even know existed. Also, there's something Professor Foley told me himself. He said that captivity is *in* these days. There are books, and there are conferences. *Now* there's a field called 'captivity studies.' Professor Foley hadn't read Clark's book because it wasn't an academic book—it was just a local curiosity—and because, eighteen years ago, captivity studies wasn't his specialty, anyway, because it really wasn't anyone's. It practically didn't exist."

"So why did Professor Foley read the book now?"

"You never met him, Leah. He was interested in everything, I think. He was like a kid. He sparkled. Anyway, he'd just been to a conference where he'd been discussing Indian captivity with someone. That's where he heard that there *was* a privately printed book about Hannah Duston. This is awful to think about, but, in a way, maybe it was partly my fault. After I asked him about Hannah, he must've called up whoever had mentioned the book to him and borrowed it from another historian or from a library somewhere."

"But if it wasn't in *Widener*—"

"Then, miracle of miracles, it might still have been somewhere else. In fact, it *was* somewhere else until Randall Carey removed it. It was in the Haverhill Public Library and at the Haverhill Historical Society. But it must have been other places, too. Maybe Widener located it for him. Or another historian let him borrow it.

Leah, if Foley was Randall Carey's advisor, wouldn't he
have had a copy of the dissertation?"

"Probably. He'd've been given one. Whether he kept
it is another matter."

"Obviously, he did. Or he got it just the way you did,
from the archives. And he compared. He reached the
same conclusion we have."

"Definitely about the plagiarism. About Jack Andrews's murder?"

"Maybe. Maybe not. In either case, I think Foley
called up Randall Carey and invited him over to discuss
the matter. Instead of blowing the whistle, he gave Randall Carey a chance to turn himself in. Professor Foley
was a gentleman himself, and I think he offered Randall
Carey a gentleman's way out. Jack Andrews must've
made the same mistake. It was fatal for him, and it was
fatal for Professor Foley. Leah, Randall Carey has killed
twice to keep his doctorate and his pride, and the second time to keep his freedom. He's like Hannah Duston. He's like the people who took her captive. His
motives are just as practical as theirs, and he's just as
desperate. Promise me that the second you hang up,
you'll take that dissertation and return it instantly. And
say nothing whatever to anyone."

"But what about you? What—"

"Kevin will be home any second. I'm going to lock my
doors and wait for him. I'm going to sit here and play
the damsel in distress."

Reversing our roles, Leah warned, "Don't open the
door for anyone."

"Of course not. Not for anyone."

Thirty-one

―――――――――――――――――――――――――――

I thought you meant your dissertation on Hannah Duston, I'd told Randall Carey. *If it's a copy of Lewis Clark's book, I already have one,* I'd also said. Now, as I waited for Kevin, I'd have given anything to take back those words. At least I hadn't mentioned Leah. Or had I? No, I was pretty sure I hadn't. Unless Randall Carey had suddenly decided to go to Pusey Library and, by wild coincidence, happened to see Leah returning his dissertation, she was safe. I suppressed the impulse to call her number. If she'd followed my instructions by promptly returning Randall Carey's plagiarized ticket to his doctorate, she'd still have had to sprint across the Yard to reach her room by now. I had no reason to believe that she was even headed there. The chances were good that she'd gone directly to the dining hall. I could imagine her surrounded by friends, swearing about chemistry, and, with a grin, insisting that the mystery meat was substandard dog food. I wished I'd made her promise to call me back.

I picked up the phone and, instead of running next door as I'd ordinarily have done, dialed Kevin's number. His mother answered. I asked when she expected Kevin home.

"Any minute now," she replied.

"Have you heard from him this week?"

"Not until an hour ago. He called to say not to worry." She again assured me that Kevin would be back any minute.

"Well, the second he gets there, would you tell him that I have to see him? Right away." Feeling foolish, I added, "It's police business."

"Police business," she repeated. "I'm writing it down." Before I hung up, she said "God bless!"

By now, Rowdy and Kimi were nosing around and *woo-wooing* in expectation of dinner. "If I feed you," I informed them, "you'll need to go out, and I would really rather not leave here until Kevin's back. So just hang on another few minutes."

Keeping Kevin's driveway in the periphery of my vision, I looked up Tracy Littlefield's number and dialed it.

She answered. "Tracy's Doggone Salon!"

"Holly Winter," I said. "Tracy, I have a question that's probably going to sound off the wall, but . . . Tracy, are you alone? Is Drew there?"

"Yes indeed!"

"Yes he is?"

"Yes."

"That's okay," I said. "Maybe you could just answer yes or no? It's not about . . . Well, okay, here it is. Shortly before Jack, uh, died . . . Let me backtrack.

Did Jack ever use the Haverhill library? Did he ever take a book out or go there to look anything up?"

"Funny you should mention it."

"Shortly before he died?"

"Very."

"Sunday?"

"No."

"Saturday?"

"Keep going."

I worked backward to the Thursday before the murder.

"You got it. Could we make this quick?"

"I'll try. What he wanted was an old book about Hannah Duston. *And One Fought Back*. It was in some kind of special collection."

"Yes."

"And did he find it?"

"Sure did!" Then she said she had to go. I thanked her and hung up. So Jack hadn't trusted his memory. Once something had jogged it, he'd gone to the trouble of taking a new look at the old book. Sometime before Thursday, he'd seen Randall's dissertation. His suspicions had been aroused. He had, however, written his report on Hannah as a schoolboy; he probably hadn't so much as seen Lewis Clark's book since then. And the charge of plagiarism was not one Jack would have made lightly. Jack had gone to Harvard. He'd have been fully aware of the extreme seriousness of the crime within the university and of the consequences of discovery for the scholar who'd stolen another's words. On Thursday, Jack had gone to Haverhill to compare the two texts, Lewis Clark's and Randall Carey's. By Thursday night, he'd had proof of Randall Carey's guilt. Four days later—two workdays later—at sometime after five o'clock on Monday afternoon, when he'd been in his office, he'd drunk coffee that Randall Carey had some-how laced with the sodium fluoroacetate that Jack him-self had obtained to poison rats and had carelessly tossed in the trash.

And, unbelievably, Kevin Dennehy *still* wasn't home. "Damn!" I told the dogs, whose restlessness was increasing by the minute. "Damn! I really am sorry. One more quick phone call, and he'll be here, and then I'll feed you."

As the words left my mouth, I heard a soft metallic jingling and a muffled bang. My heart pounded. The dogs silently moved to the kitchen door. Even more eagerly than usual, they stood there wagging their tails. Rita's high heels clicked reassuringly on the floor of the back hallway. The jingling: her keys. The bang: the opening of the outer door. Rita's heels tapped up the stairs. Overhead, Willie, her Scottie, barked a welcome.

"Truly, guys, I'm sorry," I said. "Any minute now."

Rita informs me that a moderate level of anxiety has a beneficial effect on intellectual performance but that terror makes you stupid. In retrospect, it's clear that I should have called Rita and Cecily to warn them to stay inside and, above all else, to let no one into the building. Instead, I phoned Estelle Grant and got stuck listening to her blather about some New York literary agent's supposed interest in *Multitudes in the Valley of Decision.* I tried to be patient. Estelle's dreadful novel was, after all, what had precipitated my call. What was it she'd said? Something about how vital it was to start with what you know. One of her characters had obviously been based on Jack Andrews, another on Shaun McGrath. The house of prostitution was a transformation of the pub-lishing house. In the novel, the house was raided by the police. The real rats appeared, as did the poison. If

Jack, Shaun, the press, the police, the rats, and the poison, why not Randall Carey?

Multitudes in the Valley of Decision. The material Estelle had gathered. The preponderant *material* in the book? *Leather.*

Breaking in recklessly, I demanded, "Estelle, have you ever happened to run into a guy named Randall Carey?"

"Oh, him! Hey, let me give you some advice. Stay away from him. He's really . . . Well, *chacun à son goût*"—she paused to translate—"to each his own and all that, and if that's what appeals to you, I don't have a problem with it, but if you ask me, he's . . . Well, of course, the literary act is one thing, and it's certainly necessary to *connect* the passion to the prose and so forth, and if that's what *you*—"

"Not me," I said.

"Well, then, stay away from him."

"You met him at Damned Yankee Press." It wasn't a question.

"He had an appointment with Jack."

"On Friday. The Friday before Jack was murdered."

"Yes. And as usual, everything there was in total chaos, and Carey ended up having to wait around in the front office. Elsie was there—I mentioned her to you—and one or two of the part-time people, and they were all supposed to be working on mail orders that, per usual, were all backed up, and Shaun breezed through and yelled at everyone, especially me, of course, because everything's always the temp's fault. Anyway, I gave Randall Carey some coffee, and he sat around, and then Jack finally got around to seeing him. And then, by the time he finished seeing Jack, it was five o'clock, and when he was on his way out, I was leaving, and he asked me out for a drink."

"You went with him."

"Stupid me. First of all, he took me to this place with leather seats, not that that's telling in itself, really, but the fact is that he was very supercilious and condescending and snide. I should've gone home."

"Did you talk about the rats? And the poison?"

"Not then. Not that I remember. We probably did while he was waiting to see Jack. We must've, because I'm sure it was Friday when Jack finally threw that poison out. And Friday wasn't even trash day! So that's where Shaun got the poison, of course, out of one of the trash barrels in back of the building. He heard us talking, and then he came sneaking back over the weekend and went through the barrels until he found the poison. I know we were all talking. In case you wondered, not a lot of work got done around there."

He overheard. He snuck back sometime during the weekend. He found the poison. Yes, he did. But *he* was not Shaun McGrath.

"After Shaun, uh, breezed through, did you talk about him?"

"Probably. I know he yelled at everyone, so we would've. Yeah, we must've."

"And after you had a drink with Randall Carey?"

"I'd really rather forget it. Art is one thing, but . . . I found it very humiliating." In complimentary tones, she almost whispered, "And I'm quite sure that *you* would, too."

"I'm sure I would. Estelle, have you seen Randall Carey since then? Around the Square? Have you ever . . . ?"

"Once or twice, but I've hightailed it in the opposite direction."

"Estelle, besides, uh, other things, that evening, did

Randall Carey ask you about Jack Andrews? His habits, his schedule, anything like that?"

"The fact is that I had too much to drink. And then later, we did some dope, and . . . You won't mention this, will you? Because once *Multitudes* comes out . . ."

"It's strictly confidential."

"The fact is," Estelle confided, "that what I can't remember I'd greatly prefer to forget."

I wished Estelle success with her novel and hung up. The Dennehys' outside lights were still illuminating Kevin's empty parking place. Rita's heels and Willie's nails clicked quickly down the back stairs. Shooing Rowdy and Kimi out of the way, I moved toward my kitchen door to warn her to let no one in. As I opened the door to stick my head out and speak to her, she opened the outside door.

Randall Carey stepped in.

Thirty-two

Rita continues to blame herself. She shouldn't. How could she have known? She tells me that it never occurred to her to be suspicious. It wasn't as if Randall Carey had had a shaved head and worn black leather studded with metal and emblazoned with the emblem of some notorious gang. On the contrary, he wasn't even wearing that stupid-looking tweed hat. His suede jacket and khaki pants were unexceptional, and the weather was cold enough to justify his leather gloves. Nothing about his appearance that night gave Rita any cause for alarm. What must have been the sudden pallor of my face might have concerned her, but by the time Randall Carey had a strong grip on my kitchen door, she and Willie had clattered down the outside steps.

I have repeatedly asked myself what I should have done. Screamed? Bolted? Hollered to Rita to run and call the police? Even if I'd tried to shriek, I'm not sure I'd have succeeded. The muscles in my throat felt frozen, and my mouth and tongue were almost painfully dry. What impeded me from barging through the door or turning around and fleeing through the front of the house was, I am sure, my ingrained habit of never, ever giving the dogs a chance to get loose. I cursed myself for following the safe practice of storing my revolver in one closet, the ammunition in another. I could, I suppose, have dashed to the side yard and shouted for help. Leaving Rowdy and Kimi to follow? Leaving them alone with Randall Carey?

He stepped into my kitchen and closed the door softly behind him. The leashes hanging there swayed back and forth. I must assume that Rowdy and Kimi sensed that something was wrong. Instead of jumping on Randall Carey or even greeting him in their ordinarily hospitable fashion, they stood calmly on either side of me.

"Hannah," Randall Carey said.

Holly, I wanted to insist. Holly, not *Hannah.* I said nothing.

"I have come to offer my most profuse apologies." Carey's customary self-mockery was missing. He looked soft, round, and harmless.

I cleared my throat. "I have lost all interest in Hannah Duston," I said hoarsely. "I'm not destined for the scholar's life. I don't have the training. Besides, the world of academe is much too gory for me." In a gesture of helplessness, I raised my right hand to my breast. In my ears, my voice sounded hollow, distant, and scared. I hoped that Randall heard it as the falling petal of a frail flower.

He didn't reply immediately, but ran his eyes around my kitchen until his gaze locked on the stack of books and papers that rested on the counter. Leah's list of references was there, of course, the list that included his own dissertation. So was the photocopy of Lewis Clark's book. Without turning his back to me, he took a couple of roly-poly, plump-boy steps across the linoleum and caught sight of the photocopied book. I edged backward. The dogs backed up with me. In teaching them correct heel position, I'd trained them to ease themselves toward me or away from me, forward or backward, as needed. They seldom, however, backed up without a reminder. In any case, heel position—*place,* as I tell the dogs—means sitting at my left side, and both dogs were standing squarely, Rowdy on my left, Kimi on my right.

Words came to me unbidden, and not pagan words, either: "And sitteth at the right hand of God the Father Almighty: From thence he shall come to judge the quick and the dead." If Randall Carey hurt me or my dogs, I hoped that whoever judged him showed no compassion. Those whose "tender mercies are cruelties," I thought. The phrase was one that Cotton Mather had used to describe Hannah Duston's captors. Its source? The Book of Proverbs: "A righteous man regardeth the life of his beast: but the tender mercies of the wicked are cruel."

I inched backward. Again, the dogs moved with me. At the edge of my vision, to Rowdy's left, was the door to the kitchen closet. Not far beyond it lay the interior hallway. In the hallway was the coat closet where I'd stowed the ax. Beyond the hallway was the front door.

Randall Carey reached into the right pocket of his suede jacket and took out a small glass bottle. From his left pocket he produced a plastic packet of what it took me a second to recognize as raw hamburger. Until then, Rowdy's eyes had been fixed on my face, and Kimi had been looking back and forth between Randall Carey and me. Now the raw meat captured the dogs' exclusive attention.

"Eighteen years ago," he said plaintively, "nobody gave a sweet goddamn about women and Indians."

Through the back window of the kitchen, I could still see Kevin's empty parking spot. My mind's eye was fixed on the image of the ax. "Jack Andrews did," I said.

Randall held up the small glass bottle and tilted it admiringly back and forth. He might have been a little boy administering chloroform to a butterfly.

Stalling desperately for whatever time it would take Kevin to get here, I said, "Just to satisfy my curiosity, how did Jack get hold of your dissertation?"

Randall Carey sneered. "Foley sent it to him. *Without* my permission. *With* a letter explaining that one of his graduate students had produced a dissertation worthy of publication that might be of interest to the general reader."

"Jack Andrews was a former student of Professor Foley's. They were old friends."

"Of course."

"So why didn't Jack Andrews just go to Professor Foley? No, wait! I know! Jack Andrews did the same thing that Professor Foley did eighteen years later. They both wanted to give you the chance to turn yourself in. They didn't want to do it."

"The expression that eludes you, Hannah, is *to rat.* Fitting, isn't it?"

Again, *Hannah!* Again, I made no protest.

"They wanted you to go and confess to Harvard yourself. They didn't want to rat. But in your own way, you sure did make them squeal."

"Your mind is unpolished," Randall informed me, "but not entirely devoid of potential."

"Speaking of potential," I said, sneaking a glance out the window, "here's the thing I don't get. Why did you bother? Why didn't you just *write* your own dissertation?"

He gave a chuckle that I think was supposed to sound British. "Money, madam! Filthy lucre! The unfortunate state of my financial affairs forced me to act in haste. In those days—perhaps the rule has changed—one had to be registered for the semester in which one received one's degree. My course work was done, my pockets were all but empty, and Harvard"—here, he stretched out his patrician vowels—"and Harvard, Fair Harvard, expected me to hand in an acceptable dissertation *instanter* or fork up for the next semester."

"How long did Jack Andrews give you to turn yourself in?"

"A fair man. A gentleman. He attempted to die like one. I watched. Common sense forced upon me that repugnant precaution. Alas, the man was an addict. All too common, far too common in one of a refined sensibility. Addicted to caffeine. On that Friday, the first of November, he called me to his offices, a rat's nest, I might comment, to grant me a week in which to settle my affairs, as he put it, and present the full truth to the esteemed George Foley, who, if the *veritas* be known, probably hadn't done more than scan the pitiful work before officiously shipping it off. On that occasion, I noticed that the fellow Andrews was hopelessly addicted to caffeine, which he consumed in the form of coffee from a large thermos. On the following Monday, supplied with the means of my salvation and having made an appointment with Mr. Andrews to discuss my supposed crime, I returned after that ridiculous excuse for a publishing house had closed for the day, I waited for my opportunity, I medicated the coffee, and I tarried to observe."

"Professor Foley didn't give you a week, I gather."

"The code of the gentleman is not, alas, what it once was. He demanded immediate action. I obliged. But enough of all this. 'The time has come,' as the Walrus said. Rats, I find, are a great convenience. One is so tempted to set out poison."

"I have dogs. I would never put out rat poison."

"Your devotion, my dear *Hannah,* is apparent."

"My devotion is very well known."

"Having accidentally killed the beasts, you would unhesitatingly swallow the stuff yourself."

I said nothing.

"I am," Randall said, "engaged in a deep internal debate, to wit, whether 'tis more fitting to dose you first and permit your stalwart guardians to stand by as you perish, or whether to let you survive to savor the sight of your hairy friends as they consume their din-din." Unwrapping the raw meat, he said, "The latter, I suppose. One is pulled in both directions." He placed the hamburger on the counter next to the copy of Lewis Clark's book. With infinite care, he unscrewed the cap on the glass bottle.

"Stay," I quietly told the dogs. The ax called to me. I could almost feel the familiar handle in my hand.

Lights. Headlights. In Kevin's spot. Through the window, I saw Kevin heave his bulk out of his car.

What did I have to lose?

Desperate to sound an alarm, I shot my arm past Rowdy to the door of the kitchen closet, the closet where I store the dry dog food. How much was left in the forty-pound bag? Half, I thought: twenty pounds of premium, meat-based kibble. Rowdy bounced and whined. Kimi yelped. As Randall Carey tipped the poison bottle over the raw meat, I wrenched open the closet door and shoved my way past the hungry dogs, who already had their noses to the bag of dog food and were already jockeying with each other. Rowdy, who'd started out next to the closet, was the first to force his head deep into the bag, but with a deep, menacing snarl, Kimi nipped at his neck and hurled herself on top of him. As Rowdy swung his head around to administer a painful lesson in the perils of stealing *his* food, Kimi took advantage of his momentary inattention to ram her head past his and straight into the bag.

I grew up with big dogs. From my earliest days, I'd been warned never, ever to tease a dog with food and absolutely never to try to break up a dog fight. Another prohibition went without saying: It never occurred to my parents that I'd deliberately trigger a dog fight. What's more, with the peaceable golden retrievers of my childhood, the task would have been difficult. Two rivalrous males would've quarreled over a female with a come-hither scent; nothing but the eternal canine triangle, however, could've persuaded our sweet-tempered kennelmates to turn on one another. I certainly hadn't had to tether my goldens at opposite ends of the kitchen to give them dinner. Rowdy and Kimi were devoted to each other. Malamute devotion, however, had *nothing* to do with sharing food.

Now that I'd started the fight, my goal was to move it out of the closet. Stretching my arms over the snarling tangle of dogs, I sent my hands flying down past the flashing teeth, got a grip on the bag, hauled it up and out of the closet, and upended it on the linoleum. As I'd hoped, when the twenty pounds of loose kibble hit the floor, the dogs switched into what malamute people call "survival mode." Ignoring Randall Carey and his deadly meat, the dogs scrambled and snatched until the two-dog melee transformed itself into a single beastly, roaring swirl of flying fur, crashing bodies, fighting jaws, and gnashing teeth.

Randall Carey, meat and poison in hand, took a step toward the battling dogs.

I turned toward the hallway, toward the closet where I'd stowed the ax. Its blade was sharp and heavy. The muscles in my arms and shoulders swelled.

"Hannah." Carey's voice caressed the name.

That persistent, mocking *Hannah* stopped me. I felt suddenly sick to my stomach. *I am not Hannah Duston!* I thought violently.

Brushing past the dangerous diversion I'd created, I grabbed a wooden kitchen chair, raised it, and, with its seat shielding me and its sharp legs projecting forward, gave a survival-mode snarl worthy of both my dogs, launched myself and my domestic makeshift weapon at Randall Carey, and drove that murderous son of a bitch away from my animals and across the kitchen until his back slammed into the refrigerator. With a quick yank, I jerked the chair toward me and aimed one of its legs directly at the center of his face.

In a reflex effort to save his sight, Randall Carey dropped his shoulders, lowered his head, and flexed his arms inward at the elbows.

"Listen to me, you bastard!" I growled. *"No one* hurts my dogs! *NO ONE!"*

Like Jael, who put her hand to the nail, and her right hand to the workman's hammer, I drove the wooden legs of my weapon forward. As Randall Carey's hands flew protectively toward his face, he still grasped the package of raw meat and the bottle of sodium fluoroacetate. As he cried out in terror, one leg of the chair, one spike, collided with the open bottle. Sisera asked for water. Jael brought him milk. Sisera drank willingly. Randall Carey swallowed his poison by accident.

Sodium fluoroacetate: A few drops can kill a horse.

But not within seconds.

Like Sisera, at my feet, Randall Carey bowed, he fell, he lay down. "Hannah," he murmured lovingly. "Hannah." A smile crossed his face. "Hannah, I have been a very bad boy."

Thirty-three

As a dust, sodium fluoroacetate is lethal to inhale. The liquid? I'm still not sure of the potency, if any, of the fumes. For what it's worth, Kevin Dennehy informs me that the bottle contained a highly dilute solution. When Randall Carey fell at my feet, however, I knew only that I didn't want to die with him. Also, I had a dog fight to break up, and, of course, I had to get Rowdy and Kimi safely away from Randall Carey before they decided to lick his face.

Kibble crunching beneath my feet, I backslid into my old role of tough alpha leader. Grabbing Rowdy's and Kimi's collars, I ordered, "Cut it the hell out!" I have spent thousands of hours training these dogs. Still, I'm always astounded when they obey.

Just as the dogs fell silent, the back door to the kitchen crashed open. In his beefy left hand, Kevin Dennehy held one of the big iron wood wedges I'd stashed by the stacked firewood. In his right, he brandished my sledgehammer. Naturally, he reminded me of Hannah Duston. By now, everyone and everything reminded me of Hannah Duston.

I nodded my head toward Randall Carey. "Sodium fluoroacetate," I said. "Be careful what you touch."

Thus it was that Randall Carey did not die alone. Jack Andrews hadn't died alone, either. Neither had George Foley. Randall Carey had lingered to eat and drink their agony. Randall Carey, too, perished in torment. For all I know, he may yet endure it. I can't help wondering whether he treated that copy of Dante's *Inferno* on his coffee table as a sort of Damned Yankee guide to his own ultimate destination. I assume that he feels right at home.

While I'm on the subject of home, let me report that, in a fashion disquietingly reminiscent of Gareth Andrews, I subsequently developed a sort of paranoia about my kitchen. Rita said I wasn't really paranoid. Rather, I was suffering from a phobia caused by post-traumatic stress. "You're bound to feel contaminated by the whole experience," she explained.

The symptom I exhibited was a terrified conviction that a lethal dose of sodium fluoroacetate had seeped into the linoleum or lurked elsewhere in the kitchen—under the refrigerator?—where, sooner or later, one of my dogs would accidentally ingest it. I explained precisely that to the insurance adjuster, a wonderfully sympathetic woman who disagreed with both Rita and me by deciding that I wasn't crazy at all.

"I know that the poison isn't going to come flying out of the floor and leap into their mouths," I told her. "But what if something spills on the linoleum? And they lap it up?"

"They're malamutes," she agreed. "They'll eat anything. I have bloodhounds myself. I'd be just as careful as you are." She reached into her shoulder bag and pulled out a wallet-size photo album packed with pictures of her dogs—not snapshots, either, but professional portraits taken by none other than Violet Wish.

The insurance company bought me a new refrigerator and paid to have the entire kitchen floor and cabinets torn out and replaced. The cream-and-terra-cotta wallpaper had turned a depressing beige and rust, anyway, and I don't miss the old flooring at all. The new colors are cherry-red and white, and I finally have real tile instead of a linoleum look-alike that never did.

Once the work was complete, my fear of hidden poison completely vanished. Consequently, Rita finally quit nagging me to spend a week at that Eastern mystical stress-reduction and lifestyle-change ashram in the Berkshires.

"Look what it did for Kevin!" she kept cajoling. Then she'd lower her voice and confide, "Kevin did some deep work there. He is making tremendous progress toward scripting his own life instead of accepting the roles assigned to him by others. His mother, for example. And male authority figures. Kevin has some major issues with authority."

"He's a cop," I reminded her. "He's supposed to have authority issues."

I weaseled the truth out of Steve when I took the dogs to his clinic to update their kennel-cough immunizations and accidentally overheard a whispered conversation between the two young veterinarians he'd hired the previous summer.

I confronted Steve. "They think it's very peculiar," I told him, "and somewhat repulsive. What I think is that it's irreverent, disgusting, and highly unsanitary. So what the hell is it doing there?"

At first, Steve tried to convince me that the carcass in his cold-storage area was the remains of a client's beloved pet deer. Pot-bellied pigs, he maintained, were on their way out. The trendy new exotic pet was—

I interrupted him. "Venison? Since when do you *hang* the body of a pet and let it *ripen*?"

I got the whole story out of Steve. The only meditation Kevin had engaged in had been premeditation: He'd made sure that Rita hadn't actually known any of the people at the retreat center in the Berkshires. Furthermore, just in case he returned with a deer, he'd made a secret arrangement with Steve to share the venison in exchange for storage space, and Steve, who was leaving for Minneapolis, had enlisted two of his vet techs in the conspiracy. Kevin's mother, as I've said, won't allow meat in her house. His plans in place, Kevin had taken off for a week with some police-academy buddies at a hunting camp in northern Maine.

The part that astounded me was the deer. *"Kevin?* Steve, I'd've bet anything he couldn't get through *Bambi* dry-eyed."

With a guilty look, Steve mumbled, "His friend Phil shot it. But don't mention it."

"Of course not," I promised. "Who am I to sever the bloodied knots of male bonding?"

Bonding reminds me: Oscar Fisch? The recovery movement? Dogs? Survivors? The inner child? The *canine* inner child? Well, when I mailed that package to Oscar Fisch, I knew it was a long shot. I mean, when Oscar stopped in to order me to quit harassing Claudia, his irrational fear of Rowdy and Kimi was palpable. There was Oscar's antidog wife, too. But who could be scared of a retired racing greyhound, for heaven's sake?

As for Claudia, the sanctuaries of dog worship teem with interfaith marriage, and it was even possible that if Oscar converted, she might eventually realize that if there's one creature on earth that's the true survivor of financial exploitation and abuse, it's a greyhound that failed as a moneymaker on the track and would have been put to death if it weren't for the greyhound rescue movement.

Oscar read the book I sent: *Adopting the Racing Greyhound*. Instead of phoning me about it, he sent a note to say, as one says in the recovery movement, that he *heard* me. "I am convinced," I wrote back, "that the best therapy for the child within is the dog without." Although Francis Avenue is only a pleasant walk from my house, especially pleasant if your walking companion is a greyhound, Oscar also mailed me a snapshot of Melody, as his new greyhound is called, together with a long letter all about the letter he and Claudia had sent to Shaun McGrath's family.

Claudia, I reflected, made a habit of marrying men who put their sentiments in writing. I wished I'd asked Randall Carey how he'd gotten hold of the note that Jack Andrews had obviously intended for Tracy Littlefield, the supposed suicide note in which Jack had actually announced his decision not to pursue the "lost cause" of making a champion out of a dog that no judge cared for. My guess was that Jack had just finished writing his note to Tracy when Randall Carey arrived in his office. If so, the last words Jack ever wrote had been meant for her: "Your disappointment is my only regret. Love, Jack." I reminded myself to make sure that Tracy saw Jack's note.

The second letter found with Jack's body had, I was certain, been written to Randall Carey himself. Remember?

It is unfortunate that society judges some weaknesses more harshly than it does others. Far from desiring to create an embarrassing public furor, I am eager that what must now transpire do so as privately as possible.

With regret,
John W. Andrews

My hunch was that Jack had mailed it to Randall Carey just after their meeting on the Friday before the murder and that Randall had received it the day he killed Jack. Or maybe, mistrustful of the mail service, Jack had delivered it to Randall Carey's house. Jack's note to Tracy would move her deeply. His compassion for Randall Carey moved me.

"I still don't understand," I told Rita, "why Randall Carey was stupid enough to write that chapter about Jack's murder. The book, I sort of understand. It was meant as a potboiler. He needed money, so he wrote a piece of sensationalist trash. But why draw attention to Jack's murder when everyone thought it was solved?"

"Think about it," Rita said.

"I have! What hits me is that the chapter was the one place I came across the idea that Jack's signature on the insurance policy was a forgery. No one else so much as hinted that Shaun McGrath had forged Jack's signature. I wondered about that. I even asked Randall Carey who'd told him, but he said he didn't remember. If there'd been some question about who'd committed the murder, then maybe it would've made sense for Carey to strengthen the case against Shaun McGrath. But no one doubted Shaun's guilt."

"You're missing the point," Rita said, "because Randall Carey's whole psychology is so foreign to you. Let's step back. Why plagiarize a dissertation he could easily have written himself?"

"He didn't have time. He had to hand it in so he wouldn't have to pay another semester's tuition."

"He could've cited the book, he could've used it, he could've acknowledged his indebtedness to it, he could've applied for a new student loan, he could've gotten a job to support himself while he finished his dissertation. He had dozens of options, and he would've known what they were. He did not have to plagiarize. If he lifted whole sentences and paragraphs, he did the same thing he subsequently did with the chapter on the murder."

"Which was?"

"He flirted with getting caught."

"Punishment," I said. "The leather, uh, fetish."

"It ain't called bondage and *discipline* for nothing. Remember what he said to you? When he gave you that collar and leash? When he—"

"I don't want to think about it."

"He said, 'I've been a very bad boy.' He said it to you, he said it in his plagiarism, he said it in the chapter about Jack Andrews's murder."

"But, Rita, when he really did get caught, when Jack found out about his dissertation, when Professor Foley found out, when I did, he wasn't exactly gratified. He murdered them, and he tried to murder me."

"Holly, he didn't want the product, the actual outcome in reality. What he was driven to repeat was the process, the seeking, the emotional brinkmanship, if you will. Where the excitement lay, for him, was in creating and re-creating a perpetual tension between fantasy and reality. Reality would have spoiled the fantasy. As I said, he *flirted* with getting caught."

"Or, as Kevin said, the guy was a real nut case."

"I can't say that I'd disagree," Rita conceded.

Speaking of disagreement! If I may quote Estelle Grant, *chacun à son goût* and all that, but I really never thought that *Multitudes in the Valley of Decision* would suit even a minuscule press that catered to readers with specialized tastes, never mind the two gigantic New York publishing houses that got into a major bidding war over the manuscript and drove the price up so high that Estelle received an advance that would support me and my dogs for the next century.

Estelle has, of course, quit temping. She now devotes herself full-time to her new book, which is about monks and morticians. According to Estelle, it's really about liberation from psychic bondage. She got the idea at Randall Carey's memorial service. We went together. Ordinarily, I will do anything to avoid funeral rites of all kinds. I made an exception in the case of Randall Carey's service because it seemed to me that if ever a departed soul needed prayers, it was his, and that even my insincere muttering about forgiveness would be better than nothing. Also, since it was a memorial service, not a funeral, his dead body wouldn't be there. What was there was his mother. Alive. Until I saw her, I couldn't imagine what sort of person would hold a memorial service for a double murderer. She was a huge woman with a fierce, hawklike face. She wore a black leather coat with gloves to match. Boots, too. Black leather boots.

Still on the topic of souls, women, and all black, let me update you on Brat Andrews. After considerable soul-searching and a consultation with Rita, I asked Tracy Littlefield's permission to tell Brat about her unknown half-brother, Drew. Tracy granted it. Brat was, naturally, more than slightly shaken by the news. She has since seen pictures of Drew and has insisted on helping

Tracy with his college tuition, but she hasn't yet met Drew face to face. I don't know whether he knows about her. Or about Gareth, either. Although Gareth is now taking his medication and is reported to be doing as well as he ever does, I can't imagine that he'll ever be ready to meet Drew. I'm not supposed to tell you anything else about Brat. Actually, I don't know any more. Rita really does respect the confidentiality of her clients.

Finally, Rita's bet. And a few words about Hannah Duston. Treat this as therapy, okay? Privileged communication. And so far I know, there really is no proof that Hannah's captors were Abenaki. That was just Professor Foley's best guess. From what I've read, it was a good one, though. The western branch of the Abenaki inhabited what are now the states of Vermont and New Hampshire. In the seventeenth century, epidemics reduced their population from about ten thousand to five hundred. The English razed Abenaki villages and paid bounties for Abenaki scalps. The survivors, Jesuit converts who sided with the French Catholics against the English Protestants, traveled in family bands that took captives. The roving bands often used birchbark canoes. They eventually returned to longhouses, in Canada, for example, but when on the move, they stayed in wigwams. So it computes. Hannah's captors. Abenaki. But here's the kicker: According to the Abenaki belief system, the Abenaki are descended from animals and retain so strong a continuing spiritual relationship that animals and people are, in essence, two forms of the same being. Every band was linked not just to animals in general but to a particular species, a totemic animal. Sound familiar? A book I read showed a present-day Abenaki woman sitting in front of her house in Vermont. Just guess what she was patting.

Now, look. There are more than fifty million dogs in the United States. Lots of people have dogs. Both before and after the seventeenth century, Native Americans of the Northeast had dogs. I have no evidence that Hannah's captors were even Abenaki. If they were, their totemic animal could've been the fox or the wolf or the badger or anything at all. It really doesn't matter.

What nags at me is an account I came across in an obscure essay by John Greenleaf Whittier called "The Boy Captives." Whittier was from Haverhill. The essay mentions Hannah Duston. Mainly it's about two boys, Isaac Bradley and Joseph Whittaker, who were taken captive in Haverhill in 1695, ended up with an Indian family near Lake Winnipesaukee in New Hampshire, and escaped. The Indians didn't just go after the boys, but, damn it, pursued them with dogs! The boys hid in a hollow log. The dogs found them and started to bark. As Whittier wrote, though, one of the boys "spoke in a low tone to the dogs, who, recognizing his familiar voice, wagged their tails with delight and ceased barking." The boy then successfully diverted the dogs by tossing them pieces of moose meat. When the Indians appeared, the dogs left with them. The boys made it home.

Boys taken captive in Haverhill in 1695. Same place as Hannah and only two years earlier. Taken to New Hampshire. Just like Hannah. Captured by people with dogs, in the plural, dogs that had socialized with the captives. I remind you that I know almost nothing about Hannah's captors. Abenaki? Abenaki whose emblem was the dog? Don't ask me! And especially don't ask whether the members of that Abenaki family consisted of twelve members in human form and a little pack of spiritual relatives that wagged their tails at Hannah Duston and licked the hands that later slew their masters. The great miser, history, reluctantly doles out stingy little scraps. Hannah Duston, Mary Neff, and Samuel Leonardson killed ten people. Hannah Duston returned to Haverhill with ten scalps. History has chosen not to tell us whether Hannah's captors had dogs. Hannah presumably killed the children to prevent them from sounding an alarm and summoning help. If her captors had dogs, wouldn't she have slain the animals for the same reason? If she slaughtered children, her tender mercies toward dogs would surely have been cruelties.

One last point. As I've mentioned, when Elizabeth Emerson was only eleven, her father, Michael Emerson, was convicted of beating and kicking her. During Elizabeth's first pregnancy, she named a man named Timothy Swan as the father of her baby. Five years later, she denied her second pregnancy. Elizabeth Emerson lived with her parents. The twins were born in Elizabeth's parents' house. Michael and Hannah Emerson were in the house when Elizabeth delivered. She gave birth alone, with no help, or so she testified. Presumed guilty, she was executed for the murder of the babies. Faced with Cotton Mather's threats of hell fire, Elizabeth Emerson protested her innocence to the end.

Elizabeth Emerson had no supporters and no defense. I wish she'd had me at her side. In the manner of her sister Hannah, I'd have pointed a finger of accusation. When those twins were born and murdered, who else was in that house? I'd have asked. Who else had already endured the shame of a bastard child in the family? Whom would Elizabeth have shielded? And who was the one person there with a criminal record of violence against children? Against his *own* child? It's possible, I suppose, that both Michael and Hannah Emerson killed Elizabeth's babies. It's even possible that the twins were stillborn. My finger of accusation, however, would point and, in fact, does point at Michael Emerson, the grandfather of the babies, the abusive father of Elizabeth Emerson, the father of Hannah Duston.

Thirty-four

So, Rita, judge for yourself. Here is my story about Hannah Duston. By my standards, it has almost nothing to do with dogs. Do I win or lose? Or are all bets off?

I've been tempted to cheat. I came close to saying nothing about the boy captives and the hollow log, nothing about the Abenaki and the totemic animals. I am still tempted. Randall Carey, however, taught me a lesson about the hazards of cheating. I wouldn't plagiarize. But without my knowledge of Randall Carey, I might fall into the sin of selective omission.

So here it is. My Aunt Cassie, Leah's mother and my mother's sister, was thrilled to hear that instead of diverting Leah from her academic pursuits by encouraging her to waste her time on dogs, I'd finally turned Leah's attention and my heretofore wasted talents to a respectable field, namely, colonial history. Aunt Cassie said as much to a relative of ours named Louise, who is something like Leah's and my fourth cousin once removed. We'd never met her. Probably because Louise isn't a dog person, my mother had never mentioned her and I'd never heard of her. Although Louise, like Aunt Cassie, dwells in dogless apostasy from the family faith, she is religious nonetheless and—there really is a point to all this—recently switched creeds by converting to the Church of Jesus Christ of Latter-Day Saints. As you may or may not know—I didn't—the Mormon Church is the world's largest repository of genealogical information. The idea, as I understand it, is that you are obligated to convert your ancestors, posthumously, of course, and that to do so, you need to know their names. An interest in pedigrees runs in our lines. My mother's obsession with family trees was, however, strictly limited to the ancestry of golden retrievers. If she'd known what Louise found out, she wouldn't have cared at all.

I was more than interested. I was outright horrified. It means nothing. It bothers me nonetheless.

My mother was. So is Aunt Cassie. So is Leah. I, too, am a direct descendant of Hannah Duston.

Author's Note

With the exception of the imaginary *And One Fought Back,* the sources Holly consults for information about Hannah Duston are real. Especially useful to the author was *Good Wives: Image and Reality in the Lives of Women in Northern New England, 1650–1750* by Laurel Thatcher Ulrich.

The Haverhill Historical Society's Buttonwoods Museum is located at 240 Water Street, Haverhill, Massachusetts 01830. For information, call (508) 374-4626.